ALL BUT A PLEASURE

ALL BUT A PLEASURE

PHYLLIS ANN KARR

*An Alternate-History Role-Playing
Romance Murder Mystery*

WILDSIDE PRESS

Published by Wildside Press LLC.
www.wildsidebooks.com

"The pain that is all but a pleasure will change
For the pleasure that's all but pain..."
      —Gilbert & Sullivan, *Patience*, Act I Finale

CHAPTER 1

"With all due reverence, honored Rulemaster," Corwin protested, "the Spanish version of the Inquisition did *not* make a habit of burning witches."

"Don Serafino," said Rulemaster Sam Imani, the portly and genial host of the Sunday rolegame parties, addressing Corwin by the name of his persona, "we're playing this game by the Lurid Legend, not the historical record."

"And I approve the Lurid Legend with the warmest and most pious enthusiasm, on the whole, at least as utilized in the present ludification. I strove merely to point out why Don Serafino would protest subjecting to even so much as arrest..." Corwin's deep brown eyes turned for an instant toward Angela..."this valuable and responsible herbalist who serves her underpopulated hamlet as its sole midwife and, in effect, physician."

"You've just lost even more points with your fellow inquisitors, Don Serafino," said Julie Whitcomb, a.k.a. Fray Paulo, gracefully patting the colorful tattoo that peeked out above the scoop neckline of her long, blood-red gown. She went on, "*We* know how many secret heretics hide out as inquisitors. Rulemaster, roll the die and let's see how many points Don Serafino has lost this time."

"Oh, go ahead and burn Old Agnes!" Angela stood up. "I'd just as soon bow out of this game anyway. I'm going to see if I can't start up a Raggedy Ann scenario with some of the others."

"Raggedy Ann?" Corwin inquired, cocking one of his black eyebrows at her.

"Yes, Raggedy Ann! And when your fellow inquisitors have finished arresting and torturing and burning you, you can come over to my game and be Raggedy Andy!"

"That might prove very restful," said Corwin. "Take good care of your candy heart, Raggedy Ann."

She thought she felt his gaze following her as she bounced through Sam Imani's big living room. At the door to the lounge, she paused and glanced back. She'd been right—he was still gazing after her—though as soon as she caught him doing it, he turned back at once to his fellow gamers in the Spanish Inquisition scenario.

Why had she even joined the silly Inquisition game in the first place? Partly, she supposed, from curiosity; partly because her other choices at the very beginning of the afternoon had been The Last Great War in the den and Gojira Attacks in the dining room; and partly because she and Corwin had been childhood friends who kept up a correspondence all through college and were finally seeing each other again in person after those five years two thousand miles apart in different sections of the Reformed States of America.

Well. Corwin Davison had always tended a little this way. Ever since at least fifth grade, his favorite author had been Edgar Allan Poe, from whom he had taken the sort of nick-surname so many people used. Of course, most children had a strong morbid streak, and their own neighborhood group, Corwin's and Angela's, used to play Feds and Klingons, Pollies and Robbers, and Savage Initiation Rites like any other bunch of kids. Only, Angela had outgrown that kind of thing. From what she'd seen of him so far, she didn't think Corwin ever had. If anything, he'd grown worse…well, more emphatic about it, anyway.

She'd been forced to grow up all at once, start looking in earnest for her adult self when her mother died of Anne Sutler's Disease the summer after Angela's graduation from high school. Angela had already been accepted at the University of Minnemagantic, but her arrival there had had to be delayed for Mommy's funeral. At the university, she found she either had to cultivate a sunny outlook, or sink into a suicidal depression. Luckily for her, her faculty advisor had been Professor of Music Clement Czarny, and if a vampire—whether he really was one or only thought he was— could live so heroically decent a life, surely Angela Garvey could grow her optimistic side to full flower.

As soon as Angela was safe at college, her father and younger sibs moved down to Miami, which was why she and Corwin had never managed to see each other again in their old home town during vacations. And, apparently, letters had not been enough to keep her aware of what was going on or—maybe—not going on inside his character. How could he still be enjoying such a totally repulsive rolegame as Spanish Inquisition?

And yet, otherwise, he seemed so gentle, so considerate, so much her old friend. Even, in some ways, improved, as people ought to improve when they grew up... With a puzzled shake of her blond head, Angela pushed into the lounge and started trying to interest players who had already been knocked like her out of their earlier games in a safe and pleasant Raggedy Ann scenario.

The quieter scenarios should be starting later in the afternoon anyway, by what Corwin had told her. And, to her delight, four of the five gamers in the lounge applauded her idea, including Hank Algood, who knew even more than she did about Johnny Gruelle's world and undertook to guide her proposed scenario from the rather unexpected role—for Rulemaster—of the Camel with the Wrinkled Knees. They decided on the library for their playing area.

* * * *

Across town, Detective Sergeant Rosemary Lestrade and her junior partner Detective Dave Clayton were staring down at a stark naked corpse.

Murder wasn't run-of-the-mill in a town of 35,000 in the safe breadbasket of the R.S.A., but this young man had obviously been murdered.

Dave, who was only twenty-eight, had already gone aside to heave and come back again, reluctantly but with his mouth wiped. Officer Kim Little Bird had probably done the same earlier—she and her senior partner, Officer Stan Vergucchi, had been the first pollies called to the scene. Stan was on the edge of retirement age and might have reasonably experienced insides.

At forty-four, Rosemary Lestrade had seen murder victims before. Enough to harden her stomach. Luckily, as far as that word ever applied in murder cases, the cold water had kept the corpse reasonably fresh, or even stronger police insides than hers might have turned. Especially at what had been done to the genitals. And other parts of the body.

Officer Little Bird said, "What a waste!"

"M.E.'s on his way," Lestrade remarked. "For whatever the old floater's opinion might be worth."

"What a waste!" Officer Little Bird repeated.

Yes. Someone Kim Little Bird might have enjoyed dating, Lestrade thought wryly, if she'd met him in time. Someone whose life she might've changed enough to keep it from ending in murder.

"They didn't have to torture him to death, on top of it!" Clayton burst out. "Bastards!"

"Watch your language, Detective. You can probably find a stronger word than 'bastards.' And I'm not convinced this was a torture murder. More likely post-mortem, I'd guess. Water's rinsed away any blood that could've made it obvious, but that doesn't look like an agonized facial expression to me. More like your plain, ordinary surprise at being unexpectedly dead."

"Devils?" Clayton suggested.

Lestrade shook her head. "Stronger than that. It's always beaten me why your Christian devils would even need to bother corrupting humanity. We do pretty well—if you want to call it that—all on our own. We humans could probably corrupt the devils of your hell. Even in this 'safe and sane' age of the R.S.A."

"What's that?" Clayton pointed. "There…near the hollow beneath his right collarbone."

Lestrade stooped for a closer inspection. "Good eyes, Dave!… Looks like a tattoo of some kind… Whirligig? All blue, I think… Maybe one of those stamped tattoos popular with semi-secret groups like fraternal lodges and rolegame clubs."

"Some kind of initiation that went too far? Bloody…bloody motherprickers!"

"Getting a little warmer with that one." Lestrade straightened up and wiped her hands on her trousers. Not that she had touched any of the evidence, but that she felt dirty just being this close to it. "Better leave all this alone until the M.E. gets here." For what he's worth, she repeated to herself.

Rolegamers in futuristic and science-fiction scenarios, and maybe forensic specialists in some of the "alternate worlds" a few bona-fide scientists thought existed, might have wonderful machinery for pinpointing things like genetic evidence, exact nanosecond of death, and so on. Here and now in the real world, a small town of 35,000 budgeted minimal funds for its police department. She and Clayton were its only two detective grades. As for their medical examiner, Doc Grumeister might have an office in the station where he was on duty "ten to four,"—a dying idiom now the whole country had been on the twenty-four hour clock about twenty-four years; but Doc Grumeister was a joke, just marking time until retirement, and probably not that competent even in the forensics of the year Rosemary Lestrade was born.

Baptized Rosemary Lozinski—with herbs and flower petals in a Wiccan ceremony—she had grown into a tall, roughhewn-looking woman who entered law enforcement less to catch bad guys than to make sure no good guys got caught by mistake. Back in second grade, she had been punished herself for something she hadn't done, and the experience left its mark. If catching the real bad guys came along with clearing the innocent suspects—and sometimes you had to catch the bad guys in order to clear the good ones—that was just an added bonus. Especially if and when the cases involved crimes likely to be repeated. Which, up to now in this town, had mainly included petty robbery and passing bad checks. Two cases of vandalism and one of arson—more than bad enough. She hoped that what she stood looking down at today wasn't the first in a string of serial killings like the ones that, once solved, had made up her mind to leave Chicago, Illinois for Forest Green, Indiana.

Doc Grumeister tottered in at last, fumbled the corpse around for a few minutes, and ruled death by violence. No surprise. Whether the genital mess, burn marks, splinted finger- and toenails, lines of criss-cross cutmarks, and stamped tattoo had come before or after death, he couldn't say and showed no real interest in trying to find out, not after the unknown number of hours the body had spent in the Vigo River. He simply ruled—also no surprise—that death had likelier resulted from torture than from drowning.

* * * *

Deep in the Deep, Deep Woods, halfway to the hot dog bush on the edge of the Lemonade Lake, the Raggedy Ann gamers in the library started hearing loud screams from the direction of the living room. One, then another…a short pause, then three more…another pause, and then one last one that sounded less like a scream than a blood-curdling shriek.

At the first scream Angela started up, recognizing Corwin's voice. Then—"It's just that stupid Spanish Inquisition game," she told the four people in easy chairs around her, as she sat herself back down on the loveseat and returned to her title role in the game.

Two or three minutes after the shriek, Corwin strolled into the library, brushing invisible dust off his black lounge suit. "That was invigorating," he remarked. "A genuinely cathartic experience."

"Lawsy me!" Pearl Mitsu spoke more or less the way she conceived her character—Beloved Belindy—ought to speak, whether Johnny Gruelle had written it that way or not. "Was that you'm we done just heard a-screamin' an' a-caterwaulin' fit to bust our buttons?"

"As unmusical as that?" He sat down on the loveseat beside Angela and stretched his arms along its back. "Yea, verily, 'twas I. They found me out and administered certain exquisite devices held in especial reserve for those who fall from their own exalted ranks. Then, for the climax, they naturally burned me alive at the stake. Thus expediting me, by their own lights, straight from a terrestrial into an infernal holocaust. I, of course, enjoy a variant eschatological interpretation, my secret heresy having been that rather arrogant species of universalism termed apokatastasis. Do I make myself clear?"

"Oh, yes," Angela replied. "To about ten percent of the members of Mind-sa."

"You sounded like they were really doing something to you," said Gerry Wu, who was playing Policeman Percy.

"I rejoice—if that is an appropriate idiom—in a singularly vivid imagination. I also strongly suspect," Corwin mused on, "that every last inquisitor in that game is secretly either heretic, morisco, or judaizer. It was simply my fortune to be found out first. I wonder why?"

Angela glanced at his nearer arm. If he dropped it just a few inches, he could have it around her shoulders. She decided to leave it where it was, for now. "Because you wanted to be found out," she told him. "You were teasing them all along to find you out. Trying to get all the non-inquisitor players off like that. And never accused even one of your fellow inquisitors, I'll bet."

"I was biding my time while gathering, sifting, and collating evidence. Alas, I bided it a bit too long. Does the role of Raggedy Andy remain open?"

"We've been saving it just for you," Hank replied. "At our dear Raggedy Ann's special request."

"Ah! This may perhaps be the place for me to interject that I have never been entirely clear as to the exact relationship between the beloved Raggedies. Are they sweethearts or spouses or —"

"Sister and brother," Angela said firmly.

"Rulemaster?" Corwin looked around to see who the Rulemaster might be. His glance settled on Hank, probably because Hank had been the one who told him they were saving Raggedy Andy for him.

"Your sister's right, Andy," Hank confirmed. "She's a bright girl, but even if she wasn't, it doesn't take genius level to know one's own brother."

"Brother," Corwin repeated, sounding a little disappointed. "Siblings." He folded his arms. "Very well, Rulemaster, if you will graciously brief me on the identities and whereabouts of our congenial cameraderie in this pastoral scenario?"

"First, Thesaurus Kid," Hank ruled, "cut the sesquipedalian gymnastics. They don't fit Raggedy Andy."

Corwin blinked, and nodded. "Hard, but I'll try."

As the evening wore on, Angela had to confess to herself that he was fitting into her scenario quite a bit better than she had fit into his. He didn't even slip into complicated vocabulary more than half a dozen times.

Of course, Spanish Inquisition hadn't exactly been "his" scenario. It had been the one Julie Whitcomb and Sam Imani and their crowd were inviting people into at the start of the afternoon. True, Corwin had fairly jumped at the chance.

* * * *

As more and more players got killed or otherwise retired from their original games, the players regrouped into four wind-down scenarios in all: besides Raggedy Ann in the library, there were Dragon Mountain in the conservatory, Wonder-Glass in the dining room; and Roly-Polies and Fence Rails—based on the French children's classic *Patapoufs et Filifers*—in the billiards room.

At length only four players remained in Sam Imani's living room: Imani himself, Julie Whitcomb, lean Paul Osaka, and Curly Friedman, who was so hefty she could pull off a convincing male interpretation if and when she chose, and whose rich, coffee-colored skin was dark enough to have let her pass for an ethnic pureblood if only her hair had been woolly instead of long and straight. "Curly" was one of those ironic nicknames meaning the opposite.

All four of them bore a tattoo like a whirligig of tiny lightning bolts stamped somewhere or other on their bodies. Julie's was near the hollow beneath her right collarbone, Sam's was just below his navel, Paul's on his inner right thigh, Curly's on the heel of her left foot.

Sam, Julie, and Paul had all played inquisitors, Curly the last ordinary Spaniard to have spent the evening wriggling out of their clutches. But after everyone else had been burned at the stake, these last four, instead of finishing the game to a single winner, drew together with a final glance around the otherwise unpopulated living room, and began to confer in low voices.

"Well, what does everybody think?" Sam began. "Any potentials for Julie's replacement?"

Julie patted her whirligig. "I believe Corwin Poe looks promising. I've had my eye on him most of the summer."

Paul and Curly nodded. "Good," Sam said, writing in a little blue notebook. "I like him, too. Anybody else? Let's see. We had Trudy Huerth…Hobart McGruff…Carmine Raincloud Jones…"

"Carmine might work," Paul tapped his nose, a habit he had that looked like he was trying to straighten the crook where it had once been broken. "He's got Cinnamon blood. Might know something about the Sun Dance."

"Yes, the way each of us is fluent in our various ancestral languages," Julie observed satirically.

"The Sun Dance was Mandan and Sioux, I think," said Curly. "Carmine's ancestry was Hopi, wasn't it? Tamer kind of dancing."

"Maybe he's got a little Aztec or Mayan blood, too," Sam suggested. "They could be fierce."

"Carmine Jones," Julie declared, "is more enthusiastic about the musical stage than his ancestral heritage, whatever the tribe. I'd say he joined our scenario chiefly because the Spanish Inquisition figures in a few standard-repertory operas, and the other two serious scenarios didn't. I vote no on Jones."

But the vote split, Curly siding with Julie and Sam with Paul. One more tie vote, on Marge Hokstra. All the rest drew a clear majority No.

Most of the Purgatorio's decisions required consensus. When they voted instead, not having a tiebreaker, an evenly split vote meant further investigation—in this case, of the potential candidates. And so it went, through six more names.

"Anyone else?" Sam said at last. "I think we've pretty well named them all."

Parting her ruby-glossed lips in a grin that showed off her even white teeth, Julie Whitcomb added, "We also had, for a few minutes there at the beginning, Angela Garvey."

Everyone laughed.

That pretty young blond was nobody any of them could under any circumstances want to hurt even marginally.

* * * *

Angela had graduated from college in June, spent the next several months working props and make-up for Hodag Crossing's communiversity summer theater, and arrived back in Forest Green in September to move in with her mother's old friend, "Aunt" Sally Fulbright, while deciding whether to rejoin Dad, Barb, and Charley in Florida—a state that had never appealed to her that much—or get a place of her own here in her old home town.

Aunt Sally's home was about a kilometer this side of the Marquette House, where Corwin had his apartment. His remaining way wound through some of the most wildscaped of the city parks, and several more blocks went past heavily wooded undeveloped lots. It was the kind of stroll she knew he doted on, especially at night.

He also loved to come in and visit, but tonight Aunt Sally had gone to a movie with a group of friends, leaving only the porch light and one living-room lamp on for Angela.

As if to postpone saying good night for just a little while longer, he asked at the door, "Have you still that birthmark above your sternum?"

"Do you think birthmarks move away to some other country?" she teased.

"May they not on occasion suffer surgical excision?"

"Well, there was never any reason to excise this one. Harmless patch of pink skin that you used to say looked a little like a heart."

"And thus, I have always hypothesized, inspired you to gravitate to the Raggedy world." Keeping himself to simple words for Raggedy Andy must have exhausted him.

She caught him looking at her chest. "Corwin Davison Poe! We were little kids when you looked at my birthmark, and you're certainly not going to have another look at it now we're grown up! Just pretend it's melted away, like Raggedy Ann's own candy heart when she fell in the water and drifted."

"Melted away to permeate her entire precious, stuffed body with sweetness. But did not our Camel with the Wrinkled Knees observe at one point that in this matter Raggedy Ann had been laboring under an erroneous opinion, which she subsequently revised with the discovery that her candy heart was still in place?"

"Maybe just part of it melted. Just the outside edges. Remember, Beloved Belindy said near the end that she thought Raggedy Andy must have a candy heart, too?"

"To which I think I responded, 'No, my stuffing is plain white cotton through and through just now, but perhaps some day I will have a candy heart."

"And our Camel complimented you on getting the words so very close to what Raggedy Andy actually says in the book. How could you remember that, Cory, and not remember about the Raggedies being brother and sister?"

"The words concerning Andy's hope for a candy heart, I suppose remained in the subliminal depths of my hippocampus from rapid and possibly superficial childhood reading of Gruelle's magnum opus. The relationship subsisting between the Raggedies… there, my forgetfulness could conceivably have an interpretation delicately suggestive of Freudian overtones…"

"Say good night, Raggedy Andy."

They were much of a height. Stepping a little to one side, he leaned close, murmured, "For old times' sake, Raggedy Ann," and put a very tender kiss on her cheek. She couldn't help reaching up and patting his night-stubbly cheek in return.

Once inside the house, she leaned against the closed door and rubbed the spot on her cheek. Thoughtfully, very thoughtfully.

What a bundle of contradictions he had grown up into!
What a bundle of dear, precious contradictions.

CHAPTER 2

MONDAY, SEPTEMBER 18

On the salary of a junior police detective in a town of thirty-five thousand—even a police detective with a nice little legacy of lands and money, the latter going into making the former more livable—Dave Clayton cut corners where he could. This morning he was at the yearly health fair in the Friends' Meeting House, where flu shots cost less than anywhere else. He was also running late for duty, thanks to uncooperative traffic lights.

"Hey!" he announced, marching in behind his identification card. "Police detective here."

"Detective!" a neat, gray-haired lady in blue tunic and trousers greeted him. "Is there any trouble?"

"None at all, M.," he answered, turning the volume down on his baritone voice. Why did people always jump to that assumption? "Just hoping I can get my flu shot and still make it to work on time."

"Of course. Are you investigating that dreadful murder right here in Forest Green?"

"We've always got a lot on our plate, M. But, yes, that one'll be taking precedence until we've got the killer in custody." Which might be a lot sooner if the Old Woman wasn't quite so tender about risking miscarriages of justice; but Dave kept that thought to himself. Solidarity before the public.

"Right this way, Detective." The gray-haired lady led him straight to the head of the line, nodding out apologies on the way. "Here you are, Detective. Nurse Whitcomb, can you take this police detective next?"

The nurse giving out flu shots glanced up from patting an adhesive mini-bandage on the arm of a little girl about nine or ten. "Surely, M. Esteridge. Right away." Handing the little girl a cookie, she shooed her off the chair and beckoned to Dave. "Next."

Quite a beauty, Nurse Whitcomb—Nurse Julie Whitcomb, he saw by her name badge. Black hair braided up on top of her head behind the white nurse's cap, green eyes with just the merest suggestion of epicanthic folds and Butterscotch skin to match, straight nose, luscious red lips, long neck…

"Smooth or rough, Handsome Detective?" Nurse Julie Whitcomb teased him as he took his seat on the folding chair and rolled up his sleeve. "You don't look like a man who's afraid of needles."

"I'm not. But make it smooth, anyway."

The time he got studying her bosom while she bent over his arm, imagining what lay beneath that neat nurse's collar and smooth white tunic, was all too brief. "Finished," she announced.

"You *were* smooth! I never felt a thing."

"Comes with long practice. How about a Bugs Bunny bandage?"

"Hey, what happened to 'Handsome'? Now you think I look like a Bugs Bunny type?"

"Oh, in features you're more a Cary Grant type. But with that mischievous twinkle in your eye…" She flicked her tongue out between those fleshy red lips just long enough for him to appreciate its pinkness. "Whoops!" she went on. "All out of Bugs Bunny. Take a Dizzy Duck instead." She slapped one on his arm and told him, "Now roll down your sleeve and head on out, Handsome Detective. Other people are waiting."

"The name's Dave. David Clayton. You in the phone book?"

"How else can I make myself available?" She gave him a wink and a shove on the back. "*Ciao*, Detective Dave Clayton."

He thought it was a joke. He was sure it had to have been just a joke. Nurses didn't have to take any extra work on the side. And even if one did, she surely wouldn't broadcast it to a pollydeck? Would she? It had to have been just flirtatious banter.

He was going to phone her tonight. Make good and sure.

Maybe that was what she wanted to make sure he'd do.

Nice thought.

* * * *

Moonlighting with local yearbooks, night Desk Officer Holly Davenport had come up with thirty-six possible matches for the corpse's face. Even thirty-six was an impressive job of weeding down, and might easily have missed the one they needed. His character, his psychomystique, the millions of big and little things that had made him unique in the world when he was alive—all had vanished after death into a corpse that could have belonged to almost any one of a quarter of the young male population in the country. Age probably between twenty and thirty, medium build, black hair, hazel eyes, probably good-looking in a generic kind of way when he was animated and happy, teeth distinctive only to the dental records.

Dentists. That was the place they'd start this morning, as soon as Clayton got in. Meanwhile, Sergeant Lestrade set Officers Little Bird and Vergucchi, reassigned to this case full time, at work with the telephone directory, phoning every family they could find for the young men on Officer Davenport's list. Then Lestrade sat down to make her own list: the dentists in town.

Little Bird and Vergucchi had found a dozen families and crossed them all off—either the young men were safely accounted for or else they had moved out of state some time ago—by the time Clayton strolled in humming.

Lestrade tapped her fingernail against the bowl of her cherry-wood pipe. Like three-fourths of the floaters who used to carry pipes a dozen years ago when it was the big craze, Lestrade's had never known tobacco. Of all the substitute flavors that were still available, she preferred anise.

"Well, Detective," she greeted him sourly. "Finding murder something to hum about these days?"

He blanked his face at once. "No, Sergeant, sorry. It wasn't the case I was humming about. It was the nurse who just gave me the smoothest flu shot a floater could ask for."

"And you made it to work anyway, a mere —" She glanced at the clock—"seven minutes late. Impressive. I don't even want to know," she added, cutting him off with a wave of her pipe stem. "You like this one that much, save her for when you get off duty. And I had my flu shot a week ago." She stood up, pocketing her list. "Don't bother sitting down, either. We're out to pick up some dentists for body identification."

Holy martyred Silverstairs! Lestrade hated getting people in to identify dead bodies. Whether it was a mere formality or, like now, a necessity.

With the third dentist, they struck paydirt. Dr. Marvella O'Connor stood there a good hundred and twenty seconds, staring down at the face Lotus Blossom Lee had arranged with the expertise of her former life as a mortician's assistant, once Doc Grumeister was through with his so-called examination. "I'm not sure…" the dentist said at last. "It could be… They look so different, don't they? When they're dead."

Even when it had been a peaceful, natural death. Both detectives nodded sympathetically.

"And then, if it is…You understand, I would've known him only as a patient…" Dr. O'Connor stretched her hands out toward the mouth, hesitated, glanced first at Lestrade and then at Clayton. "Do you mind, Detectives? That is, I wouldn't be…corrupting the evidence, or anything?"

"Whatever you need to help us identify him, Doctor," Lestrade replied.

The dentist touched the lips, jerked her hands back from the shock of dead flesh, reached again and, using just her fingertips, eased the mouth open for a look inside. "Ahh!" she breathed. She turned her head to look from a slightly different angle. "Ahh! Yes…yes, I've worked on these teeth. I remember the gap between his upper left lateral incisor and cuspid—tiny, but distinctive. And I put that big filling in the lower right second molar just a few weeks ago. Thought…I thought it'd last him for years. I remember the day he got it, he was talking about maybe getting a real tattoo, if he could figure out a design that'd work for both his Hallowe'en costume this year and the rest of his…life…afterwards. Yes…what was—is?—was?—his name? Sorry, I've got so many patients… Jack… No, Harry…Harry Jackson…Harry Carter Jackson! Oh, dammit to hell, Harry Jackson!"

"Thank you, Dr. O'Connor," Lestrade told her gently. "We'll have to check your dental records for our official books. But when we catch whoever did this, it'll be largely thanks to you. If they still watch us from…whatever name you give it…Harry must be cheering for you now."

"Sergeant Lestrade... They said on the news...it was torture? Not just murder, but..."

"We don't know that for sure," Lestrade replied, swearing the news media out in her mind. "Long as his body lay leaching out in the water, all those marks could just as well have been made post-mortem."

Thank the Lady the damn media had at least cooperated far enough to keep that tattoo out of the news. A secret Lestrade refused to break now. Not even to draw back the white sheet and get the dentist's opinion whether or not it could have been the one the late M. Jackson had talked about maybe getting.

Somehow, she didn't think it was.

* * * *

The body definitely identified, next thing Lestrade did was make a call to Chris Grunewald back in Chicago. Chris was out of town. Some kind of forensic examiners' conference in Denver, followed by a few vacation days to visit a brother in Chillicothe. Try again Thursday.

All right. Body into coldest possible storage for a little longer before it could be released for burial. Another unwelcome job for the family. Who had to be told right now. The "formality" identification.

Of everything Lestrade hated about her workline, this part was the worst. She'd cheated a little by trying to sneak in her call to Chris first. No more excuses to put off notifying the family.

They had a nice house in the Joliet Park area. Turned out the late M. Harry Jackson had been re-alighting at his old home nest while he sent out feelers for a position that could use his brand new Ph.D. in Astrophysics.

The Jackson-Carters had thought their second-born was over-nighting with a young lady downtown. They hadn't started worrying until news of the murder hit the media. Another hour without at least a phone call from Harry, and they'd have called the police station themselves.

People reacted in different ways. Harry's mother turned white, left her husband to ask the usual questions of shock and disbelief and "no possible mistake?" and walked slowly out of the room. To return in a little under ten minutes, carrying a thick book that could have been from Ward and Roebuck but turned out to be a sample book of tattoo designs.

She looked back and forth a couple of times between Lestrade and Clayton before handing her burden to the junior partner. "Just last Wednesday," she told them numbly, "he borrowed this from a local tattoo artist. I don't know which one. We…we've always been tolerant about it, it's so popular what else do you do? but never really interested, nobody else in the family. Except Linda, who got a tasteful little rose last year. Along with the rest of her graduating class. Harry thought he had narrowed it down to Egghead McJones, the solar system as an atom, or…or…"

Linda Jackson of the tasteful rose tattoo supplied, "Or 'Love and Peace' in Elvish script."

"Or 'Love and Peace' in Elvish script. I think he may have decided, forgotten to take the catalog back. It should go back now. This catalog. Harry was always so careful to get his library materials back on time. This should go back, too. I'm sorry, I don't know which…body artist. Somebody local. I know it's somebody local."

They thanked the family, explained about releasing the body as soon as they could…it might be two or three weeks, maybe even as long as a month, but it was absolutely necessary for them to keep it until it could get a second examination. Not necessarily a full autopsy, no, and everything would be kept as integral as possible, but these things needed a second opinion, and it'd be much better if they kept the body now instead of having to exhume it later. Meanwhile, could they have one or two recent photos of Harry?

And, very sorry about this, M.'s, but some member of the family would need to come in to make the formal identification.

Some families liked to hold memorial services right away, even if full interment had to wait.

While Lestrade took her turn driving, Dave sat silently for a couple of miles through city traffic, the sample book in his lap. She knew he didn't like informing the survivors any better than she did. Any polly who liked that duty, wasn't fit to serve as a polly.

At last, halfway to the station, Dave said, "Egghead McJones, the solar system as an atom, or 'Love and Peace' in Elvish script." Her peripheral vision caught his slow headshake. "Nope. I can't connect any of those with the one he actually has."

"I can't either, Dave," said Lestrade. "I can't, either."

* * * *

Chicago had a body artist on every corner, but Forest Green had four to serve the whole town and surrounding area. Tattoos were usually permanent, and people had only so much skin area to cover, no matter how popular good body art might be among about forty percent of the population. And then, there were some groups, like rolegamers, who as often as not preferred the paint-on or peel-off versions, so as to change their body art with the scenario.

Three of the town's body artists were as legitimate as their business. Only two of the fifty-five Reformed States had ever outlawed tattoos—Rhode Island, which probably did it to be quaint, and Texacali, which probably did it to give her tattoo enthusiasts the thrill of mild and harmless lawbreaking.

Lestrade hated having that kind of law on the books. Helped blunt the force of the real laws, the laws every society needed. The law against murder, for one. The law against what had been done to Harry Carter Jackson.

Come to think of it, about the only thing Rosemary Lestrade liked about her workline was getting to clear the occasional innocent party.

Sydney Naismith was known only to his clients and the police. Thirty-eight years ago, when he was starting up in Toronto, he'd been a little too careless about sterilizing his needles, and tattoos had gotten infected. Three people needed hospitalization, one of them died, and Naismith ended up blacklisted for life by the International Association of Body Artists.

Lestrade had decided to tackle Naismith first.

Moving farther and farther down the ladder as his hair got thinner and grayer, he had sunk into a one and a half room basement apartment in what Forest Green liked to think of as its slum district: four square blocks that any self-disrespecting skid row in Chicago or New York would have labeled lower middle-class without a second thought. His bed was a fold-up, his kitchenette was on the street side of his living room, and…

"Where are you hiding the equipment now, M. Naismith? Lestrade asked him, more curious than anything else.

"We know you haven't gone out of business," Clayton added. "We ran one of our regulars in just last week, with a new flower on her ankle in your distinctive lack of style."

"Art. That's why they call it 'body art,' Detective, and I don't like you blighting it just because you don't understand it. That's why I ever got into the business in the first place. To practice art. Then one effing mistake and they try to kick me out for life. You don't bottle art up, Sergeant Hatchet Face." (Lestrade noticed with wry amusement that Naismith had slid from her junior partner to herself without a pause.) "Or it eats you alive from inside out," he went on. "Like it says in the Gospel of Thomas, if you let out what's inside, it'll save you. If you don't, it'll destroy you. I'm an artist, pollies. You want the tools of my art, get yourselves a warrant and search the place. Shouldn't take more than half an hour. Take you longer to get the warrant than it'd take for me to give this dump a whole new paint job, floor to ceiling, maybe put in new wood trim, too."

"I see you still like to go on talking half an hour after making your point," Lestrade told him. "As it happens, today we aren't interested in ferreting you out for the benefit of IABA."

"You're safe enough in this town," Clayton added, "until whatever you let out of you destroys somebody else."

"That was thirty-eight years ago, Pollydeck."

"Make it another thirty-eight, and we'll get you into a museum," said Clayton. "And don't call Sergeant Lestrade 'Hatchet Face.' Here." He produced the sample book. "This yours?"

Naismith took it, riffled through it, shook his head. "Nope. Looks likes what's-his-name's style. Where'd you get it?"

"Turned in at our Lost and Found," Clayton lied easily.

"Well, better try my...colleagues." Naismith said the last word like an insult. "Especially...what's-his-name, the one lording it off uptown."

"Okay, Detective Clayton," said Lestrade. "Show him the design."

They hadn't brought a photograph of the tattoo. A photograph would show part of the dead body. So they'd brought a tracing made from a photograph, using a pencil almost the same shade of blue.

Naismith glanced at the tracing and said, "Looks like one of those effing stamps."

"Took a whole lot of time weighing that decision, didn't you?" Clayton asked him.

"How much time you think it takes to recognize a piece of mass-market crap?"

Lestrade took over again, and deliberately used a term she guessed he wouldn't like, just to feel him out a little more. "And you can tell how it's punched in from a tracing?"

"Why'd any self-respecting body artist take the time to really tattoo anything that's going to end up looking like one more piece of mass-market crap? These stamps, you can call *them* 'punching,' if you want. I'd call it worse. But don't you ever say 'punching' when you're talking about real tattooing. You want respect from me, Pollydecks, you give my art some respect, too."

"I take it," Lestrade commented, "you wouldn't be caught dead using one of these tattoo stamps?"

"Call that respect, Sergeant Hatchet Face? Leonardo ever use rubber stamps in his pictures?"

"Stop calling her —" Dave began, but she caught his eye and shook her head. Let it pass, hot beaver. It isn't that important.

"Then let me put it to you very respectfully," she went on to Naismith, more sternly than respectfully, "you wouldn't make one of these stamps even if somebody requested one? Offered you a lot of money for it? You wouldn't see it as a challenge?"

"I'd see it as an insult. Like I hear you insulting me, Sergeant Hatchet Face." Naismith glanced around at his third-hand furnishings and the pitiful stock of generic canned goods in his open shelves. "But if I ever did make an effing stamp for the money, even if I ever thought getting the equipment to make it would be halfway worth the expense, you can bet it'd have a lot more style than this piece of crap." He took another glance at the tracing and thrust it back at Clayton. "It'd be something you could almost mistake for art. It wouldn't be crap."

Lestrade signaled her partner with a nod.

He held out the two photos they had gotten from the victim's family. "Ever see this floater before?"

Naismith grunted and examined the first photo. Shuffled the second one out on top and examined it as well. Finally shook his head. "Guess I could've seen him around town. Yeah, I get out and around town sometimes. Never been in here to buy any tattoos from me, if that's what you're getting at. Why, what kind of rap you trying to pin on him?"

"Missing person. Just asking everyone we see. Routine. Well, thank you, M. Naismith." Queen Hatchet Face deliberately bestowing mercy on a peasant. "I think that's all. For today. We'll see ourselves out." Standing in the middle of the room, they were all of two steps from the door. Where did Naismith put his clients, whenever he had any?

Once outside, Dave smoothed the tracing out and studied it. "Doesn't look all that bad to me."

"Lady save us from the artistic temperament," said Sergeant Lestrade. "Let's hope the others are practical business people."

CHAPTER 3

STILL MONDAY, SEPTEMBER 18

Closest to Naismith on the town grid was Elias Hammer, who was both legit in every sense and reasonably prosperous, with a two-story building to himself just off the main business district. Parlor downstairs front, looking out on the street like a police interrogation room. Office and supply rooms downstairs back. Living quarters upstairs. Everything clean, neat, and antiseptic as a hospital.

When Clayton gave him the sample book, he hesitated, took a second look at it, and said, "How come you're handling this without gloves, Officers?"

"Offering to let us take your fingerprints, M. Hammer?" Lestrade replied experimentally.

They had in fact dusted the volume, cover and pages, for fingerprints first thing, and had the prints safe on file. But fingerprints helped with identification only when the parties' prints were on record or could be readily supplied for comparison. And there were laws about whose fingerprints the police could take under what circumstances. The mere fact that a victim had borrowed a sample book of tattoo designs shortly before being murdered wouldn't have constituted evidence for demanding to take the prints of any tattoo artist who might be the owner, unless the book had been found on the murder scene, preferably splattered with the victim's blood.

"Sure, Officers," Hammer said with a grin. "I'll let you take my fingerprints if you'll get a tattoo from me."

Clayton said, "Gratis?"

But Lestrade said, "Why would we wear gloves to handle a lost-and-found item?"

"Yeah," her partner hurried to add. "The things people find and turn in at the police station! As long as we were coming out to see body artists anyway, we just thought maybe we could bake two cakes in one oven."

"Yeah, good thought," Hammer agreed. "But what've we done to deserve your attention today, anyway?"

"Just looking for information, M.," Lestrade told him. "What can you tell us about tattoo stamps?"

"Tattoo stamps? As much as any other tattoo artist, probably more than some."

"Not above making the things, then?" she pursued.

"Sure, I make stamps. There's a lot of tridols to be made out of 'em and I'm not above making tridols. Someday I plan on making enough of 'em to move out somewhere as posh as the Dupont-O'Toole establishment."

"Ever seen this one?" Lestrade nodded at Clayton to show him the tracing.

He studied it a long time, glancing back up at the detectives every so often. Finally he handed the paper back and shook his head.

"Not mine, no. Maybe one of O'Toole's. Not Fleur Dupont's, I don't think. Doesn't quite look like her style. Maybe Naismith —"

"Who just told us he never debases his art with stamps," Clayton remarked before Lestrade could cut him off. He was overdue for another dose of Why We Play Our Cards Close to the Chest. Did he have his whole mind on the job this morning? Or was part of it still on that nurse who gave the smoothest flu shots any floater ever enjoyed?

"Naismith told you that?" Hammer was saying. "Don't believe him. He likes to eat. Or that —" He waved at the paper in Clayton's hand—"could be one of those mail-order things. I can't tell you who designed it…if you can call it a design, looks more like a frou-frou for cocktail napkins—but I can give you a guess who'd be likely to use it."

"For cocktail napkins?" Clayton asked, with another look at the tracing.

"Cocktail waitresses?" Lestrade pushed Hammer. "Who?"

"Even a town this size has its population of perverts and smasters, Sergeant. They're the ones you want to be looking hard at when you're looking for murderers. These so-called 'inferno clubbers,' these violent rolegamers—they're the ones you want to be looking at. Hard. Really hard."

Lestrade didn't even cock an eyebrow. "And they'd be likely to buy tattoo stamps, would they?"

"Without even blinking. They like to identify themselves. A different design for every subgroup—subhuman group, I'd call 'em. I've seen a few marked with three or four different stamped tattoos—that's the expression, Detectives: a tattoo stamp makes stamped tattoos—showing themselves off as members of three or four smaster dens, sometimes all at once."

"Hmm," said Lestrade. "Thank you for the tip, M. Hammer. And you've seen these people how?"

"Some of the…some of them come in here to get an old stamp removed or covered up with real tattoo work. And I've also seen them around, Sergeant Lestrade. You wouldn't believe the respectable places—the respectable covers—some of them use to pass themselves off as normal. But once you get an idea where to look, what to look for…" He let his voice trail away.

Lestrade repeated, "Hmm."

Clayton pointed out, "Respectable people get tattoos, too." Lestrade happened to know he himself had Yosemite Pete tattooed on one of his upper arms and Gargoyle Gertie on the other.

"Oh, yeah," Hammer agreed. "Very respectable people. Doctors, bank presidents, school teachers, sweet little debutantes wanting flowerchain necklaces and bracelets in time for the Big Prom. Not many murderers there. The respectable people tend to want real, stencil tattoos."

Lestrade decided to remark, "I hear you saying, Scratch a stamped tattoo and you'll uncover a murderer. So why do you make any of these stamps at all?"

"Hey, Sergeant, I'm sorry if I gave you that impression. I've made 'em for high-school honor societies and graduating classes, service groups, bowling teams, once even a Presbyterian confirmation class, for Pete sakes! No, the stamped tattoos you want to check for murderers are the ones on these young floaters with sick, sick hobbies. I try never to make any for unwholesome types like that, but —" Hammer shrugged—"you never know. One or two might get past me. They can dress up like respectable people, when they want to."

"That's twice you've mentioned murderers," Lestrade observed.

"And I'll go on mentioning 'em until you start finding 'em. If you pollies aren't out looking for whoever murdered that poor kid—what's his name, Jackson?—who's been all over the news today, what the hell are we paying you for?"

"Okay, fair enough." Lestrade gave Clayton a nod to ask his prepared question.

"These stamps, M. Hammer. All the tattoos each one makes are identical as gingerbread bears, but what about the stamps themselves? Are any of them mass-produced?"

"They'd darn well better not be. Not if there's any ethics left in the profession. Even the mail-order houses have got to live up to their promise of 'every stamp unique' if they want to keep their legal standing with IABA."

Lestrade tapped her chin. "Two artists ever come up with the same design by serendipity?"

"Yeah, that'd be possible. Like it'd be possible to find two snowflakes identical. The Association keeps all the legit stamp designs registered to keep accidental duplication from happening, but there could always be a slip-up. Or an illegal copycat rip-off. And the more popular these things get, the more of them get on the market, the more likely you're going to find two exactly alike." Hammer paused. "Of course, sometimes you find two stamps similar enough, you've got to look real close to spot the difference. See here—let's see that one you brought in, again."

Clayton handed the tracing back over. Hammer squinted at it with a deep frown. "Yeah. Yeah, look here. These little lines petaling out. Each one of 'em's got a couple of jags. Like little lightning bolts. Take a swirl with smooth curving lines, or just a single jag per line, and at first glance your average eyeball probably wouldn't pick up on the difference. So round up all the smasters and perverts you can find, but check their symbols real close once you get 'em down to the station house. Not that the whole lot of 'em shouldn't be put away, anyway. Anything else you'd like to ask me?"

Fielding her partner's glance, Lestrade pretended to think for a few seconds. "Yes. Oh, yes. Missing person. We're checking with everybody. Routine. Detective Clayton, show him the photos."

Hammer took them, looked at them. Looked at them very close-ly. Very closely. Gave Lestrade a sharpish glance. Took another long look at the photos. "Still missing, you say?"

"That's right. Ever see him around?"

"Maybe…like you always see people around…but never close enough to say hello. Sorry, Officers, can't help you with this one. But I'll tell you this—he looks like the type perverts and smasters go for. Even in a 'safe' little city like Forest Green. Anything else?"

Lestrade shook her head. "Not at this time. Well, good-bye, M. Hammer. Thank you for your time. We'll remember everything you told us."

* * * *

"Sheboygan!" Dave remarked once they were on the way to their last stop. "I think I preferred Naismith. At least he didn't put most of his energy into badmouthing his list of potential clients."

"Naismith may not have enough clients and potential clients that he can afford to insult any of them." But Lestrade's mind was only half on Sydney Naismith even as she answered Dave's com-ment.

* * * *

The area nowadays called Vadnais Estates had been built in the Gilded Age as the neighborhood of the rich elite. After going through various hard times and slummy generations, it had been reborn, remodeled, redeveloped, repainted in the flower garden of colors they now called the true Victorian fashion, and once again occupied by the richest local elite. "Sheboy!" Dave remarked as they drove through. "Anybody hurting here, they sure don't show it!"

"They might not, Dave. Could be people living in quiet despair here, like anywhere else. Every spare tridol going into keeping up appearances, none into the pantry."

"And if they lose weight, they pass if off as fancy spa treatment they're not really getting?" Dave shrugged. "What price economy? Not all of them, though. Plenty of these have got to be rich in fact. Let's see…" He read the names above the addresses, usually displayed in custom-brass signs. "Lang…Van Geldman…Imani… Fletcher-Symthe… Ah, here they are! Dupont and O'Toole."

One more fenced estate of half a dozen treeful acres. The husband and wife team's tasteful plaque, mounted on their glazed blue brick gatepost, read: "Dupont & O'Toole: Fine Body Art. By appointment only."

"Guess these floaters aren't hurting for tridols, anyway," Dave remarked.

Lestrade replied. "One of them could have inherited wealth, maybe both."

"And they just tattoo for the same reason Narjinski paints and Lulabelle dances?"

"Art is where you find it, Detective." On the gatepost opposite the one with the plaque, Lestrade located an unobtrusive black doorbell button. She tabbed it. If the power line to the front door was still in operation, fine. Otherwise, they'd give it five minutes before walking up unannounced. There was a dog the size of a seeing-eye pony just lying there beneath the birdbath, looking at them lazily. A mixed breed, like ninety-five plus percent of the population, canine and human alike. Lestrade guessed this one was predominantly Labrador and Saint Bernard, spiced with almost everything else in the Big Dog genetic line-up. It looked friendly and, if it wasn't, Dupont and O'Toole were due a crippling fine for leaving their front gate latched instead of key-locked.

"Speaking of body art," she went on to her junior, "when and where did you get yours, Dave?"

"Yosemite Pete to mark my high-school graduation back in Rensselaer, Gargoyle Gertie to celebrate getting out of the Navy. Did you know I've also got a third one, Sarge?"

Hearing a 'bet you can't guess where' implied in his tone of voice, she said, "Ivy vines circling round and round your navel?"

It was pure irony on her part, but he stared openmouthed. "Wow! Sergeant Lestrade, you scare me sometimes."

The dog got up, shook itself, and came over to the gate to lick Lestrade's hand through the wrought-iron grille.

"It isn't ivy," Dave went on. "But it does circle round and round my navel. Actually, it's a dragon spread over my chest with his tail circling around my belly button. Nobody could mistake it for ivy, so I know you didn't sneak my shirt up and spy on me when I was napping. But…sheboy, you guess good!"

"Maybe I just know you better than either one of us was aware, Dave."

Three minutes after Lestrade rang the bell, a mid-age blond woman in brown culottes and a green jacket-blouse with big pockets came strolling down the path and called out to them, "Eet ees by zee appointment onlee."

"We don't need an appointment, M.," Lestrade told her. "We're police detectives on official business."

The dog looked back and forth between them, and whined a little. The blond sped up so fast her phony French accent dropped off. "Good boy, Pango. Officers?" She swung the gate open. "Whatever have we done?"

"Police business includes soliciting expert opinions, M.—Dupont, you'd be?"

She nodded. "Actually, it's Hilga Strudelmeyer. 'Fleur Dupont' is my professional name."

"What about your husband?" Clayton asked. "How many names does he have?"

"Just the one. He really is Lyman O'Toole, all the way through. I'm afraid he's in Indianapolis today, getting supplies."

"We may come back," Lestrade told her, "if we find we need to. Meanwhile…" She tossed a pointed look at the mansion among the trees. Like pretty well every residence in Vadnais Estates, that place had lots of room inside.

"Oh!" said M. Dupont-Strudelmeyer. "May I ask you in? Offer you coffee or…or tea?"

"Coffee will be very welcome, M.," Clayton replied, probably hoping for a sandwich or something else it could wash down.

Pango padded up to the house after them, probably hoping pretty much the same.

Indoors, they sat around coffee and cookies on the table in a breakfast nook big enough for zoning and bright enough for the Fourth of July, looking into a kitchen where every square centimeter that could be stone was marble or highly polished granite, and the rest was stainless steel rubbed down to a soft gleam. Probably kept up by housecleaners coming in at least every other day. Like Clayton had said, big tridols at work here. And Lestrade guessed more of those tridols came from inheritance or shrewd investments or both than from body art, no matter how exclusive and expensive.

Pango lay under the table obviously waiting for crumbs. Very biblical. What was that passage Christians liked to quote? Something about the dogs eating the scraps that fell beneath the table… "All right, Detective Clayton," she said, "we might as well start with our missing person."

M. Dupont-Strudelmeyer gave the photos a polite scrutiny and shook her head, more in helplessness than negation. "I think I've seen someone who might have been him, going into one of the houses where gamers meet. Mostly rolegamers, though the Cartiers host weekly bridge parties and the Orlovskies hold a chess tournament every couple of months. This boy…looks more like one of the rolegamers. One we've seen from time to time during the summer. They have a big rolegaming party at M. Imani's every Sunday, very orderly and well-behaved young people, some oldsters as well. The Langs, and the Forester-Joneses, over on the other side of Vadnais Park, also hold rolegame parties sometimes. But this boy…he just looks like so many other young men his age, doesn't he? You say he's missing? How long?"

"Not long at all, M. Dupont," said Lestrade. "Just long enough to make us ask everyone. Routine. How about clearing our lost and found item out of the way next, Detective Clayton?"

He put the catalog down on the table. The body artist examined it and shook her head. "Not ours. Very neatly done, though. I'd guess M. Hammer's, though it could be M. Naismith's. I'm afraid I don't make as thorough a study of our fellow artists' styles as I probably should. Or it could belong to somebody from out of town."

"Thank you, M. Dupont." Lestrade kept her voice carefully neutral. "Detective Clayton, our last item?"

Again he got out the tracing, unfolded it, and slid it across the marble tabletop to M. Dupont-Strudelmeyer. She picked it up and studied it for several seconds. "My professional opinion on this, Officers?"

"If you'd be so good, M.," Lestrade replied.

"Well…it's pretty enough, but is it Art?"

Lestrade pressed on, "Any thoughts whose style it might be?"

"Any competent tattoo artist could… Some of them might not want to, but almost any of us *could*… I take it this is a— Oh, dear Lord in Heaven!" Dupont exclaimed. "This wasn't—could this be connected to that—that horrible murder just this past wrap-around?"

Seeing Clayton open his mouth, Lestrade beat him to the punch. "We're always investigating several cases at a time, M. Dupont. Even in a town this size. So. Can you rule out any of your fellow body artists who wouldn't soil their hands with something like this?"

"Well, we wouldn't, Ly and I. Fortunately, we have enough money as it is. Unless…" Her hand trembling slightly, she laid the tracing flat on the table and studied it again. "As one element of a larger picture…or even by itself, with a few individualizing touches… Yes, it could have some possibilities, after all."

"Could it be a stamped tattoo?" Clayton asked.

"Certainly. In that case, we couldn't legally use it if we wanted to. Not unless the client already had it and asked us to incorporate it into a larger picture. All stamp designs are registered."

"How do you check?" Clayton said curiously.

The body artist sighed. "With great difficulty, Officers, with great difficulty. The literature speculates that someday we may have electronic brains to file and sort through things like this automatically, but for here and now I'm afraid it's still pretty much the old honor system. Resting mainly on what the client tells us. And since these stamps became so popular, the annual IABA directory has gotten as thick as the New York phone books."

Lestrade asked, "Anything to stop an individual artist from turning out two identical stamps of his or her own design?"

Dupont-Strudelmeyer took a minute to answer that one. "Not legally, I don't think. No, the design would be the individual artist's, to re-use at will. It'd be more a matter of commercial ethics. You wouldn't want to annoy any client who bought a stamp from you by selling one with the identical design to another client."

"Not even two officers of the same club?" asked Clayton.

"Well…a case like that could be an exception…but I still don't think it'd be very wise. Any kind of a club or association can break up, and then you could see rival organizations wearing the same design. No…it might work for something like a graduating class, where the membership never changes no matter what internal politics may develop. Then you might see two or three identical stamps—say, one for the class president and one for the faculty advisor. But otherwise…you've got to understand, Officers, you've caught me more or less in a blind spot here. Ly and I don't design stamps, don't even have the right equipment."

"But you do have those annual directories?" Lestrade wanted to know.

Dupont sighed. "Yes, we've got the directories. IABA guide-rules. Every year adds more designs, and once they're there, they're there forever."

"How do you keep updated on the designs being made between editions?" Clayton rubbed Pango behind the ears.

"Honor system," Dupont repeated.

"You might get a 'Friendly Dog' sign for your gate," Lestrade observed.

"We have one. We decided to take it down after somebody was murdered here in Forest Green. We've even talked about getting a watchdog that isn't so friendly."

"Let's not panic, M. And we'd like to borrow your latest direc-tory." Lestrade didn't make it a question.

She noticed Clayton smothering a sigh, probably thinking he was going to end up checking the thing page by page. Well, maybe she'd help him out there. She didn't have anything more important in her plans for this evening, and he was hoping to snag a quick date. Talking about this nurse he'd just met, the one who gave flu shots so smoothly a floater didn't even feel it.

CHAPTER 4

STILL MONDAY, SEPTEMBER 18

Julie Whitcomb lived alone in a moderately priced four-room apartment in Pankhurst Heights, one of Forest Green's most respectable upper middle-class neighborhoods. The Pankhurst Arms—lodge-style lounge, changing rooms, and bar downstairs, four tidy apartments upstairs—was a piece of pleasantly retro-style architecture only two degrees removed from imitation Frank Lloyd Wright, set down with an artificial pond pretending to be a lake on one side and a small but rolling park on the other three. "Pankhurst Lake" really could accommodate rafting and oar-boating, though neither full-sized sailboats nor anything motorized. They even kept it stocked with pan fish. Both pond and park were free and open to the entire Pankhurst Heights subdivision: four blocks of duplexes and single-family residences on each side of the park.

Thirty years ago, Pankhurst Heights had been both posh and somewhat less respectable than it was today, with—local legend whispered—a high-class courtesan house in the building that had been "saved," like any other poor sinner, into a nondenominational community church with angels in stained glass windows and a real organ. Thirty years ago, Julie Whitcomb could never have afforded an apartment in the Pankhurst Arms. The big reason she could afford it now was because activities in the lodge lounge and bar just below the apartments, as well as Theater in the Park and the various school picnics, family reunions, summertime rowboat races and wintertime skating parties, Fourth of July and New Year's Eve fireworks over the pond, and so on, while good, clean family fun, were both frequently scheduled and frequently on the raucous side. Not like the weekly wraparound activities at Sam's house, which never disturbed the neighbors.

Also, the management gave Julie an additional discount because, as a trained nurse, she could be on call in case of need for these races and parties and other affairs, whenever she got enough advance notice to juggle it with her hospital hours.

Her life sometimes made it challenging to sandwich in her Life, but what was Life without a challenge?

Anyway, someday—probably soon, seeing she was already twenty-seven—her prince would come and she'd leave all this behind, both life and even some of Life, without a second thought, move on to her next incarnation as wife and, sweet Jesus willing, mommy.

Maybe that prince of hers had come already. Not, of course, Paul Osaka, who had the apartment catacorner to hers. He was a great floater, only he swang the other way; and, besides, Dante's Delight Purgatorio had its guiderules, which let out Sam as well. But maybe, just maybe, the one she'd met this morning... Well, if not, she'd give that prince just six more years to reach her. If he didn't, at the symbolic age of thirty-three she was phasing on alone if necessary: adopt an orphan or two grown to the age where they were hard to place, maybe get herself artificially inseminated, find a bigger apartment or even a nice little house...sweet Jesus knew where she'd get the money, but sweet Jesus should know, providing for the birds of the air and the lilies of the field and all that!

And then, she'd already budgeted and bought the last big expense she expected to want until age thirty-three, anyway.

She closed her bedroom drapes, turned on her nightstand lamp, peeled off her garments down to the last stitch, and studied her naked body in the mirror. Not that it actually looked naked any longer. Not since a month and a half ago. Her fellow Purgatorians understood; Curly even approved. Not that Sam or Paul would ever see the whole thing in all its glory. That was reserved to serious candidates for her prince.

A blue and crimson dragon, puffing out roses and daisies instead of flames, rose up across her belly to her breasts, the tip of his pointed tail just touching her pubic nest, while his wings shelled her nipples and continued around her torso to her back, where they helped disguise her scars, at least to sight. The symbol of Dante's Delight danced with its lower half resting in an interlinked host of blue snowflakes and frostlike patterns that wove from just above her right breast, around her upper arm, and back across her shoulder blade, incorporating more of the old scars, left from before they'd gone over exclusively to rubber hoses and beading needles. And high time, too! The bodies of those earlier Purgatorians must have ended downright embarrassing after years of scourges, votive flames, and the woodcutting tool they used to use for the old scarification symbol, before they intelligently went to a stamped tattoo.

Julie smiled. These last five had been good years, useful years, and she felt she'd done her little part in polishing the old Purgatorio and its good work. Still, she was definitely feeling the need to move on. She might not even stay with it all the way to age thirty-three, whether her prince showed up or not. But that meant they really needed someone to replace her. Four was the minimum functional membership, six the maximum—on paper. They'd never actually had six in practice. Five, once, for a while, but that had been before her time.

When her prince showed up, she'd know. She'd know by the way he looked at her naked for the first time and saw, not a one-night stand, but a good piece of art on a body he would be proud and happy to spend the rest of his natural life with. For his eyes and hers only, from that hour on.

She patted the still-blank hollow between her collarbone and left breast. This area, she was saving for when she had her prince to decide what should grace it. Maybe by then she'd be able to afford—or maybe he'd afford it as a wedding gift—to go to the very best, to Dupont and O'Toole, who attracted clients from all over the fifty-five states.

Her phone chimed. She hurried over and snatched it up from the nightstand. "Hello?... Oh, yes! Oh, yes, I remember you..."

A long exchange of smalltalk-type feelers. She was amazed, glancing at the clock, to see it had lasted almost ten minutes. Then:

"Yes, yes, I think I can make it tonight.... Scoops and Bottles? Fine!... Yes, I know the place, it's very versatile. Ideal for a first date.... You know, I always like to go doubles on a first date.... No, you can leave that to me. I'm sure I can line someone up on short notice.... Yes, yes, I've done it before. My friends know me."

After another several minutes of sweet talking about how she'd better get busy lining up that double date before the notice got *too* short, she finally signed off with him.

"My prince?" she wondered again, cradling the phone receiver. Cautious, girl! You've been stung before. That's the reason for doubling on the first date, also for leaving each potential prince on the doorstep until at least the second date. If he *was* the prince, he'd call for date number two. If he didn't, he wasn't.

Now, who could she recruit this time? She thought Sam met with his Shriners gang on Monday evenings. Curly tended to be a little too boisterous for times like these. Paul's apartment was just down the hall, and he never minded going with Lizette or Pearl for the sake of appearances and good conversation.

Or... Julie exchanged a grin with herself...why not bake two cakes in one oven? She looked up the number, lifted the receiver again, and dialed.

* * * *

Should she get a place of her own here in her old home town...a large apartment or tidy little bungalow for one...and maybe find some kind of service job? Money was not a problem for the Garvey-Johansens, but idleness was, at least for a person like Angela, who liked to feel both busy and of some social usefulness.

She'd had some thought of...but now it appeared to be just as well she'd never hinted anything about that. Maybe if she'd come home to Forest Green right away after graduation, hadn't left him all summer to get acquainted with Julie... Well... Friends, best friends—she hoped, for life. Don't spoil it by reaching for anything else. Besides... Best friends was good. Very good. And he had been fine as Raggedy Andy. She couldn't help chuckling when she thought about that game...

Just then, the phone chimed.

"Hello?" she cried, snatching up the receiver. "Angela here.... Raggedy Andy? I was just thinking about you.... Yes, it does resemble mental telepathy, doesn't it?... Tonight?" (Too eager? Too flustered-sounding?) "...Oh, oh, I see.... Oh, yes, yes, I can stop by for you at eighteen hundred hours.... Yes, it'll be nice to see Scoops and Bottles again. Is that place still as good as it used to be?... They've actually improved it? Oh, I can't wait!... Yes, as you say, 'copacetic.'... Well, good-by for now, I'll see you in—oh, my, in less than an hour!... Yes, yes, I'm as good as ready now. See you soon."

She cradled the receiver, stood for a moment with her hand resting absently on the telephone, and heaved a great huge sigh, just as Aunt Sally came into the living room.

"Who was that, Angie?"

"Corwin."

"Oh, good. He's a nice boy—young man, I should say."

"No, Aunt Sally, I think maybe we should stick with 'boy.' But, yes, he is nice. A little strange. But...nice."

"Well, they say that no males and only ten percent of all females ever really grow up. What was he calling about?"

"He asked me to go out with him and Julie and a floater named Dave Clayton. A sort of blind date for me. I've never met this Dave, but Cory said he's a police detective, so it should be very safe. Besides, Cory will be with us. And Julie Whitcomb. So I told him I'd go. We're going to Scoops and Bottles. We're all meeting there at eighteen hundred thirty. I'm picking Cory up at the Marquette House. "

"Angie, are you sure *you're* the one they've set up with this Officer Dave...Clayton?"

"Oh, yes, Aunt Sally, I must be. Cory and Julie hit it off so perfectly yesterday at that stupid Spanish Inquisition rolegame."

"But are you *really* sure? How, exactly, did Corwin phrase it?"

Angela closed her eyes and concentrated. "Well...let me see... 'I am the recipient of an urgent supplication'—you know Cory—'from M. Julie Whitcomb, under immediate pressure for a second lady to assist one David Clayton, police detective, herself, and me in comprising a congenial foursome this evening.'"

"And you're sure that was the order he named you all in?"

"Yes...yes, reasonably sure."

"Well," said Aunt Sally, "to me, it sounds a little ambiguous. As if the one they've set up with Dave is this Julie...?"

"Whitcomb, Aunt Sally. Julie Whitcomb. Oh, if you'd seen them yesterday, you wouldn't be in any doubt. I think they must have been made for each other!"

"And yet, didn't you tell me that he got out of that game shortly after you'd left it yourself?"

"Only because it tickled his fancy to be the first inquisitor caught out as a secret heretic and tortured and burned to death. That was the way he was playing it from the very start of their stupid game, before I even left it."

"And promptly came over to join your Raggedy Ann scenario?"

"As Andy. Raggedy Andy." Angela sighed again. (She would *not* cry, not about this!) "Best friends."

Good old Angela—he'd never word it like that, of course, but that'd be the boiled-down gist—here's a nice, staid, respectable, maybe slightly boring polly who should make the perfect blind date for good old Angela. Yes, she could easily imagine Julie Whitcomb wording it something like that. "Best friends," she repeated to herself in a whisper as she headed for her guest room, not to change, exactly. To re-accessorize. "Best friends for life. Like brother and sister. That's better than nothing."

It might even turn out to be better than whatever Corwin thought of as hot romance. Did she even want to know?

She was already wearing her apple-green trousers and tunic, with lightly flaring legs and sleeves. She took off her daytime headband and substituted one of pale gold wire mesh with an enamel Mourning Cloak butterfly on each side—very fetching against her blond hair, which was almost exactly the same color as the gold wire. She shed the white silk scarf at her throat and replaced it with her favorite pin-necklace: a white kitten on each of her collar points, the one on the right fondling a ball of yarn and the one on the left holding one paw out to catch it, with the "yarn" stretching loosely between the kittens, glowing because it was strung with pearls only just large enough for the bead holes. She exchanged her white leather belt for a golden yellow silk sash. Last, she changed from white shoes with laces into white driving slippers. No high heels. She didn't even own a pair of high heels. She didn't intend to throw her body out of alignment and have later-life problems because of it. Besides, Cory was one point six eight meters tall, and she was one point six five.

Julie Whitcomb had been wearing spike heels in red Sunday. It had made her taller than him, and he didn't seem to mind.

Well, there was still the danger of later-life posture problems.

Julie was a nurse, wasn't she? If high heels posed a health danger, shouldn't she be aware of it? Or did nurses think they were immune and could do anything when they were off duty?

Angela threw one glance at her reflection in the full-length mirror. One point six five meters of slim blond woman—very wholesome, very girl-next-door—dressed well enough for a blind date at Scoops and Bottles, unless the place had grown a lot more formal than it used to be.

* * * *

She knew that once Patrice Davison Hawthorne and Mike Olmstead Dickinson—Corwin's "mater" and "pater"—had seen their first child, Corinna Olmstead Casanova, safely settled down in Arbor City as a University of Michiana librarian, and their second, Corwin, safely graduated from Astoria State, they had taken off on a world tour for their "second" (actually about their fifth) honeymoon. Money was maybe even less of a problem for the Davison-Olmsteads than for the Garvey-Johansens.

Angela had known the pleasant Davison-Olmstead family home in the Joliet Park area almost as well as her own, but had not yet had a chance to see the apartment where Corwin was living for at least as long as his parents took exploring the world: two years or longer, if they chose. After what she had seen of the newly graduated Corwin so far this fall, she approached his door just a little apprehensively.

Instead of his name, the sign on his door, right above the lion's-head brass knocker, read: "Arnheim." At least it didn't read "The Dungeon" or something like that. She lifted the ring in the lion's mouth and dropped it against the sounding plate, once, twice —

And the door was open, and he was smiling at her. "How expeditiously you located me! And how exquisitely those sable-hued butterflies set off your hair, how congenially the kittens disport themselves on either point of your collar! Have you a moment to glance over my perhaps temporary abode?"

He seemed eager, and she didn't see anything so very lurid or "outre" over his shoulder, so she said, "I'd be delighted, Cory," and went in.

To see at a glance that it wasn't at all what she had feared it might be. The walls and ceiling were painted a sort of silver-gray like mother-of-pearl, the carpet was one of the richest greens she had ever seen, the couch and chairs were rattan with bright gold cushions, there was a round rattan coffee-table that held a few leather-bound books almost glowing in the soft light of a Tiffany lamp. In front of the white drapes along the far wall, one of those miniature waterfalls kept the water circulating in an aquarium of goldfish, seaweed, and white sand at the bottom. Surrounding the aquarium, Corwin's old bonsai collection, still alive and, she thought, expanded, grew like a tiny forest, with more ordinary houseplants—geraniums, ferns, azaleas, coleus, and so on—crowding one another in a healthy-looking way on the floor around the aquarium table's legs. Beside and above it, a canary sang in a large white cage. The mantelpiece over the gas fireplace held a row of clothbound books between one bookend with a small antiqued globe of the earth and a matching bookend with a globe of the night sky. A small, antique roll-top desk held the phone beside the doorway to the apartment's back rooms. The pictures on the walls were Currier and Ives landscapes.

"Kept in order," Corwin explained, "by thrice-weekly visitations of the Vermeer Domestic Service. They minister to my rooms each Monday, Wednesday, and Friday, in return for which invaluable service I endorse their enterprise whenever opportunity presents itself." He went on, indicating the canary, "Not 'Nevermore'—as being a bird of quite a different feather than a raven—but 'Evermore.' With an additional courtly bow to Longfellow's 'Birds of Killingworth': 'Somewhere the birds are singing evermore.' And here —" He scooped up a tortoiseshell tabby who had appeared out of somewhere, "soliciting in her aloof feline fashion the favor of an introduction to you, is my estimated Caterina, veteran of Forest Green's highly-to-be-recommended Animal Shelter."

"Very pleased to meet you, Caterina." Angela stroked the tabby's soft head. Caterina yawned, purred, and snuggled into the crook of Corwin's arm. Angela took another long look around the apartment.

"Cory, it's—it's beautiful!"

Maybe he heard surprise and relief in her voice, because he answered her with an ironical half-smile, "You anticipated, perhaps, metal-plated walls 'rudely daubed in all the hideous and repulsive devices to which charnel superstition has given rise,' with a circular black rug in the center symbolizing a pit, a scimitar-pendulum depending from the ceiling in lieu of chandelier, table of rough-hewn lumber bedecked with various species of restraints, papered floor-border thick with portraitured rats, the whole illuminated only by the fitful and wavering glare of thick black candles?" He shook his head. "Such scenes are well enough to while away the coveted idle hour, but not to reside within clockround."

"But all this —" She made a gesture to take in the whole room. "It just doesn't look very Poesque, somehow."

"Oh, Angela, let me reassure you that in fact it is. Not slavishly, I confess, but in spirit, which is why I style it 'Arnheim.' The Venerable Edgar did not dwell exclusively in settings of horror and decay, as popular opinion would have it. He was—or would have been, if in possession of sufficient pecuniary resources—a well-rounded gentleman of wide-ranging literary tastes, with a keen appreciation of both the sublime and the ridiculous. Alas, his works in the former category tend to be overlooked *in toto*, and those in the latter all too often misread utterly by persons determined that if Edgar Poe wrote it, it *must* be horrific in sober earnest, no matter its clearly humorous extravagances.— I have been soapboxing, dear Raggedy. Why did you not remind me of the hour?"

"You were doing it so well, Cory. I almost understood most of it. You should be a professor."

"I should bore half my class into cherubic slumber, whilst maintaining the other half in wondering suspense as to what strange foreign tongue, nameless to their syllabi, I was employing in my lectures."

"Well, Cory, as nearly as I've figured your rules out, they include: Never use a three-syllable word when you can find one of four or five syllables that works almost as well, and never miss a chance to throw in a long or unusual modifier whether you really need one or not."

Grinning, he spread his hands and replied, "What can I do save plead extenuating circumstances? I relish words." Tossing Caterina gently onto the cushion of the wicker chair, where she curled up, meowed, and set to licking her paw, Corwin offered Angela his arm. "Madam Raggedy Ann, shall we venture forth to our joint assignation?"

CHAPTER 5

STILL MONDAY, SEPTEMBER 18

Dave Clayton had been right on time. Julie liked that in a man. They got to Scoops and Bottles and chose a table for four where she had a clear view of the door. He wouldn't have known so well who to watch for, never having to the best of his knowledge met either of the others socially; when off-duty, the best of pollies was no more omniscient than anyone else. While they waited, Dave entertained Julie by spearing a couple of toothpicks into mint-jelly beans from the courtesy dish on the table and making them "dance" on the tabletop, twirling and kicking like tiny legs. Something he'd seen, he said, in an evening course he'd taken a couple of years ago in classic cinematic literature.

Another point in his favor. She liked cine-lit, too. It was so graphic, such a solid diving board for the imagination.

She happened to look up just as Corwin and Angela came through the door. Another instance of E.S.P.? "Ah, here they are now," she told Dave as she half stood and waved her arm to catch their attention.

It worked at once. Threading their way through the crowded sweet bar and grill, they soon arrived at the right table. "Angela, Corwin," she began the introductions, "meet David Clayton. Dave, Angela Garvey, M. Corwin Poe."

"Angela" he replied, half rising to shake hands. "Honored. 'Angie' to your friends? M. Poe?"

"It is a privilege and an honor to make your acquaintance, sir," Julie's prospective recruit replied, somehow making the outdated formula sound cordial. "And 'Corwin' will be fine."

Angela, meanwhile, after glancing around the table, seated herself opposite Julie, at Dave's other hand. Angela really was a dear, sweet little thing, thought Julie: fresh, clean, and wholesome as a spring morning in a meadow. The kind of dear child you simply wanted to hug and protect forever from hurting or being hurt. The kind any nurse would inject as smoothly and painlessly as possible, without even asking.

Corwin, now. Him she would ask first, and wouldn't feel at all surprised if he said, "Rough, if you would kindly be so accommodating." Which might not fit the needs of Dante's Delight so well, after all. Since nobody was here for flu shots or blood draws, and she was as much off duty as a nurse, as Dave was as a pollydeck, she would have to feel out her potential recruit with conversational clues.

They placed their orders: for Julie, mixed salad with cilantro chicken and a glass of white wine; for Angela, a shrimp omelet with a glass of iced tea and a chocolate soda to follow; for Corwin, filet mignon rare and V-9 juice on the rocks, to be followed by the establishment's featured ice cream drink of the day; for Dave, the half-pound house specialty cheeseburger and whatever Chinese beer they had on tap.

Julie liked to see her dates enjoy their food, and a lot of it. It gave her a sort of vicarious pleasure. It also suggested a hearty appetite for other things…though she always saved that for at least the second date. If he looked like a really strong candidate for her prince, she would test by making him wait until date number three.

She thought Dave Clayton looked like a solid third-date candidate. He made her laugh. He made them all laugh, telling jokes like a stand-up comedian while somehow making his meal disappear without ever letting a bite get in the way of a punch line.

Yes, he did monopolize the mealtime chit chat, a little, but nobody complained or seemed to mind. The jokes were too good and he told them too well. After one especially humorous shaggydog, Angela remarked that he should be doing this some place that had a fifty-tridol cover charge, and how lucky they were to be getting the floor show free.

"Why, shucks, ma'am," he drawled in stage-comic Western, "keepin' jest too blame busy with mah reg'lar workline." It was the closest anyone had yet come to the subjects they had banned for the duration: their workhour occupations, and the weekend's sad local news.

This was one of the best rules for life that the Purgatorio had taught Julie: no grave conversation at mealtime.

They saved more serious sessioning for over their coffee cups, when the minted jelly beans were the only solid foodstuff remaining on their table, and the other tables were starting to empty without being re-occupied. Then Julie remembered she also had designs, of quite a different kind, on the other fellow at the table, and turned to ask him, "So tell me, Corwin, are you really a universalist, or was that only part of your Don Serafino character?"

"Don Serafino character?" said Dave.

"In a rolegame they were playing last night," Angela told him, her voice studiously neutral. "Spanish Inquisition."

"Hmm," said Dave. "I enjoy a good game myself, now and then. But give me Mount Doom or Star Trek or good, old-fashioned Dens and Dragons like they played it when I was a boy, back when we called the dragons 'dinosaurs' and watched 'em trample our lawns."

"Oh, Dave," Angela protested. "You can't be as ancient as all that. I'll bet you aren't even thirty!"

"Twenty-eight," he grinned. "But I've got a long white beard for when I play Gandalf. If I happen to have it with me at the time the game strikes."

"In my observation," Corwin interjected, "twenty-eight may prove a perilous age of life, fraught with angst and a nattering sense of calendrical time marching inexorably on, to leave oneself stranded on the barren shores of unfulfillment."

"And you would know this, how?" Dave asked, eyeing the last speaker whimsically. "You're all of—what—twenty-three? Twenty-two?"

Corwin inclined his head. "To the charge of excessive youth, I must plead guilty as charged and fling myself on the leniency of the court. You were—presumably—twenty-two yourself once on a time, in the dim light of the primordial dawn. I base my hypothesis on painstaking attention to divers instructors encountered during my late, unlamented collegiate career."

"None of which," said Julie, "answers my original question. Well, Don Serafino?"

Looking like he had lost track of her original question, Corwin took a sip of coffee and, seeing that they all remained silently waiting, replied, "For the sake of filling what appears to be one of those curious periodic cessations occasionally befalling even the most animated of conversations… Yes, I suppose I must likewise plead guilty to entertaining a somewhat universalist outlook. Not—please understand—that I should ever argue, as Don Serafino might, the notion that some quality in ourselves obligates our Creator to save all of us in despite of our sins; but that I cleave to the more orthodox conception that the Divine Mercy might not elect of Its Own free will to maintain us in existence for the sake of subsequently damning any portion of us to an eternal perdition of unspeakable and horrific pain."

"You're very lucky," Dave remarked, "or very lacking in imagination, if you've never run up against the hard cold fact that there are some scuzzballs in this world who deserve eternal horrific pain."

Seeing how close the conversation was skirting to the murdered body found yesterday, Julie held her breath. None of them spoke for a heartbeat or two.

At last the younger man inclined his head again and said, sounding apologetic, "It would be grave presumption to deny the actual existence of Hell. But may I nevertheless entertain some hope that the damned are tortured, not by God, but by one another, of their own free choice?"

Julie held back a grin. Yes, maybe they could work with this one.

"Yeah," Dave was saying, "okay, I might be able to go along with that. More or less. But look here. If God is maintaining us all in existence every minute continuously, why doesn't God just stop maintaining the scuzzballs, let them fall apart into nonexistence?"

Angela said, "Where would it stop? 'In the worst of us, a seed of good—in the best, a seed of bad.'"

"'The purest soul may yearn for blood, the sanest go a little mad,'" Julie finished the famous quotation. "Gilbert and Sullivan's last, most serious, and some say greatest, 'The Drood Solution.'"

"Well, if we're onto Gilbert and Sullivan," Dave said, and proceeded to sing in a nice light baritone, "'When the felon's not engaged in his employment—his employment—or maturing his felonious little plans—little plans—his capacity for innocent enjoyment—'cent enjoyment—is just as keen as any honest man's."

Everybody still left in the restaurant, diners and staff alike, applauded.

Dave having left off, Corwin continued, speaking, "'When the hatter's finished jumping on his mother, he loves to lie a-basking in the sun'—a reference, no doubt, to some notorious contemporary episode since fallen into profound obscurity."

Dave sang again. "'Ah, take one consideration with another—with another—a policeman's lot is not a happy one.'" Speaking again, "But that's the only Gilbert and Sullivan I know. I sang the Sergeant of Police in a college production. Back when we had all that trouble with dinosaurs trampling our lawns. You know, 'The Pirates of Penzance' is too strong for the Old Woman—that is, my immediate superior—that is, a certain impressive lady I know. Who doesn't want any kind of entertainment that has anything at all to do with crime or criminals. No matter how light and innocent."

Corwin opined, "I find that admirable in its way, little as I might personally care to emulate her obvious nobility of soul. Wait! I have perchance encountered her at the Wallace Public Library. A statuesque woman of encroaching maturity, hazel eyes, dark brown hair besprent with silver, nobly sculpted features and dignified mien?"

"Sounds like her," Dave replied. "Just a hint—don't put it that way to her face. She'd call it flattery, and she can't stand flattery. What kind of books was she checking out?"

"Light and frolicsome volumes replete with pleasantries and notable artwork."

"Well, okay," Dave went on, apparently sensing he wasn't going to get any further hints about the Old Woman's reading tastes. "But I still don't see...all right, admitting all this philosophy about a seed of bad in the best of us...so why can't this merciful God just stop holding the bad seeds in existence, make all of us good all the way through?"

"Oh, how boring!" For the first time that evening, Julie felt just a little twinge of doubt as to whether Dave could really be her prince. "I mean—that is—yes, dissolve the really evil stuff, Dave, by all means, but leave us a few little streaks of...mischief. Just enough to keep life interesting." And you on a regular payroll, she added to herself.

Angela said, "Wouldn't fires and floods and tornadoes, accidents and diseases and other things like that be enough to keep life interesting?"

Corwin began quoting, softly at first, his voice gradually gaining power:

> *"...In me lived a sin*
> *So strange, of such a kind, that all of pure,*
> *Noble, and knightly in me twined and clung*
> *Round that one sin, until the wholesome flower*
> *And poisonous grew together, each as each,*
> *Not to be pluck'd asunder.'"*

"As nearly as I can follow that," said Dave, "it's gobbledygook."

"It is Tennyson," Corwin answered quietly. "His *Idylls of the King: The Holy Grail*. You see, I am capable of quoting other authors besides the Venerable Edgar."

"Tennyson or not," Dave persisted, "it's still gobbledygook."

"Oh, I understand it," Julie said, looking at Corwin and thinking, Yes, I really think here's one we can work with.

"And I'm with Angela here," Dave went on. "Natural disasters, accidents, and sicknesses would give us all plenty of excitement, without the crime and moral guilt. You should know that, Julie."

"I should," she agreed before he could break their rule against mentioning worklines, "and maybe I do. But if we never knew anything about crime, Dave, we wouldn't be able to enjoy 'The Pirates of Penzance' or 'The Drood Solution' or most of Shakespeare, or almost any of the world's great literature. You can't make very many good jokes and witticisms about cancer and tuberculosis, or even about broken arms."

"As...that lady I know...would say, 'And you can about crime?'"

"Well, not about real crimes," Julie backed down a little. "Not about crimes that really hurt real people. But about crimes that everybody sees are never going to be committed..."

"Or ludicrous mock-illegalities," Corwin added. "*Exempli gratia*: flirting in Titipu, or 'forging one's own will.'"

"Or—sometimes—things that happened in ancient history?" Angela suggested. "No," she corrected herself at once, "I guess we probably shouldn't joke about those, no matter how long ago they happened, or far away."

Gazing at Angela, Corwin said, "Unless, indeed, the humor is utilized as psychomystical methodology for coping with the horror."

"Well, all right," Dave argued, "why couldn't our knowledge of crime be completely historical?"

Julie said, "People forget."

"Moreover," said Corwin, "our own milieu will relegate itself to the historical tomes of subsequent generations. What grounds may we claim for appropriating to ourselves privileges denied our ancestors?"

"The grounds that we should've learned better by now," said Dave.

"We do forget," Angela said, returning to Julie's last comment. "That's why we have to take years of courses in social history before we can really understand the ancient Romans, for instance, or the Bible."

"Or even the near-contemporary era of our own parents' juvenile days," said Corwin. "Although, as touching the scriptural documents of the various religious persuasions, a certain degree of re-interpretation, even re-symbolization, would appear not only permissible, but actually commendable. I should propose, as one example among many, the Crucifixion and Resurrection as a remarkably apt template of the shamanic initiation of Christ the Great and Wounded Healer."

Oh, yes, thought Julie, we can definitely work with this one.

* * * *

Only yesterday, while they were all roleplaying so happily at Sam Imani's, that horrible murder had been discovered just on the other side of town. So Angela took full advantage of her driver's seat and drove right on past Aunt Sally's to drop Corwin off.

"This cuts both ways," he argued. "Are you to wet-nurse my security, and I to be prohibited against concerning myself with yours?"

"It's only twenty-one thirty, Aunt Sally's house has a built-on garage with an automatic door opener, and I'll drive with all my car doors locked. You'd want to sit visiting with us for a couple of hours—keeping me up past my preferred bedtime, I might add—and then walk home melodramatically at midnight."

"And you would prefer not to sit visiting so much as half an hour in Arnheim? Caterina would be yours to stroke for the duration, dear Raggedy Ann. She evinced an immediate affection for you."

Fighting off temptation, Angela gave a determined shake of her head. "No, I'll just watch from the car till you're safely inside."

"Where, peradventure, the heinous monster lurks concealed amidst the interior shadows, awaiting his newest victim."

"Cory, don't make jokes about it!"

"Forgive me," he said at once in a properly chastened voice. "Certainly, it was no joke to M. Jackson." The victim's name had finally been mentioned on the afternoon news. "Let us employ your schema, then," Corwin went on, "with the unique proviso that you telephone the moment you are safely inside, with all doors leading to the exterior securely locked and bolted, and Aunt Sally in the kitchen—should she so elect—preparing bedtime cocoa."

"You have a deal," Angela agreed. "It'll have the lagniappe—you aren't the only one who knows a few fancy words—of reassuring me that the heinous monster wasn't lurking in the shadows waiting for you, after all."

She pulled to the curb in front of the Marquette House and parked the car. It was now, or never. "Oh, and Cory…"

"I attend your forthcoming utterance with bated breath."

"Cory…please…don't set me up with any more blind dates."

"Angela?" By the bafflement in his tone, he must have been so pleased with himself, so sure he'd found exactly the right man for her!

"Dave Clayton is really very nice," she hurried to add. "I never meant to imply he wasn't! It isn't that at all. I'm sure he'll make a wonderful prize for some other woman. He just…doesn't appeal to me, not that way. And…some people don't like surprise parties… I simply don't like blind dates. I never have, not really."

"I…see," Corwin replied slowly. "That is… Yes, certainly, I perceive the inexorable justice of your point, and accede as gracefully as possible to your wishes. I hypothesize that I can confidently indemnify you against ever finding yourself alone on a solo date with the much-to-be-pitied M. David Clayton."

She heard the handle chunk as he turned it to open the passenger-side car door. It was on the edge of her tongue to say, Why don't you speak for yourself, John Alden? But Corwin was Julie's romantic prize. Julie was such a perfect match for him! And Julie obviously thought so, too— Angela had seen the way she kept eyeing him. So all she said this time was, "Before you go, Andy, how about a good-night kiss, Raggedy style?"

He paused in the middle of opening the car door. "Sisterly and brotherly?"

"Best friends-ily."

He leaned over and kissed her forehead. She kissed his cheek. Then, just barely touching, they exchanged one kiss on the lips. Light as it was, Angela felt a warm deep stirring and thought, Oh, darn it anyway! Why *Julie*?

Then he was out of the car, up the walk…he reached the door, went in…after a dozen heartbeats, he leaned back outside and gave her an "all safe" kind of wave.

She felt that he went on watching until her car was out of sight around the curve. She would give him that phone call the minute she reached Aunt Sally's.

* * * *

Julie and Dave had driven their own separate cars and met at Scoops and Bottles. When the foursome finally separated to go their different ways, Dave turned up waiting in the Pankhurst Arms parking lot when Julie drove in.

She parked beneath one of the lamp posts, got out, and stood leaning against the closed door of her old red Ford. He got out of his Nash Rambler and crossed over to join her.

"Well, Dave?" she remarked, looking up at him. She was fairly tall, especially in her spike heels, but he was taller. The lamplight, half behind his head, haloed his sand-brown hair; and while she couldn't see the color of his eyes—had to go by the memory that they were gray—she could see them shining.

"Well, Julie?" He seemed to be appraising her the way she was appraising him.

Then, just like that, they were kissing. Tight in each others' arms, and enjoying long, deep, tongueful kisses.

The first time they came up for breath, she said, "How did you beat me here? Come to think of it, how did you know where to come?"

"Hey, darling, I'm a pollydeck. We know how to use city directories. We also know all the short cuts."

"Good enough for me."

Another kiss. This time, even longer and deeper. Eventually one of his arms loosened from around her shoulders, snaked in between their two bodies, found her breasts…

What would he think, she wondered, this fine, upstanding, straight-arrow police detective, if he could see what she had tattooed all over those breasts? She was tempted…yes, she really was a little bit tempted…but she had her own guiderules. Darn it. If there was one thing the Purgatorio taught you, it was playing by guiderules, especially your own. Anybody else's that you thought good, but especially your own.

So she shook her head free of their latest kiss, and planted a teasing little shove on his chest. "Sorry, Dave, boy. Never on date number one."

"Never?"

"Never. Never with any floater on date number one."

"Oh, I get it. You want to make sure there'll be a date number two."

"On date number two, yes, if the floater is just good enough for a fling. If he shows real promise, it's date number three."

"The better you like him, the longer you make him wait?"

"Now you, Dave, are definitely a date number three."

"Oh, the agony! How many have you had? Two's and three's?"

"Enough to know my way around a man's body. Nowhere near enough to get jaded. Two's—one or two. Three's—just one so far, but he fizzled out and moved away. You…I hope you've got plans to stick around awhile."

"One of these dates down the road, I'm taking you out to see my country home." He kissed her again. Both arms snug around her. They felt good. Guiderules, Julie Whitcomb. Discipline. Guiderules.

"Well," he said at last, "here's hoping I break that rule of yours. Here's hoping I'm the number two you decide to keep."

"Mmm. Maybe. Maybe, if I decide you're worth it." (And if you decide I'm worth it, she added in her thoughts.) "Meantime… Dave… Never, never on date number one."

"Hmm. Oh, okay. One more for the road?"

She gave him one more, for the road. Then, because of the murderer who might still be prowling around town, he insisted on escorting her into the Pankhurst Arms. Then… Dave actually left. Without further argument.

Deep inside, she wasn't entirely sure how happy she was about that. If he wanted to set a precedent, why not start with date number one?

Well, he was obviously a good polly, and good pollies knew how to respect guiderules. They had that much in common with Dante's Delight Purgatorio, whether or not they would ever admit it. Actually, his leaving like that, with no more argument, was one more point in his favor.

She guessed she'd see it that way in the morning. Even be happy about it. In the morning.

CHAPTER 6

TUESDAY, SEPTEMBER 19

It was Tuesday morning, and Lestrade was plotting strategy with Clayton, just the two of them alone in their office before joining the uniforms in the briefing room.

Murder was rare here and now, Lady be praised. Especially rare in Forest Green, listed for almost half a century among the safest cities its size or smaller in the whole country. A big part of the reason Lestrade had chosen to move down here from Chicago. Gave murder some priority if and when it happened. But the regular stuff still had to be taken care of—traffic tickets, the occasional shoplifting or small burglary, petty crimes, misdemeanors, and—the part Rosemary Lestrade envied the uniforms on patrol—finding lost children, giving emergency ambulance service in a police car, and otherwise just helping out good people in no-fault trouble. Sick as it was, Forest Green's first murder in seven years was still a single incident, and Chief Grayling refused to pull more than two officers off regular duty to assist the detectives full-time until the case was either solved or buried beneath a dozen weeks, whichever came first. The rest of the force—eighteen uniforms and the station staff—would be briefed on anything special to keep their eyes open for, in case it happened to flutter past them during their regular workload.

"See if we can't get Chris Grunewald down here from Chicago," Lestrade told Dave. "No matter how many hours in the Vigo River, I still think there should be some way a competent forensic specialist can at least make an educated guess when those apparent torture marks were made, before death or afterwards."

Clayton took a sip of coffee. "How much difference does it make, Sarge, really? Either way, we're looking for a real sicko."

She sighed. Sometimes he seemed too junior to remember his own street address. "Strenuous date last night, Detective?"

"I was in bed before midnight, Sarge. My own bed. Alone." He sighed.

"But still thinking about her. Never mind— I don't want to know, I just want your mind back on your work. Believe me, how long and far you swung or didn't swing last night makes considerably less difference than whether those marks on M. Jackson's body were pre- or post-mortem. Which, by the way, made a little bit of difference to Harry Carter Jackson. Pre-mortem, we're looking for a sicko who just likes hurting people. Post-mortem, we're looking for a sicko who for some reason or other wanted to make it look like torture. Motive, Dave. It goes to motive."

"I guess I meant, probably pre-mortem, because who'd want to just make it look like torture instead of mutilation after the fact? Oh, you're onto your old 'looking at a frame-up' hobbyhorse again? Noticed lately how rare frame-ups are in real life? As opposed to fiction and screenshows."

"Rare, Dave, rare. 'Rare' means that sometimes they happen. Anything that never happens at all, we don't even have any word for it." Well, maybe that funny young floater she saw every so often at Wallace Public Library did. The rest of society didn't.

"Okay. Get in touch with your Chicago examiner, see what Chris says... Sergeant, what I just said, about it not making any difference... I guess all I really meant was, the poor floater's dead now anyway. Out of his pain, however much it was or wasn't."

"And that makes it any better?" said Rosemary Lestrade. "Lady God! If it doesn't matter anyway—if anything that ever happens to anybody, we can just shrug off an hour later and say, 'Well, they're dead now anyway and out of their pain,' then what the hell are we in police work for, Detective Clayton? Why is anybody in firefighting, or ambulance and medical, or teaching—any workline at all that tries to help people—what the hell good is any of it?"

"Okay, Sarge, okay."

"Anything that happens, Detective Clayton, it stays happened. Yesterday, last week, last century, ten thousand years ago—makes no difference. On some plane of existence, some world, somewhere, it goes right on happening. That's what we call 'Eternity,' Detective. 'Eternity.' And the best we can hope for is that the Gods in their mercy have some way of soothing it over even while it goes right on happening. Since we can't be sure, all we can do here and now is try to set things right according to whatever it is we call 'justice,' and work our damnedest to keep more bad things from happening."

"Whew!" Clayton gulped more coffee. "I guess that scorches me well and truly."

"Scorches? You call *that* a scorching? Detective, that was idle theological chit-chat. Better pray I never feel the need to scorch you for real."

"Don't worry, Sarge, I'm praying to every god, saint, and/or angel I can find out about."

It must have been more her tone of voice, she thought, than her actual words.

* * * *

They didn't really have all that much to brief the general force on. Just be extra watchful, look out for suspicious characters, the usual blah, blah, blah that should stay in a good polly's clockround observation anyway. When the rest of them had filed out to their rounds of regular duty, Lestrade turned to her special-assignment uniforms, Officers Kim Little Bird and Stan Vergucchi—one the next thing to a rookie and the other one the next thing to retirement, but the pair who had been first on the scene when that poor bunch of beer-party-in-the-park teenagers spotted the late Harry Jackson floating in the Vigo. "Officers Vergucchi, Little Bird. Start checking the hardware stores, sleaze shops, every other place in town where our sicko could conceivably have gotten his equipment. Whatever he used on Jackson, whether pre- or post-mortem. Don't forget to try verifying whether any of these places peddle tattoo stamps on the side—but be careful how much you say about that. We don't want anybody outside this station aware what exact stamp we're looking for, and why."

THURSDAY, SEPTEMBER 21

Thursday morning. Lestrade put in another call for Chris Grunewald, got a "Try Chris at home later this afternoon."

Nothing yet on the tattoo stamp, too much on the other stuff: the sicko could have used almost anything to mutilate Harry Jackson's body. Probably either stashed away by now to look innocent, or lying somewhere at the bottom of the Vigo. Meanwhile, with nothing but mutilation marks to go on, no photos to show around town except the victim's, garbage cans picked up and emptied Monday morning before they could have even tried to get a garbage-can search warrant through the Privacy Privilege and Private Communications Acts laws—and even then, the only area they could possibly have gotten one for comprised the neighborhoods along the banks of the river itself... No, barring some accidental find out of the blue, that end looked almost as dead as the corpse.

Right after lunch, a call to Chris's home number. Thirty rings. A few big-wheel floaters here and there were getting wire-recorder answering machines, but the gadgets hadn't filtered down yet to very many ordinary folks and, anyway, it wasn't an answering machine Lestrade needed to talk to. Four more calls between 1300 and 1600 hours, sandwiched between whatever else she could find to do that might possibly tie into the case...still nothing but rings.

Finally, at 1737, more than an hour and a half after she should have checked out of the station—she was on her own time now, off the record and unpaid—she caught Chris, who had just stopped at home to drop off suitcases before heading out for dinner.

"Rosemary! Rosemary Lozinski Lestrade! Good to hear your voice again. Say, what about that gruesome little murder this week down there where you moved for some peace and quiet after our big-city mayhem? Out of the frying-pan, huh?"

"Not quite that bad yet, but our 'little' backwater murder is what I'm calling about."

"Aww! Not my charm?" Sounded like the very long week wraparound had really buoyed Chris up.

"Yes, okay, your charm, too. Look, Chris, sounds like you've read something about it. What I need to know is whether those apparent torture marks are pre- or post-mortem."

At least Chris didn't waste time asking why it might be important. "Tricky, Les, tricky. I'd almost say, based on what I've read in the papers, next to impossible to say for one hundred percent sure, body having been in the river for—how long was it, again?"

"Last seen 1930 hours Saturday, when he left Bernatelli's Pizza on Second Street with four friends. Peeled away from them at the door, talking about getting in an hour at Wallace Library. Body spotted in Vigo River about 1530 hours Sunday."

"Up to eighteen hours in cold, flowing water. More than long enough to wash the wounds clean, assuming they bled. Sharper M.E.'s than your Doc Grumeister would let this one slip as 'Uncertain.'"

"I want an opinion from somebody really competent in the field. At least an educated guess. If not about the pre- or post-mortem question, at least about length of time in the river, help us target actual time of death a little closer. I seem to remember you've got tests and equipment in your Chicago big-city lab that we couldn't afford even the catalogs for down here."

"Well, as long as you're sweet-talking me…" Chris hesitated. "I could drive down there tomorrow, use up one more vacation day and hit my big-city lab Monday morning when God designed workweeks to start anyway. Or you and I between us could arrange to get the body shipped direct to my Chicago. Me coming down would be quicker but guessier. Shipping it up here would let me educate my guess a little more, but would take longer, depending how much work's been piling up for me."

"How about if you came down here for a preliminary look? Maybe give you a wedge for shoving Jackson's body to the head of your examination list?"

"For a fairly high-profile case coming out of a safe heartland burg like Forest Green… Yes, I think I could do that."

"Good," said Detective Sergeant Rosemary Lestrade. "See you tomorrow."

FRIDAY, SEPT. 22

Chris matched Lestrade's memories pretty well: a little older, a few more gray hairs, maybe a kilogram heavier, same attitude of slightly mischievous competence. "Rosemary Lozinski Lestrade, you old hammerhead shark!"

"Chris Grunewald, you old marine zoologist. Unwound from your drive down?"

"Hey, slave driver, I'm still technically on vacation. Give me a cup of coffee, a donut, and a little chew about old times in the big city. Then we'll get down to the serious stuff."

Chris had always been very good at boxing the serious stuff away from the happy-hour stuff. Chris also had a long-standing game of "Make Rosemary Laugh." Once in a while, it worked.

Three quarters of an hour later they stood in the examining room—about the same size as a medium-income family kitchen—of the Forest Green Police Station, Lestrade watching Chris go over the remains of the late Harry Carter Jackson. Eventually the Chicago forensic examiner straightened up and said, "Educated guess?"

"Educated guess."

"Post-mortem, but not by long, and too much margin of error for any court. If only the poor floater hadn't spent up to eighteen hours in the river. Well, you're right about us having tests and equipment up in Chicago that would help me whittle down that margin for error."

Lestrade said, "You'll have the body by Monday."

* * * *

Friday evening, and the regular weekly gathering of the members of Dante's Delight Purgatorio at Sam's house. Tonight's promised to be especially intense. After this week's murder—they must have been pulling Harry Jackson's body out of the Vigo even while Sam's weekly rolegame party was going on—the air needed purifying rather badly over all of Forest Green.

"Julie?" Sam asked, turning to her. "You've put in more than your share over the years."

"So have you, Sam."

"Different for me. As grandson of the founder. My point is, do you want a turn as penitent this wraparound, too?"

"Badly as we need it, after this…this thing that happened here? You bet I do!"

Paul said, "We should have put in one or two special sessions already this week. We could've juggled our regular schedules around."

"Who knew how edgy the town was going to get?" Sam excused the group. "It was nowhere near this tense seven years ago."

"Much different kind of murder," said Curly, "the one seven years ago. Well, we can't start any earlier than now. Add a session tomorrow afternoon, and we can all have our turns at both duties this wraparound."

"Good floaters!" Sam's grin was grateful, genuine, and proud. "All right, then, we all know the drill. Julie and Paul start fasting tonight." He and Curly were fasted and ready to go now, tonight having been their regular every-other-week turn for penitent duty.

They skipped the meal completely, Julie and Paul sucking hard candies for the energy they needed. They lit their candles—purple for the penitents, white for the angels—and started in procession up the three flights of stairs, Julie in the lead, Sam and Curly next, Paul last, to the Purgatorio in Sam's shuttered tower room.

Sam showed himself grateful for their community spirit. Julie felt grateful for having had that date with Dave while the news of the murder was still so fresh that the initial shock hadn't quite had time to settle into the fear that ate away at the whole town and surrounding countryside.

Dave had wanted another date for this evening. She'd had to put him off, explaining that she had a long-standing engagement on Fridays. Let him think it was a bowling group or something. Then he'd wanted one for tomorrow night, but she'd seen far enough ahead to make him another excuse, already guessing that they'd add one of their rare Saturday afternoon sessions this wraparound and tomorrow night she'd be too sore even for a platonic kind of second date. Sunday night...yes. For Sunday night, she'd said yes. The weekly rolegame parties were light refreshment. She could easily play from two to four and skip out early. Or skip out on the rolegaming completely for one week, and just spend Sunday afternoon resting and recuperating alone in her apartment until date time. Depending how she felt after her Saturday session.

She suspected she might have to hope Dave was enough of her prince to wait for bedtime until date number three.

* * * *

Curly was initiated to the sixth level and Sam, who had passed through levels two, three, five, six, and seven over and over down the years, experimented by making Julie insert beading needles beneath his right-foot toenails. Nobody ever took the initial level more than once, and as soon as they reached level four—angel duty—they all naturally fulfilled it every other meeting.

Afterwards, when they had come downstairs again— Sam limping and Curly still stretching her hefty limbs—and when tonight's penitents had broken their fasts, and when they had retired to the living room for serious talk, Sam harked back to their discussion of last Sunday night. "Well, what do you think, gang? Anyone had a decent chance to sniff out our possible new blood, free Julie up to go emeritus?"

Paul shook his head—failure, not negation. "I don't think Marge Hokstra would work out, after all."

Curly grinned and chuckled. "Carmine Jones neither, not in the clinch."

"Curly! You know the rule."

"And I never broke it," Curly explained. "You know me, Sam. I just teased him with a little kissing, a little necking, a little love-tapping, and he bruised like a scared bunny. We never went a pat deeper, not until I had him crossed off the Dante's Delight list for good and all."

"Well… Okay, Curly, we'll take your word for it this time, since you bent the rule before tonight. But now you're ready for seventh level, make sure you give it the full seven days between crossing-off and whatever else you feel like doing with the ex-candidate."

Then the three of them turned to Julie. She smiled. "Oh, yes. Yes, I believe there's quite a strong potential in Corwin Poe."

CHAPTER 7

SATURDAY, SEPTEMBER 23

Saturday morning in downtown Forest Green. The trees along the walkways were putting on their fall colors—orange and gold, crimson and peach and some still bravely green—all glowing against the clear blue sky. There seemed to be a relaxed, cheerful feeling among the early shoppers enjoying the glorious weather and colorful window displays, and Angela felt happier than she had since... Well, it might have been since Monday evening, if she could have appreciated being set up with a blind date. Dave Clayton seemed like a nice floater, yes, she hadn't lied to Corwin about that—but for some other woman. So, say happier than she'd felt since Sunday night, the Raggedy Ann game, and not yet knowing anything about that horrible murder, the first they'd had here in seven years, when she was just midway through Riley High, and that murder had been almost plain, near-accidental manslaughter.

Well! At least things seemed to be getting back to normal now, after a week of gloomy weather and gloomier spirits. Angela gave her mind a little shake and went into Barb's Boutique for a closer look at that lovely autumn-colors silk tunic in the window.

They had one her size. She tried it on, stepped out of the dressing room wearing it for the clerk's opinion, and stood stock still, thinking for an instant that somebody must have moved a mirror in front of the dressing-room door.

There she was! Nearly heart-shaped pale face framed in gold-blond hair, broad forehead, medium-thick curving eyebrows, nose slightly upturned, small rounded chin, surprised expression...

Then both young women started to laugh.

"I beg your pardon!" Angela exclaimed. "You're wearing my face!"

"And some ladies," the other young woman cried, "get all out of alignment if they see someone else wearing the same tunic and trousers!"

* * * *

"Her name is Gaia Soderstrum," Angela explained to Corwin several hours later, when they met for lunch at the Sorrento. "We helped each other accessorize our new outfits, and then had coffee together at Queequeg's. She's thinking about getting a necklace-style tattoo. Then we'll look less alike, at least when she wears a low collar. The Soderstrums only moved to Forest Green about a year ago. That's why we never happened to run into each other before."

"Another Angela! But does not Raggedy Ann have numerous sisters identical to her in every physical attribute?"

"So does Raggedy Andy. Brothers, that is."

"From my vantage, there must always be room in the world for an additional Angela Garvey. I am not, however, entirely persuaded but that a single sublunary Corwin Poe might be one too many."

"Oh, Cory, now you're fishing for compliments."

"Am I?" He paused and seemed to consider the question. "Well," he said at last, "It is hypothesized that each and every individual of us has somewhere on this terrestrial globe a doppelganger. Why should not yours be here in Forest Green whilst mine, with any luck, resides in Timbuctu or Manchuria?... Wait! Have I veritably caught stray glimpses of her at some little distance— M. Gaia Soderstrum, you said?—imagined her to be you, recollected that you had yet to return to us here, concluded my eagerness to have misled me, and erased the episode from the immediately active regions of my cerebrum?"

"Besides, I don't imagine men and women go into all the same kinds of places."

"There might prove to be greater overlap than our residual cultural stereotypes frequently appreciate. Still," he added, "unless she were another haunter of the hushed and hallowed catacombs of Wallace Public Library, which seem to have been devouring the bulk of my own hours in the greater megalopolitan shopping district of Forest Green..."

"Oh, yes! How is all that coming along?" Angela knew he had been turning his hours since graduation into research for two classmates who aimed at writing novels and one already more or less established author whom he had met during his years at the University of Astoria on the west coast.

"Diana desires to embark upon the Tyrrhenian Sea with the antique Etrurians, Atramentacia's latest communication was specific in its nonspecifity— 'Just whatever *umwelt* looks fruitful to you' constituted her directive, allowing me rather more considerable scope than truly desirable—and Harve discovers the absolute necessity of further jots and tittles to round out his essential acquaintanceship with the Spanish Inquisition."

"Just a hint, Cory. Don't try applying them to the game if you play that scenario again. You managed to get yourself eliminated quickly enough as it was."

"True, alas. Rather agonizingly so. I spare you additional details."

"Please do. After what really happened to poor Harry Jackson."

Corwin nodded. "You are entirely right. I spoke in the poorest possible taste…" His voice died away and they sat in silence a few moments before he resumed, "And last Sunday I had before my eyes that distracting carrot of a plum role awaiting me in your scenario in the adjoining room."

"Good. I think maybe we should just go back to Marcella's nursery right away tomorrow."

"One of the few guiderules *chez* Imani is the avoidance of utilizing any scenario two weeks in a row. They prefer, rather, to let them lie fallow at least one Sunday, after the method of crop rotation, and with much the same motivation. Meanwhile, how fares your quest for a socially beneficial avocation?"

Angela sighed. "Slowly, Cory, slowly. I wouldn't want to use up a paying job somebody else might need for the salary, they already have too many pink ladies at the hospital—the best they could do was put me on the waiting list—and they don't even need another volunteer at any of the thrift shops just now. In another month or two, they all said, when the Christmas season gets underway. And then I can ring a bell at a Salvation Army bucket, too. But that'll last only until New Year's."

"And would in my humble opinion squander your university education. Why not embark with me among the epochs and by-ways of historical research in quest of Atramentacia Scrivener's 'fruitful *umwelt*'?"

"Oh, no, that sounds too much like schoolwork! I'm still in recovery from my university education. Now I just want to do something— 'socially beneficent.'"

"True, too true. What are we, after all, but social drones, those of us who delve away in the dust of an earthy yesterday ferreting out arcane lore for others to fashion into dry and scholarly fictions—or overripe bestsellers, for that matter—destined to molder away into the earth of a dusty tomorrow." By his tone, she couldn't tell whether he was being playful or a little serious about his supposed uselessness to society.

She decided to treat it as playful. "Well, you could be wasting your own education just sleeping all day and partying all night like a playboy."

"I do in fact, since graduation, follow my natural proclivity to sleep half the normal person's day, rarely arising much before luncheon, save when Sunday forces me into activity at the ungodly hour of ten. Thank Saint Martha's for an eleven o'clock Mass!"

"And then you lug home satchels of books and work away half the night. You're not really a lazy idle drone, Cory, you've just gotten your clock schedule slipped a little around."

"Whereas you... Are you still astir with the roseate dawn, Angela?"

"Most days. I love mornings the way you love words. I always have."

He gazed at her thoughtfully. The waiter brought their plates of spaghetti. When he had left again, Corwin resumed, "Have you ever meditated on how well our schedules might mesh? Each having an approximately equivalent number of hours—early in the morning or late at night, respectively—for personal consumption, whilst enjoying time together for mutual interests from luncheon until the earlier of our slumber-hours?"

She sprinkled Parmesan cheese over her spaghetti while thinking what to say, how to respond. Could she just be hearing things the way she wanted to hear them? That must be it. If there was one man in the world who would never try to keep two women on his string at the same time...

"I've been thinking," she said. "I may try to set myself up for a date with...with Hank Algood. Yes, Hank. Will he be at Sam Imani's again this week?"

"Ah!" said Corwin. "I assume so, considering that to the best of my knowledge he has been in attendance every Sunday... I speak erroneously, every Sunday but one, in July...throughout this estival season just passed."

"Oh, good, then.... What do you think, Cory? Is he my type?"

"Angela, you hardly stand in need of my permission. As a woman of legal age and superior intelligence, you are at indisputable liberty to arrange whatever assignations you may please. At the least, this will not constitute a *soi-disant* 'blind date.'"

He must really have been disappointed that his and Julie's plan to set her up with Dave Clayton hadn't panned out. "No, really, Cory. I'm not asking your permission, just your advice. You've had all summer to get to know these people. I haven't. Would you have chosen Hank as a blind date for me, if I liked blind dates? Is there anything I should know about him, other than that he started teaching at Riley High the year after we graduated?"

Corwin shut his eyes a little longer than the average blink, then started twirling spaghetti up onto his fork. "Insofar as my observation of and acquaintanceship with Hank Algood extend, he is an estimable gentleman whose erudition ought to prove congenial to your own body of knowledge and personal tastes. No, I know of absolutely no evidence to adduce in Hank Algood's disfavor. May you enjoy your date with him, and bless you, my children, bless you!"

CHAPTER 8

SUNDAY, SEPTEMBER 24

They were back at Sam Imani's big old Victorian mansion of a house for another rolegame Sunday. This time Sam, who Angela thought seemed to have a slight limp that she hadn't noticed last week, began the afternoon by settling his group in the living room for a rousing scenario of Christians vs. Lions—the lions usually won, but just enough element of doubt remained in this rolegame version of history, Corwin assured Angela, to add a piquant flavor of ambiguity.

Angela looked around at the rest of Sam's circle as it had gathered so far. Curly Friedman and Carmine Jones and Paul Osaka and Trudy…what was Trudy's last name? Began with 'U'? She really ought to make more of an effort to apply Corwin's mnemonic tricks for remembering names. Gerry Wu and Pearl Mitsu this time, too—Policeman Percy and Beloved Belindy in last week's Raggedy Ann. And several others whose names Angela didn't know at all yet. And, of course, Julie Whitcomb, sitting in the big old cushioned armchair, looking a little…drawn out, somehow? Angela hoped she wasn't just imagining something her deep, subconscious psychomystique wanted to believe about Julie. Pearl was sitting in the closest sofa space to Julie's left. There was one straight chair left, just to Julie's right. Corwin looked around once and claimed it, indicating his desire to play a Christian called Nichomachus. Angela announced that she was going to see what other scenarios might be grouping.

She found Hank Algood in the library again, this time talking about a good, rousing game of Topsyturvydom. It had been one of their favorites back in high school. Corwin used to play a superb Ruthven Murgatroyd, quite a fair Reginald Bunthorne, and a really good John Jasper, who in Gilbert and Sullivan's version turns out not to be a murderer, after all, but dies at the end anyway. Taking dibs on Pirate Ruth, Angela darted back briefly to the living room, hoping perhaps to entice Corwin over to the G&S scenario right away.

She found that even more players had gathered for Christians vs. Lions, so that now there were two staggered rows of filled chairs between him and the door, and Sam was already rolling the die. So she just called over, "Topsyturvydom in the library, as soon as you've teased the lions into eating you!" and hurried back to be Pirate Ruth.

* * * *

Julie pulled out the little folding chalkboard they were pretending was a Roman wax tablet with stylus, and told the rulemaster, "Lavinia would like to pass a message to Nichomachus."

Sam tossed his die, gave it a glance, and said, as he would have said, according to the mysterious power of rulemasters, no matter what number turned up, "Granted, Lavinia, and successful."

She opened the chalkboard, chalked in, "When & where can we talk privately a.s.a.p.? R.s.v.p. as Corwin," and passed it over to Sam as rulemaster, who looked at it briefly and passed it on to Nichomachus.

He opened and read it, gave Julie an inquisitive glance, rubbed out her message to chalk his answer, and turned to the rulemaster. "Shall security and success crown my striving to return my own epistle into Lavinia's hands?"

Again Sam rolled his die, looked at it, and nodded. "*Vero*, Nichomachus."

Nichomachus passed it back to Lavinia. She opened it, read, "Tomorrow, 1400, late luncheon at Wallace Library coffee shop?"

She gave him a nod and poised the eraser above the chalkboard.

"Well, Lavinia? Sam rumbled in his deep voice. "Whether you can tell any of the other players or not, you've still got to share it with the rulemaster."

Aware that Corwin, watching closely, knew by now that Sam was in on the planned appointment, Julie refolded the chalkboard and submitted it to the rulemaster. He read it, erased it, and passed it back. "As Pope Eusebius, I rule that Lavinia may invite any others she wishes to the *agape* in her house. As Emperor Diocletian,

I warn all Christians that any such meetings are liable to be raided and every attendee arrested, and all of you know what being arrested means in such cases." He flipped his die a few times from hand to hand.

Lavinia looked over the ranks of Christians still remaining after the first feline feast in the Colosseum. She signaled about a third of them, and play continued.

Her *agape* went off safely, but fifteen minutes later, both she and Nichomachus were arrested for refusing to burn the pinch of incense to Caesar, and sentenced in short order to the arena.

"What?" Nichomachus protested. "Not subjected to strenuous interrogation even with the ambition of extracting from us the names of our *confreres* and *consoeurs*?"

Sam rolled his die, studied it, and shook his head. "Nope. Sorry, Nicco my chap, Emperor Diocletian says the lions have got to be fed right now."

So Lavinia and Nichomachus were hustled into the Colosseum, which they found crowded with tier upon tier of hooting non-player characters. A gate opened at the far end of the arena...the lions roared into view...they came charging across the sands of the arena straight toward the bravely quivering Christians...again the rulemaster rolled his die...

"Sorry again, Nichomachus, that lead lion has just bitten off your head. Nice bite, Lion."

Curly-as-Lion growled, nodded, and bent back to her dinner.

Nichomachus sat stunned for a heartbeat before registering his protest. "But is that actually conceivable, anatomically and naturalistically speaking? *Is* the oral apparatus of even the largest lion available outside the fabulous monster genre of cinematic literature truly capable of engulfing the entire head of an adult *homo sapiens*?"

"Okay, it just snapped through your neck at the first bite. Either way, death was instantaneous. Apologies, Nicco," the Emperor Diocletian repeated.

"That was...abrupt," Nichomachus conceded. "Very well, then, appealing to Pope Eusebius, have I garnered sufficient virtue to linger behind awhile lending spiritual and possibly a modicum of material assistance to those of my Christian sisters and brothers who still remain in the sublunary veil of tears?"

Pope Eusebius consulted his score booklet and shook his head. "Apologies again, but Pope Eusebius says, Not quite. Best you can do is reassign the points you've got to your surviving fellow Christians."

"All to Lavinia, then." Corwin rose. "*Vale et bene, omnes.* Nichomachus may as well translate himself at once into the celestial abode coveted by Pagans as the Elysian Fields and known to us more accurately informed Christians as Heaven. My palm of martyrdom, if you please."

Pope Eusebius pantomimed handing him a palm visible only to spiritual vision, Nichomachus pantomimed brushing it across Lavinia's head while wishing her better fortune than his, and the first lion fed while the second waited in envious hunger, pawing the bloodied white sand.

As the new martyr crossed the living room, Sam gave the die another role and said, "What's this? The second lion has attacked the first one, and they're fighting for the prey that's already dead. Looks like the emperor may have to send in the soldiers, here. Hmm…or maybe the gladiators."

The late Nichomachus never looked back in his progress toward the hall. Julie guessed he was headed for Heaven in the library, and gave herself a little smile, thinking about Dave Clayton.

* * * *

Like most games of Topsyturvydom, this one started in Victorian England, where more than half the Savoy Operas were set. Also like most games in this particular scenario, it moved rather quickly into one of the other settings, most often starting with Titipu, especially when the rulemaster adopted the role of the Mikado, like Hank Algood.

"Oh, by the way, Angie," he told her while Pearl Mitsu (who had been devoured in the lions' first banquet) as Katisha and Mickey Patinkin as Bunthorne were planning their next action, "you know we're doing 'Foggerty's Fairy' this week at Riley High."

Her date with Hank might be easier to arrange than Angela had feared. "I never miss a 'Foggerty's Fairy' if I can help it. Next to 'Iolanthe,' I think it's my favorite. Are you asking me to go with you, Hank?"

"Well, not exactly. I was going to offer you and Corwin a couple of complimentary tickets for any evening Thursday to Saturday, or the Sunday matinee."

"Corwin?" Was it that obvious to everyone but Corwin himself? "He's like—like a brother to me, but sometimes, you know, a woman likes to go out with somebody who isn't her brother."

"Even an old, avuncular type like me?"

"Oh, Hank, you're only—what—about thirty!"

"Thirty-four, but thanks for the compliment. Well, Corwin's right there in the doorway, Why don't we ask—Whoops!" Hank added, even as Angela jerked around in her chair to look. "He just ducked out again. Maybe to get a sandwich before joining us."

"I never heard him scream this time. I've heard others screaming their way out of Sam's and Ike's scenarios this afternoon, but not…"

"I did a pretty doggone good scream when the lions ate off my leg," Pearl said proudly, "if I do say so myself."

"How odd." Angela shook her head. "I don't mean your scream, Pearl. It was a good scream. I mean, about Corwin."

"Maybe he hasn't been thrown into the arena yet," Hank suggested. "Maybe he was just on his way for a sandwich to fatten himself up for the lions. As an English teacher at Riley, I can get you in for the Wednesday night dress rehearsal, and you can decide about those comps from there."

* * * *

Back in the living room, Lavinia gave a most satisfying scream as the *secutor* prodded the lion closer to her while the *retiarius* cast his net over beast and lady together. Emperor Diocletian cast his die and pronounced her properly martyred. Pope Eusebius consulted his score book and announced that, adding in the points she had inherited from Nichomachus, she had enough to hang around and help the living.

"But Saint Lavinia," Julie replied, "chooses to distribute all her points among…let's see, who's still alive?… Flavia, Marcus, Jubilatus, Cornelia, and Petrus Argentus. Saint Lavinia chooses to follow her companion Nicco's example, take her palm in hand, and flit to Heaven right away. *Vale et bene*, everyone! Convert those lions if you can, and if you can't, may you give them all galloping indigestion."

Reaching the hall, she bumped into Corwin, who was just backing out of the library. She gave him a quizzical look.

"Angela," he explained, "appears to be in extremely comfortable *tete-a-tete* with Hank Algood. Their happiness ought to remain unalloyed."

"Angela's and *Hank's*?" said Julie.

"She earlier confided to me that she desired to arrange a date or two with him."

"She did? Well, your age is the best time for playing the field." Unlike mine, Julie thought, which is the best time for settling down with a single partner.

"Is it? That's some modicum of consolation. Here—Hobart!" Corwin went on, catching Hoby McGruff on his way back to Topsyturvydom with a sandwich in one hand and bottle of cola in the other. "Could you kindly be so accommodating as to convey to Angela my felicitations, along with the intelligence that I have departed prematurely under the spur of...of a raging headache."

"Yo!" Hoby acknowledged, moving on into the library.

"A headache?" said Julie.

"A hardly unanticipated side effect, I conceive, of having that appendage masticated by a ferocious beast of prey. Are you also among the blessed by now, Lavinia?"

"Even though I doubt my screams are quite as entertaining as yours, whenever you get a fair chance." She winked. "But, yes, I'm on my way to Heaven now, and without even the trace of a headache. Guess my lion went straight for the heart. Can I drop you off on my way?"

"Utilizing the occasion to broach the topic of our platonic—I trust—assignation tomorrow?"

She considered that a second or two. This afternoon she just wanted to finish resting up for date number two with the front runner for her prince. And she didn't think it would hurt a bit to keep Corwin in the dark overnight. She shook her head. "No, I think we'll leave that till tomorrow at fourteen hundred. It'll work out beautifully—I have the night shift Mondays right now, I can just go on to the hospital from the library. All I'm going to tell you for now is that you're right: it's perfectly and absolutely platonic. Want that ride anyway?"

"No, thank you, I shall appreciate the walk. A mere four kilometers, give or take an insignificant number of steps, traversing certain of the most aesthetically pleasing sectors of Forest Green, on an autumnal afternoon of rare clarity; and having for companionship this anticipatory conundrum to mull over *en route*. Yes, all this ought to clear my cranial neuralgia quite nicely. Should you, however, desire gentlemanly escort as far as the door, I stand obedient to your most gossamer whim."

"As far as the front door." She hooked her hand through the crook of his elbow, and they made their way outside, where they said, "*Au revoir*" and parted, she for her car and he for the footpath.

CHAPTER 9

STILL SUNDAY, SEPTEMBER 24

Topsyturvydom came to its usual solid conclusion, almost every character happily paired off, not necessarily with the same party they got in their original operas—this time Katisha got Dick Deadeye and Princess Ida got the Duke of Dunstable while Ko-Ko ended with Lady Jane—and then everyone joined in the rousing final chorus from "The Tuppenny Prince" with which the scenario traditionally ended.

And Corwin never had come back after that one time Hank glimpsed him in the doorway.

Angela had never heard him screaming, either. But she did hear singing in the living room, an enthusiastic rendition of "Triumph, Christian Martyrs" to the tune of "Onward, Christian Soldiers," the traditional way to end that rare game of Christians vs. Lions when events had unfolded in just the right way, the number three turned up on the last roll of the rulemaster's twelve-sided die, and the last batch of Christians converted the lions, much as Saint Francis was to convert the wolf of Gubbio a thousand years later. Was it possible that for once Corwin's character had actually survived to the end of the game? She went into the living room, hoping to find him there.

No. There were only two Christians left, Paul Osaka and Carmine Jones. The lions had joined the singing, to make it sound fuller.

"Corwin?" said Sam Imani, the host. "Oh, yes. He never had a chance to scream because he got thrown to the lions before ever being interrogated, and then one of them bit through his neck first thing."

"He got up and said he was translating himself into Heaven," Paul Osaka added. "I assumed he meant your scenario in the library."

Carmine said, "Julie's character got eaten just a few minutes later and she left for Heaven, too. Didn't she?"

"Maybe the snack table," suggested Curly Friedman, one of the converted lions.

So Angela tried the snack table. He wasn't there, either, but Hoby McGruff was, getting himself another hot dog.

"Corwin!" Hoby exclaimed, slapping his forehead and getting a little mustard on it. "I forgot! I saw him with Julie in the hallway. He said to tell you he was going home early with a headache. I got the impression Julie was giving him a ride."

"Oh," said Angela. "Thank you."

Well, if she was going out with Hank, she couldn't very well blame Corwin for going out with Julie, could she? Except...wasn't that the whole reason she had decided to date somebody else in the first place, just *because* Corwin was hitting it off so well with Julie?

And Angela had been so open and aboveboard with him about her decision to try dating somebody else. Why wasn't he being as open and aboveboard with *her* about Julie?

Still, she only had his message at secondhand—"hearsay," the courts called it. Maybe Hoby hadn't remembered it exactly. Corwin *might* have said, "Tell Angela I'm going out with Julie."

Or he *might* really have gone home with a headache, and let Julie drive him rather than pull Angela away from her game. Acting like a good, easy old friend. Not some kind of...of romance espionage agent.

* * * *

Julie was still sore from yesterday's penances...didn't spring back quite as quickly at twenty-seven as she had at twenty-two. It really was high time she found a replacement and went emeritus from active duty. We couldn't all be Sam Imani's. And if you married your prince, didn't you owe it to him to keep yourself ever ready for love?

Date number two was nicely taken care of, anyway: pizza at Rivelino's, Cary Grant double feature—"Guys and Dolls" followed by "Arsenic and Old Lace"—at Cineclassics, then sandwiches at the moviehouse's own nostalgia-decorated coffee shop, where Julie ate cream cheese and watercress on whole-grain rye and watched Dave polish off a jumbo-sized ham and Swiss and a slice of peach pie half hidden under a generous dollop of whipped cream.

Oh, yes, she did like to see a healthy appetite in a man. Especially when he was her potential prince.

"Cary Grant really was beautiful, wasn't he?" she remarked. "Suave and funny both at once. I can't even imagine anyone else playing Sky Masterson in that movie.... You know, Dave, you remind me a little of Cary Grant."

"My hair's too light, I don't have any cleft in my chin that I'm aware of, and I'm not even going to ask 'in what other way.' Too much like fishing for compliments. Just let me wonder."

"And make up the compliments for yourself?" She grinned at him. "Your facial expressions, for one thing—and that's all I'm going to tell you!"

He grinned back and swallowed a jumbo-sized bite of sandwich. "Y'know, the Old Woman—using that as a title of sincere respect, Sergeant Lestrade is my senior partner—she could never enjoy either one of those movies. If a show has anything at all to do with crime and/or lawkeepers, she just can't take it as plain entertainment."

"Yes, I think you mentioned that last week, that double date we had with Angela and Corwin."

"Well..." Dave amended slightly, "I did catch her chuckling once at a Three Phunny Inspectors cartoon, so I guess maybe she doesn't too much mind us pollies getting spoofed, as long as it can be done without laughing at crimes and criminals at the same time."

"Not the easiest thing in the world to do. I see her point, though. Crime—real crime—surely isn't anything to laugh at. But I'm very glad *you* can laugh with me, anyway, at such absurd not-for-real 'crimes' as in those two old movies we just saw.... There can't be too many comedies and musicals left for her to enjoy. What about 'The Wizard of Oz'? I can't remember any actual crimes there..."

"Miss Gulch threatening to sic the sheriff on Toto—she hates to see law and lawkeepers misused like that. And, of course, the

Wicked Witch tries to murder Dorothy and all her companions, and ends up getting murdered herself for her pains —"

"To be technical, I think we'd have to call that an accident, not murder."

"I'd call it self-defense." Having finished his sandwich, Dave lifted his pie plate into place and brandished his fork above it. "Anyway, even with all that, it's one of the few screenshows she actually can enjoy. I've even heard her chuckle when the water hits the Wicked Witch of the West. I think maybe the Old Woman sees the Witch as a parody of herself."

"Dave," Julie asked suddenly, "do you see your Sergeant Lestrade as a mother figure?"

He thought about it while chewing and swallowing a bite of pie, and at last shook his head. "Nope. Definitely not a mother figure. A father figure, maybe…"

"Good." Smiling at him, Julie reached across the table to scoop a double fingerful of peach goo out of his pie.

"Hey!" he protested jokingly. "Order your own."

She shook her head and licked her forefinger. "Don't want to stretch my girlish figure." She licked her middle finger and reached for her napkin. "But I do love cooked fruit." She folded the napkin around her hand and wiped carefully.

"Umm? You a jelly or a jam person?" Putting a whimsically protective wall around his pie with his left hand, he forked another, larger bite into his mouth.

"A jam person, given the choice. With nice, large chunks of fruit."

"Strawberry, plum, or raspberry?"

"Oh, raspberry," she replied. "I love to crunch the seeds."

"Hey, so do I! I'll bring you a jar or three—just stirred up a batch last week."

"Wonderful! I shall live for the day. I like a man barefoot and panting in the kitchen."

"I do a pretty fair chicken cacciatore," he offered. "And a Hungarian goulash that has won rave reviews from certain knowing friends."

"If that's an invitation for next time at your place," said Julie, "the answer is yes."

"Friday night?"

"Fridays are tied up for me, remember?" She closed her eyes and considered. Angel duty for her again this Friday, thanks to what yesterday's special session had done to the rotation; but if things continued calmer in town, there should only be the one regular session per week again. "I think I can make it Saturday night, unless something comes up."

"Yeah," he agreed without question. "I guess nurses have it pretty much like pollies that way, don't they? All we can do is lay plans and hope nothing comes up to change them."

"Both our worklines take flexibility," she agreed, aiming a finger at the peach goo that still remained on his plate.

This time, grinning back at her, he laid his fork down and dabbled his finger alongside hers to mop up the last of the sweet stuff, gliding their fingers together as they did so.

* * * *

The days were already shorter than the nights. Not that it mattered that much. Now that the equinox was past and the country was back on Winter Clock, it would have been dark anyway by the time Angela left Sam's, after—with great determination and resolution that ought to make her proud of herself—she had stayed for a quick game of Snapdragons and a last plateful from the remains of the refreshments table, until she was one of the last people to leave.

She started out on the straightest way to Aunt Sally's, which lay between her and the Marquette House. At Van Buren she suddenly turned left. At Fourth she resolutely turned and got back onto Riley Drive. At Carmichael she turned left again. And so on until she had bypassed Aunt Sally's and found herself pulling up in front of the Marquette House, after all.

She parked her old tan "Mason jar"—only an auto as good as a Mason could have lasted this long in good working condition—and sat inside, going over and over things in her mind. There! Up there! Isn't that a light on in his apartment? He could have just left it on to make it look like someone's at home. Look here, Angela Garvey, what are you thinking? Friends since childhood gives you some sort of exclusive dibs on him? Something that lets you go out with other people and him, not? All the same, he *could* have looked in on our Topsyturvydom scenario long enough to tell me himself he was going out with her! Even if he really was just going straight home to nurse a headache, he could every bit as easily have told me *that*... Well, I suppose, if I can't find out for sure, I may never get any sleep tonight. Twenty-one hundred hours already!

Finally, at 2110 hours, she got out of her car—just remembering to lock the door because, after all, it was only a week ago today that they had pulled poor Harry Jackson's body out of the Vigo—and marched up the lawnwalk to the front door of the apartment building.

In ordinary times, the front door—the public door—was only locked between 2200 and 0600. Tonight she found it already locked. She thought for a minute, looked around for the row of chimer buttons, and tabbed the one labeled "Arnheim."

He answered within two seconds. "Currently in residence."

"Cory? It's Angela."

"Angela!" The front door snicked to "open" at once, and by the time she was through it, he was halfway down the stairs to meet her in the lobby.

"Looks as if that headache isn't crippling you *too* terribly, Cory."

"The headache? Ah, my headache! No, my preprandial perambulation homeward proved quite salubrious in that respect. It's... Your concern gratifies me deeply."

"You *walked*? They said you left with Julie."

"They did? They garbled the message, then. But how..." He thought a moment. "Ah! We did egress Sam's abode at the same time, but only coincidentally. She spoke of preparing for a keenly anticipated assignation with...with a gentleman who appears to have captivated her quite auspiciously."

"Really? Julie? Oh, Cory, I'm...I'm sorry."

He blinked. "Sorry? Why?... But perhaps I should confide in you the identity of the gentleman in question. Understanding his failure to...shall we say, enthrall?...you, Julie elected to essay her own date with Dave Clayton. This meets your approbation?"

"Cory, it wasn't that I didn't like Dave. Just not in any romantic way. For me, I think he'd be fine as a friend."

"As a friend. Even as you and I?"

"Never 'as you and I'—wherever that comes from, I know you're quoting something, probably the Venerable Edgar."

"Actually, on this occasion the citation originates in Kipling. Would I be fishing to solicit an explication of your rejoinder, 'Never as you and I'?"

She chuckled. She couldn't help it. "I think I could be plain friends with Dave, Cory. I'm sure he could never be 'best friends' with me. It takes years to become *best* friends."

"I think I comprehend, and…feel honored beyond my merit. And you? Has success crowned your ambitions regarding the discretionary time of M. Hank Algood?"

"He's taking me to the dress rehearsal of 'Foggerty's Fairy' at Riley High this Wednesday. Cory…he's offered to get us a pair of complimentary tickets for one of the regular performances."

Corwin shut his eyes as if he were overcome with emotion. He'd always been good at that kind of play-acting. It was what made him such an excellent rolegamer. "Ecstasy!" he breathed. "Friday evening?"

"Copacetic." She ventured to brush a kiss across his cheek.

He shut his eyes again, drew a deep breath, and suddenly exclaimed, "But you found the door locked! Here." Reaching into his pocket, he pulled out his keyring and worked two keys off it, fumbling a little in his haste. "The key to the public front door… the key to Arnheim. Should you ever need a refuge, this house is available to you whether or not I myself am at home."

"What about you?"

"I have duplicates in my possession."

"But will you be able to get back into Arnheim tonight?"

"Affirmative. I believe I left my door on the latch but, even should it prove otherwise, that light above her door informs me that our admirable concierge, M. Florsheim, is immediately available on the premises. She has a skeleton key lending *passe-partout* to every apartment."

"Why don't you just run upstairs and check your door right away?"

"Because it is my duty and my privilege to escort you to your automobile." He offered her his arm.

"All right, but only if I get to sit in it and watch till you're safely back inside again."

"So stipulated."

The night was warm for late September, and the soft glow of the street lamps washed out fewer stars than the half moon did. Really, Forest Green seemed almost as safe as it always had, all these lingering precautions just a little bit overdone.

"It may behoove me to confess," Corwin said as they reached her old Mason, "that Julie has in fact solicited a conference with me tomorrow, a late luncheon at the library coffee shop, on some matter as yet mysterious to me, but which she has guaranteed to be strictly platonic."

Oh, thank you, Angela thought, thank you, thank you! You *did* tell me! Aloud, she said, "Cory, why should it make any difference, between best friends, whether she wants to be 'strictly platonic' or not?"

"...True. We are still at an age, are we not? you and I, where a certain degree of window-shopping remains appropriate behavior. Your car doors *are* locked?"

"This whole time."

Nevertheless, he peered extravagantly through the windows, and even double-checked the back seat after she had unlocked her door, before finally allowing her to sit down and buckle herself into the driver's seat. Last, he made sure all the doors were still or again locked.

She rolled the driver's window down, unwilling to let the moment slide past quite so soon. "Cory, do you remember that day in fourth grade when you brought yourself to Show and Tell, announced that you were an 'octoroon' and if we took a time-travel bus back to the Antebellum South, you'd be liable to being sold as a slave?"

He chuckled. "And proceeded to strip to the waist, place myself on an imaginary auction block, and knock myself down for the remainder of the school day to the highest bidder." Another chuckle. "Who eventually proved to be Ralph Abernathy. Does he return to your memory?"

"As a sort of a bully."

"Something of an understatement. Albeit, with all his faults, not utterly lacking in generosity. An entire bagful of Smackworth's mixed-flavor jelly beans he plunked down for me on the barrel head...and what hoops he put me through until my automatic manumission by the dulcet tones of the end-of-the-school-day chime!

Why, twice or thrice, gleefully portraying Simon Legree, he even attempted demanding the return of his jelly beans!"

"Thank goodness you'd had the foresight to bank them with me."

"I was somewhat astonished and more than a trifle disappointed that you had held yourself aloof from bidding on me, Angela."

"I don't think I had anything as grand as a whole bagful of Smackworth's mixed-flavor jelly beans. Besides…I don't know… it seemed a little wrong, somehow, to treat it all so lightly."

"I was trebly blessed, then, in that you condescended to serve as my banker, and partake of those jelly beans with me after the completion of the school day."

"Of course, you were the only kid in class who knew what an 'octoroon' was. I think you even stumped M. Finestein."

"Was that not the purpose of Show and Tell: to assist in the education of one's peers? They may have been unacquainted with the word at the commencement of my little demonstration, but they comprehended it to denote familial pride in my Chocolate great-grandmother, born and bred though she was in Canada, and thus never in her life menaced with the auction block." He sighed happily. "It is invigorating to be not entirely Vanilla, but marbled or swirled, as it were, with a richer flavor."

"I've thought ever since that day that it must be where you got those wonderful, dark eyes of yours."

"Whereas your eyes are wondrous blue, even as the deep sky of a spring day over the Painted Desert."

"And yet I have an 'octoroon' of Cinnamon in me from a Native American great-grandfather. I think I could register with his Tribe, only it's so far away, down in Oklahoma. I have a Native great-grandmother, too, though she was only a step-great grandmother, that great-grandfather's second wife, and it was really a son by his first wife, his Vanilla wife, who helped eventually make me."

"I feel less than persuaded that such connections count."

"Have you ever traced your family heritage past great-grand-parents?"

He shook his head. "Never subsequently to that fourth-grade assignment. What would be the purpose? Sixteen great-great-grands…a mere one-sixteenth of an individual's genetic material from each…and which line to prioritize? And then, what further genealogical revelation could conceivably prove aught than anti-climax to the discovery of a pure Chocolate great-grandmother?"

"A real Spanish Inquisitor somewhere among your ancestors?"

"No, that blood would be far too diluted by now. In the ultimate analysis, we are what we are, each one of us, as they were what they were, each vital one of them, and life is for living each generation anew, rather than overemphasizing the lives of so many individuals connected with oneself more or less incidentally, and who approached their daily tribulations and celebrations with no prognosticatory sense of their descendents as definitive forms and faces."

"That disposes of genealogy in a nutshell."

"Rather a jumbo-sized nutshell?" He grinned. "Consider in what an unenviable situation over-attentiveness to genealogy embroiled the Murgatroyds of Ruddigore."

Laughing with him, she hummed a little of the ghostly chorus, then said, "And from then on, all through fourth grade, your favorite rolegame was Uncle Tom's Cabin, and escaping on the Underground Railroad."

"The slavering jaws of those voracious bloodhounds could clamp down rather sharply on whichever limb came within their enthusiastic reach. Amazing how the creatures could scent out even an octoroon! Though occasionally I did attain Canada and liberty. Once or twice, by negotiating floes of ice. Yes, I would play Uncle Tom's Cabin again. Would you find that scenario at all more congenial than Spanish Inquisition or Christians versus Lions?"

"Maybe…a little. Cory, I'm afraid you'd better be getting back inside where it's safe."

"I protest astronomical odds against our being in any grave jeopardy here and now. Still and nevertheless, the hour is late—by your schedule—and a longer distance home faces you than me." He bent his head to the open car window.

She lifted her face to his. Their lips touched. One quick, light good-night kiss of friendship had no business doing such things to her insides! "Good-night, Raggedy Andy—now scoot back safe inside."

"Stipulating that you roll up your window, Raggedy Ann, and that you telephone me as soon as you too are safely within doors,

I hear and obey." A sort of mock-sloppy salaam—mixing his game scenarios rather badly—and he turned back to the apartment house. Rolling up her car window, she watched him go. When he got inside, he turned again and gave her a triumphant wave through the glass panel beside the door. Waving back, she started her car, smothered a sigh, and determinedly thought about seeing "Foggerty's Fairy" with Hank Algood.

* * * *

"Mmm," said Julie, coming up for air. "Handsome, what have you been wasting your time on all my life?"

They sat in his red Rambler in the Pankhurst Arms parking lot. He had slid over from behind the steering wheel, and she in from the window, to meet in the middle of the front seat for half an hour or so of necking, petting, and smooching like teenagers.

"Mundane stuff," Dave answered her question. "Like helping bring bad guys to justice."

Another long kiss. Then, "What is 'justice'?" Julie asked.

"Justice is not buying a car with these new armchair front seats."

Another kiss, and hands up and down each other's torsos. A few more minutes, and Dave suggested, "I hear the back seat can be pretty nice, too."

"So can bed, sweetheart." She drew back teasingly and laid two fingers lightly on his lips. "But not tonight. Not quite yet. You're definitely a date number three man." Besides that, while so far his touch had been very pleasurable, she didn't want the kind of pressure on her sore spots that real lovemaking entailed. "Think about it," she added.

One more kiss, and he wanted to know, "Maybe tomorrow night?"

"Can't. I'm on night shift Mondays just now, remember? Shall we make it…let's see…Thursday?"

"Thursday it is. Even though it's going to be a very long first four days of the week this week." He hugged her tight enough to draw out a little gasp, which she hoped he'd hear as pleasure rather than pain.

Strangely enough—which had never happened to Julie before—this time, beneath his unaware and passionate arm, the pain was…almost sweet.

Definitely, it was time to go emeritus from Dante's Delight.

CHAPTER 10

MONDAY, SEPTEMBER 25

The coffee shop of the Lew Wallace Public Library was a pleasant place, its indoor area hung about with portraits of Midwest America's favorite literary sons and daughters, its outdoor terrace overlooking a pleasant bend of the Vigo River...kilometers away from the place where Harry Jackson's body had been found. A cafe of any kind might not have been Julie's first choice for the coming interview, but it was better than strict—and therefore suspicious—privacy; and at 1400 hours they should have it almost to themselves. She got there about 1345, bought tea and a salad at the food counter, and, seeing how warm and sunny the day was for late September, carried her lunch to a table on the terrace, where they would be out of even the kitchen staff's easy earshot.

Corwin joined her promptly at 1400, with a sandwich plate in one hand and cup of coffee in the other. "*Ave et bene,*" he greeted her, taking his seat. "Salutations and felicitations."

"*Aves* of the heartiest," she returned. "You know, every time I've seen you, you've been wearing black. Do you always?"

"Since millennia before our recent prejudices came to associate darkness with undesirability, black was the symbolic hue of life, the earth, healing rest and salubrious slumber. Rendering it vastly more appropriate for our clergy than the common rather vague associations of mourning for the sinfulness of the mortal condition and renunciation of the world as perceived in Manichean theology. Moreover, I do not wear black exclusively. Today, if I remember, I donned a turtleneck undertunic in tawny amber."

"So you did!"

"But for how much longer do you purpose to balance me in suspense regarding the subject of this conference?"

"First, let's eat our lunch. Recreational talk only during the meal. Serious conferring afterwards."

He pushed his plate to the center of the table and folded his arms across his chest. "Can you truly expect me to small-talk my way through the tenterhooks of anticipation? I refuse to partake of a mouthful until you have elucidated the enigma."

She decided, just for once, it might be more in the spirit of the guiderule to bend it a little. "Tenterhooks," she said carefully, feeling her way. "Now, that's an interesting choice of words. Let's look back about half a century…"

As she spoke, she watched his expression move from astonishment to admiration, his sandwich forgotten and his coffee cooling untasted. Never a hint of outrage, censure, or willful misunderstanding. By the time she finished, his face fairly glowed with enthusiasm.

Nevertheless, after finally taking a few bites of his sandwich and swallowing a little coffee, he said, "The invitation honors me, very likely, beyond my merits. Still, you understand, I shall require a few days of meditation preliminary to signing the consent form."

"Of course. We wouldn't want you if you didn't take time to think about it first. I don't even have the consent form with me."

She had sipped her tea away between sentences, and he pronounced his coffee too tepid for proper appreciation. He replenished both their mugs, bringing back a plate of petits fours at the same time, and the rest of the hour passed in pleasant chat about ancient philosophy and recent films.

THURSDAY, SEPTEMBER 28

The Geldhoffer was the swankiest dinner club in Forest Green. It dated from late Victorian times, when it had been the Geldhoffer Mansion, built on a rounded hill that might be an Indian mound— or might not: the legal skirmishes between the present owners, the archeologists, and the Tribes threatened to outdo the plot of the Dickens novel *Bleak House*, providing job security for a lot of civil lawyers. For the foreseeable future, the Geldhoffer Restaurant was safe where it was, overlooking a bend of the Vigo River; and the present owners had promised that, if a court decision favoring either the archeologists or the Tribes ever forced them to do so, they would move the historic old building to another site, plank by plank and brick by brick.

To dine at the Geldhoffer on the salaries of a police detective and a nurse marked how deeply Dave and Julie felt about their third date. Dave's Sergeant Lestrade, who knew the sous chef from when they both lived in Chicago, had made the reservation in Dave's name, and their table sat by itself in a cozy alcove papered with crimson flocked arabesques on an ivory background, accented by striped draperies in the same colors, mock gaslights in translucent shades, and crimson candles in silver holders on the creamy tablecloth. Enough dark shades for richness, enough light tones for cheerfulness.

They settled into their antique mahogany chairs with petit-point seat cushions, and their waiter produced a bucket stand holding a half-magnum of champagne on ice, "compliments of a friend," whom both guessed to be Sergeant Lestrade again.

"I can hardly wait to meet her," Julie told Dave.

"Some have said it's easiest to admire her from a distance," Dave replied in a cautioning tone, and took a sip of champagne. "But I'm proud to be working with the Old Woman."

"Maybe...if we should decide, after tonight, to take things... farther, I should ask for her permission?"

"Hey, I'm my own man, I make my own decisions." He chuckled. "However, if you need somebody to walk you down the aisle..."

"Let her walk *you* down the aisle! Last I heard, my folks are still sound enough of wind and limb to walk all the way in from Albuquerque if they have to. And if we give them enough advance warning, of course." Three sips of champagne, and already she was feeling pretty happy. She guessed that it was more than the champagne, that just plain water might have gone to her head tonight.

Must have to do less with the champagne itself than with the reason they were drinking it.

The soup—a light fruits-of-the-sea bisque—arrived in a tureen, complete with portly waiter bearing a silver ladle. Before the waiter started ladling, Dave said, "Time to open your napkin, pretty lady," and unfolded his with a clothy kind of wannabe snap.

The napkins were folded with an elegance she would probably never be able to learn in this lifetime. Opening hers fold by fold, savoring the process, she heard something clunk down into her plate.

She picked it up. A single lustrous black pearl, the size of a small, perfect pea, in a teardrop-shaped setting on a fine silver chain.

"I know in the wine or the souffle is traditional," said Dave, "but I couldn't see gumming it up and having to wash it off before we put it on you. You won't get any other piece of jewelry from me exactly this way, though. Maybe some other way…"

How deeply he must have dipped into the money she knew he had banked away for the house he was remodeling! Julie felt her throat lumping up a little. "Dave…if you'd fasten it around my neck for me?"

He did so, moving around the table on the side opposite to where the waiter stood ladling out the soup. The waiter, a merry-looking fat man of advanced middle age, wore a smile soft as candlelight on his pleasant, round face. People liked to see lovers, Julie thought dreamily. Nice, to give people so much pleasure.

Once the waiter had glided away and the lovers sat smiling over their ear-handled china soup cups at each other, Dave lifted his champagne flute again and said, "To Date Number Three!"

"Date Number Three," she whispered back, raising her own flute. "You could even have been a Date Number Four man, but *I* couldn't wait that long."

"Your place or mine?"

"Oh, mine. It's closer. After dinner, of course."

"After dinner. Of course. And eat up, my lady. You'll need all the energy you can get."

* * * *

They spent no time in his parked car this evening, but they did on her living-room couch, necking and cuddling and generally making with the preliminaries of really earnest foreplay. Julie's heart pounded in more than passion. The Moment of Truth was near. She had been able to put it out of her mind all through dinner, but now…as it grew closer and closer… Should she insist on undressing in her darkened bedroom, slipping between the sheets at once, never letting him view her naked body until afterwards? Or should she display herself to him beforehand? How often had she preplanned this, making her mind up so often one way and so often the other way that now, with the seconds melting away…so very pleasantly, she in his arms and he in hers…she still had the decision to make, all over again.

Beforehand, she decided at last, just before they reached the point of uncontrollably tearing the clothes off each other. Beforehand was more honest and aboveboard. If he really was her prince, he'd respect her more afterwards. And if he wasn't, she'd lose him anyway, whichever way she did it. That was the argument that finally won out.

Using two spread fingers, she pushed him away just far enough for tickling his face with her words. "Bedtime, Handsome Detective. Just give me three minutes alone to…change. Then you come in and see the surprise I've got for you."

"Three whole minutes? What'll I do for three whole minutes?"

"Be imaginative, my Handsome Detective. Be imaginative." She slipped out of his arms and ran across the carpet, her shoes already shed.

In the shuttered bedroom, she tabbed on the light and peeled every stitch of clothing off her body, tossing it all in a neat—well, reasonably neat—pile in the far corner. The only thing she left on was the black pearl he had given her tonight. She got herself naked in something under three minutes, positioned herself to give him a full frontal view the minute he opened the door, glanced back once at the bed—still not quite too late for Plan B—No, let him have the full force of it right away and, Sweet Jesus! how she hoped this one was okay with really big tattoos. "Ready when you are, Handsome Detective!" she called with as much of a purr as she could get into her voice.

He whammed the door open and froze in the doorway. For a moment or two, they just stood staring at each other.

He had used those three whole minutes to get himself naked in the living room. And—he had a tattoo, too! Not quite as large as hers—but it also was a dragon, breathing fire between his pectorals, spreading its wings over his male nipples, circling its tail around his navel to end with the arrow-shaped tip pointing straight down…

"Hey!" he cried. "We match!"

And into each other's arms they rushed, Dragon Prince to Dragon Lady.

* * *

"Hey, Dragon Lady," Dave asked, kneading his fingers over her shoulders and back, "what's this here? Feels like some kind of scarring."

"Oh, those!" She tried to laugh it off. "Say the dragon nipped me playfully."

"Okay. If that's your cover story. What really happened? Didn't get this done by Naismith, did you?"

"Who?"

"Old renegade tattoo artist hiding out from his association here in Forest Green."

"Oh, yes! Think I heard about him."

"If he's been getting careless again —"

She laughed louder and longer. "Hey, nurse's pay isn't quite that bad. I could afford to go a few steps higher than Naismith! No, I got those scars years ago on vacation at Michigan Beach. Slipped on some rocks and landed on a broken beer bottle. Pretty traumatic at the time, but the damage turned out to be only skin deep."

CHAPTER 11

Of the last four Gilbert and Sullivan operas, "Foggerty's Fairy" was regarded as the fluffiest, the one most nearly resembling "H.M.S. Pinafore" and the other early pieces. While literary criticism tended to bypass "Foggerty's Fairy" with a few grudging words, it remained one of the most popular for amateur revival, and even professional companies usually made money on it. In games of Topsyturvydom, Angela had sometimes enjoyed role-playing the Fairy Rebecca. Corwin had once in high school days essayed Foggerty, but found it not entirely to his taste and switched in mid-game to John Wellington Wells, until that point in the session a non-player character.

After this Friday evening's show, while waiting for their order at the Klondike Ice Cream Emporium, Corwin remarked, "It seems all but psychedelic, accustomed as we are to seeing the two roles conjoined for the showcasing of a single actress, to find the initial act's Delia Spiff and the concluding act's Malvina de Vere portrayed by two young performers of radically diverse physiques."

"They did that because so many girls always try out for high school theatricals. Hank told me at the dress rehearsal Wednesday. So they decided to go for contrast."

"Pray don't misconstrue my observation. A feisty though diminutive Miss Spiff contrasts with a statuesquely willowy Miss de Vere to truly excellent effect. The experiment could well bear repetition in professional productions.... How did you find your date with Hank?"

"Very nice. Like going out with an uncle."

"Ah. Avuncular."

"Hank's own very word.... And your date with Julie last Monday?"

"Not precisely a 'date' in the generally recognized popular connotation of that amiable metonym. Why do you persist in applying that term? A simple 'appointment.' She proffered me a pregnant—strike that, it was an unfortunate selection of modifier, allow me to recogitate…"

"Oh, I'm glad even you have to grope for a word sometimes! It mak—renders you a little more nearly human."

He grinned back at her. "Well, this time let us settle for a mere 'interesting' invitation. About which I am zealous to impart further details…" He glanced around the crowded dessert parlor… "whenever a more convenient occasion for privacy occurs."

"You've been putting it off all week! I'm beginning to think you're planning a three-act melodrama."

"Oh, trust me, I lie under no necessity of embellishing *this*."

Three quarters of an hour later, Angela pulled Aunt Sally's borrowed new model Bakersfield Panther up beside the curb in front of the Marquette House, turned off the engine, used the fancy new tab that locked all the car doors at once, and, keeping her finger down on it, turned to him in the glow of the street lamps to say: "All right, Cory, we're not going to find a much more convenient occasion for privacy than this." And found herself thinking it might have been nice if Aunt Sally had settled for a model with the smooth door-to-door cushion instead of these new individual armchair seats.

She didn't have to work very long putting that thought out of her head. What he told her did it right away. Whatever she had been anticipating, it was not this!

Julie Whitcomb belonged to a group that called itself the "Dante's Delight Purgatorio." They had existed in Forest Green for almost half a century, new members joining as older ones retired or "went emeritus," always between four and six active members. Six in theory—in actual practice, it had never been more than five. And no wonder! How had they ever found as many as five? From what Angela combed out of Corwin's description, they spent their get-togethers taking turns torturing one another. And Julie had brought him an invitation to join them!

"Good God, Cory, they're *smasters*!"

"Not smasters," he replied, sounding a little hurt and stiff. "Purgatorians."

"Oh, really? What's the difference?"

"Purgatorians participate in these activities not for titillation, but rather to assist in the penitential purification and spiritual balancing of our world."

"Whatever fancy excuses you give it, they're still smasters."

"Angela, don't you understand? Not even you? Purgatorians are in all significant ways the diametric opposite of smasters. Purgatorians have this motto: 'Pain enjoyed is hardly penitential.'"

"It's still wrong. Why, it's sinful!"

"In what way sinful?" he argued. "In what way less meritorious than the fastings, hair shirts, and thorn bushes of the honored saints? The cilices and hard beds of Opus Dei? The scourges of the flagellants? The pious practices of the Penitentes, those who voluntarily participate in the Triduum by passing several hours of Good Friday affixed to crosses?"

"All of which we're busy outgrowing! What do you think Madre Eleanor would say about this in Reconciliation?"

"What purpose would I have in confessing meritorious activity? The sacrament was never designed for boasting."

"*Boasting?*"

"Are not the penances allotted us in sacramental Reconciliation mere vitiated echoes of the more stringent practices once enjoined on all notorious sinners and voluntarily shared by our greatest saints?"

"And shouldn't we all have learned better by now?"

"What of the veneration still universally accorded to stigmatics? What, indeed, of the Passion and Crucifixion of Our Savior Himself—with Whose sufferings we are all bound to consider ourselves conjoined in mystic union? For what purpose does Holy Church so strenuously admonish us to eschew 'Risen Christ' and 'Christ the King' images on our crucifixes in favor of the writhing and bloody corpus portrayed with at least quasi-realism?"

"Oh, Cory, Cory, Cory, all that just *happened* to them. They didn't do it to *themselves!* Not Christ and certainly not the stigmatics."

"Not even through the purity of their prayerful self-identification with the suffering Savior? It's a moot point—arguable. And does not the Pauline Epistle to the Romans beg us 'through the mercy of God to offer our bodies as a living sacrifice holy and acceptable to God'?"

"That's misquoting—misinterpreting—making it mean something it shouldn't! Offer our bodies in the ordinary way of everyday living—that's what it has to mean!"

"And what of the famous Roman Martyrology and its still more famous successor in the Protestant branch of our joint creed, the magnum opus of John Foxe? Are we to adulate and strive to imitate our saintly sufferers, without aspiring to emulate their pangs? Are the merits and blessings of holy agony reserved strictly to those who can tease their enemies into administering them, never—outside the walls of certain religious orders and the Purgatory of eschatological contemplation—to those who serve one another thus in amity?"

"Oh, Cory, you're getting it all twisted! Don't you know—haven't you even stopped to think—there are people all over the world suffering—*really* suffering, *really* being tortured—without ever signing any silly 'consenting adult' forms—look at poor Harry Jackson—and you—I mean, people like your so-called 'Purgatorians'—just want to make a sort of—of *spoof* of it!"

"On the contrary," he said, for the first time sounding more than just a little stiff and hurt. "Purgatorians are all too keenly aware of the involuntary sufferings of all these others. It is *why* they willingly choose to undergo similar treatment: in the hope of alleviating in so far as they can some small part of the world's pain."

"They're idiots, then! Think, Cory, *think*! How can you alleviate the rest of the world's suffering by adding your own to it?"

"Through some mystery of Cosmic Balance," he replied slowly. "They met last Friday, and did not the atmosphere throughout Forest Green seem more relaxed already on Saturday? They held another, a special-need meeting on Saturday afternoon, and by Sunday the city felt almost returned to that sense of secure normality which has rendered it notable for almost half a century—the same half-century of the Purgatorio's existence."

"Coincidence!"

"*Is* it? Something of the need for Cosmic Balance of grief and joy, good and evil, we have sensed ever since the primordial awakening of our human awareness. The ordeals of shamanistic initiation, the blood sacrifices of native cultures—those pre-Columbian kings who drew spiked cords through their own tongues —"

"Oh, Cory, don't—*don't* tell me these people do anything like *that!*"

"Angela, please be reassured. The members of Dante's Delight employ none but safe techniques, leaving neither scar nor permanent trace, excepting a single tasteful stamped tattoo in lieu of membership card."

"Safe? *Safe?* How can you be sure —"

"Two of the Purgatorians are trained paramedics, Julie a nurse —"

"Julie!" Up till now, Angela had been so appalled by the rest of what she was hearing, that she hadn't even remembered—"Isn't Julie dating Dave Clayton? He's a police detective, isn't he? What does *he* think about all this?"

"That, I conceive, is between them. In any event, the work of the Purgatorio has no bearing on the…amorous activities of its members, who are bound in honor to engage in no such relationships among themselves and to regard the…procreational areas of the human body as sacrosanct."

"Would Julie ever even dare tell Dave about it at all?"

"I entertain some suspicion that Julie might be in quest of a replacement, enabling her to go emeritus from purgatorial activity. Angela…I am honored by this invitation to join in their efforts."

"*Cory!*" Reaching across the armrest, she clutched his upper arm. "Cory, it's one thing to rolegame all this kind of thing in your imagination, but this—to *really* do anything like this—it's *sick!* Whatever you say, whatever holy-sounding arguments you come up with—it's sick! Think how I'd feel —"

"You would witness nothing of it. Attendance is strictly limited to the membership."

"And *that* doesn't tell you anything? But think how I'd feel, just knowing you were being hurt, *really* hurt, not pretend hurting—I don't care how 'safe' and 'no scars' it is!"

"How you would feel…as a friend?"

Angela hesitated. If Julie really was with Dave Clayton, now… should she? "Cory…as your oldest friend, your best friend… maybe, someday, even more than that…I'm begging you, *don't,*

DON'T ever get yourself involved in anything like this, this 'Purgatorio'!"

"As…someday…'even more than a friend'?"

"Promise me! Promise me you won't."

He pulled her hand gently from his arm, lifted her fingers to his cheek, his forehead, his lips…then laid his other hand on top to sandwich hers between. "Angela…you have my solemn promise. Now—now, I think, lest matters precipitate over-hastily, I had best seek the solitary sanctuary of Arnheim. Apprise me by telephone when you are safe at Aunt Sally's domestic abode."

"You didn't even need to ask. The library coffee shop tomorrow?"

"*Bien sur*—no, wait. Tomorrow is Saturday. The Sorrento?"

"At two."

She watched him safely inside his building, and drove away with her head in a whirl.

Had she really hinted…? And had he really jumped on the hint? *Pounced* on it? And didn't that mean…?

Not Julie. Not Julie at all. Why so slow on the uptake, Angela Garvey? Monday…till today…five full days…no, maybe Monday shouldn't really count, she—Angela—hadn't seen him at all that day, because of Julie, because of…

Why, she wouldn't really have had to extract that promise from him, at all! They had to do these things *to one another*, didn't they? And Corwin would never have been able to handle hurting anyone else like that! All she'd really had to do was remind him…

But she was glad she *had* made him give her his solemn promise, because that was the way she'd hinted, and he'd hinted back…

Wallace Library itself was open on Saturday and Sunday, and you could even get into the coffee shop and out on its terrace to use the tables, but only for vending-machine beverages and snacks, because they didn't have enough volunteers to staff the kitchen on the wraparound days of the week. Angela had her name on that volunteer waiting list, too. Maybe somebody else would sign up, and then they'd have enough volunteers to keep it open all seven days. Then she'd be right in the same building where he researched things for his writer clients. Maybe she could get in touch with Gaia…Gaia what?…again, talk her into volunteering, too. What fun, if they were staffing the place at the same time and tried tricking him sometimes as to which was which, each pretending to be the other one!

There was the Forest Green Community Theater, too. She was on the list for their behind-the-scenes work.

And he'd hinted back! "'As...someday,'" he had said, "'even more than a friend.'"

The big, overgrown boy with his Peter Pan ideas about pain and manly heroism!

"'Even more than a friend.'" Of all that last argument of hers, those were the words he'd zeroed in on, the words he'd repeated back to her, the words that must have clinched his promise. "'As... someday...even more than a friend.'"

It wasn't until she was pulling into Aunt Sally's garage that she remembered he never had told her who the other three were, the ones in it with Julie.

Well, it really made no difference, did it? He wasn't going to join the...silly group—maybe I really shouldn't call it anything worse, that might be like throwing stones—the silly, stupid group of fools. Ever. He'd made her his solemn promise.

If she found herself looking at people suspiciously, wondering, "Is he or she one of them?" to the point where it made social functioning awkward, then maybe she'd have to ask Cory. Otherwise, "Judge not, lest you be judged." Judge not. Unless maybe to call them silly, stupid idiots.

"'...even more than a friend.'"

Being alone in Aunt Sally's car just now, Angela hugged herself.

CHAPTER 12

Guiderules insisted that a bow kept constantly strung lost the resilience needed to shoot arrows, and therefore everybody had to take time off for "rest and relaxation," the resemblance of people to bowstrings being so obvious. Much as Rosemary Lestrade hated her workline, she hated her mandated time off even more. How the heck did a floater put away thoughts about people suffering injustice, long enough to perpetrate personal "rest and relaxation"? Shouldn't mealtimes and sleep hours be plenty? Who the hades had ever come up with the thirty-hour work week, anyway? Not that Lestrade had ever felt herself bound by ten-to-four—ten hundred to sixteen hundred hours as it was now—five days a week, but national as well as local guidelaws limited the amount of overtime anyone on salary could put in, even voluntarily and without pay, except during emergency conditions. Called the "Anti-Sweatshop Laws."

Well, even in Forest Green, the Department apparently didn't count just one murder victim grounds for letting any of its members stretch "emergency conditions" out longer than the first week. And, thank the Lady! almost two weeks and they hadn't found a second victim. Forest Green continued one of the safest small cities in what was considered a pretty safe era in the fifty-five Reformed States of America.

But it left Rosemary Lozinski Lestrade feeling not only unstrung, but unraveled these two wraparound days when last week turned into next week.

She dozed in bed as long as she could, with her radio tuned softly to a jazz station. It was about the only kind of music she could rely on neither to mention somebody doing somebody else wrong criminally or otherwise, or to remind her of the various kinds of soft music—slow classical, gentle Big Band, lush and moody, or the quieter sounds of nature—the guiderules made them pipe into their interrogation room at the station. Not that Lestrade had ever agreed with those of her fellow pollies and of the general citizenry who complained about coddling criminals. Better coddle twenty real perpetrators through the preliminaries, she always felt, than make one innocent party squirm by mistake. Her fallen-away Wiccan heart applauded every guiderule designed to guard people under arrest from the police brutality of the bad old days. But her psychomystical head felt that, if you were going to be reminded of your workline, you might as well have been out on the job.

She finally got up about oh seven hundred, made coffee (not as well as they made it down at the station), scrambled herself a couple of eggs, read a couple of children's picture books from Wallace Public, surprised herself with a chuckle or two at that eccentric just-home-from-college floater who had a reserved study carrel there, always dressed in black, let the fanciest words anyone could find in Webster's Unabridged flow out of his mouth like a waterfall, and was still about the only person she had yet encountered who seemed to understand how a middle-aged polly might like to check out children's picture books for her own consumption. Everyone else, fellow patrons and librarians alike, tended to ask her about the sons and daughters and nieces and nephews and neighbor tykes they assumed she was reading to.

She was flipping through a Dr. Seuss when her phone chimed.

It was Chris Grunewald. "Les?"

"Chris."

"So you actually spend some quality time at home, after all."

"I *serve* time at home. What 'quality' it is, I couldn't say. What have you got for me?"

"The full report is in the mail, second copy on its way back with the corpus delicti. Just thought I'd make triple-sure with a phone call. Also one more chance to hear your dulcet tones."

"Skip the flattery, Grunewald. Just give me your best guess."

"Okay. Best guess. My educated opinion: most of the marks were inflicted post-mortem, with a high enough probability to satisfy most courts. Impartial courts, anyway."

"If you can ever find any such thing as an impartial court in cases like this one."

"First, you sort of have to find a viable candidate for defendant, don't you?"

"Mmm. You said 'most of the marks.'"

"Almost an equally high probability that the tattoo was stamped on pre-mortem."

"Interesting."

"Exact figures, probability percentages, and other pertinent details in the report."

"Didn't by any chance check for poison?" Lestrade asked without much hope, already knowing the probable answer.

"Les, Les, Les!" A couple tsks of the tongue. "There are some limits even to my wonder-working powers. You know before we can start running tests for poison, we've got to have *some* idea what kind of poison we're looking for. Otherwise, more different toxins out there, than there are tissue samples in a body or minutes in a year. I had to sneak Jackson's corpse in for you on my own time, as it was."

"Some injectable poison."

"Want to ship Jackson back and wait a century or two?"

Lestrade sighed. "I just thought you might have some new testing stuff in that up-to-date big-city lab of yours."

"No such luck, Les. No such luck."

"Okay, Chris, thanks. You've been a big help here. Blessed be."

"Wow! A personal blessing from the high priestess of the Earth Mother herself!"

"Never exactly 'high,' Chris, and defrocked for years." Rosemary Lestrade had sold her soul to the police force in order to clear innocent people, and ended up sneaking in unpaid overtime, only to see too many get put away in spite of her best efforts. Thanking Chris again, with the promise of coming back up to Chicago sometime for a flower show on Navy Pier or something, she signed off and cradled the receiver.

* * * *

Julie had two phone calls Saturday morning before lunch. The first at 0930 hours, from Dave, anticipating tonight's Date Number Four with an hour of checking her menu preferences: after their splurge Thursday evening, they were economizing a little with an early dinner of his cooking at his place, followed up with an early and long night in his bed. The second call was from Corwin at 1115 hours—for him, as she understood, very nearly the crack of dawn. With most sincere apologies and heartfelt appreciation of the honor, he grieved to tell her that he must decline her highly commendatory and gratifying invitation into Dante's Delight Purgatorio, in order to fulfill a solemn promise he had pledged the evening before to one whose happiness he prized above all lesser considerations.

"Angela?" Julie guessed.

"Angela." His tone of voice left no doubt that his own happiness far outweighed his disappointment.

So that was that. She congratulated him, got his reassurances that he would honor the privacy of Dante's Delight, and signed off. Well, she consoled herself, cradling the receiver, a few more prayers to sweet Jesus to send us somebody else, a little sharper lookout—in a population of 35,000 last census, there had to be at least one somebody else. After all, they had kept it going for almost half a century. And she really was ready for emeritus status. Especially now, with Dave so much in the foreground of her picture.

Meanwhile, last week's Saturday session had flipped the regular schedule, putting Julie and Paul on angel duty last night. She was ready and willing for whatever tonight had to offer. A glitch might have gotten into the long-term outlook, but at least the short-term view offered plenty of consolation.

* * * *

Angela thought Corwin seemed as giddy as she still felt from the promise of last night's goodbyes. They decided to be adventurous at The Sorrento today: instead of their usual spaghetti, she ordered layered spinach mostaccioli and he chicken fettuccine alfredo. And wine—house wine, because in spite of never having had to worry about money, neither of them was old enough to have learned how to connoisseur wine, and they felt no special interest in pretending to know anything about it, so it was best just to trust the restaurant.

Over the menu, she found herself humming the Fairy Rebecca's famous "Colonel Culpepper's Favorite Dog" patter song, and remarked, "I wouldn't mind seeing that production again tonight."

"Shall we? Riley High boasts a theater sufficiently commodious to sell out only occasionally, and should the penultimate performance prove the exception—to our disgruntlement, but the enrichment of the educational institution—Hank might be persuaded to tuck us, as cognoscenti, into some inconspicuous corner of the wings, thus affording us an unusual view of a production that we will not see again this side of the Akashic Records. For 'Foggerty's Fairy' we may have always with us, but never again in this unique production."

"Actually, in live theater, every single performance is unique, always a little different from all the other performances. That's one of the things that make live theater so much fun. But tonight wouldn't be our last chance. There's the matinee tomorrow."

"Sunday. That would necessitate our arriving tardily at the rolegaming…"

"But there will always be more rolegames."

"True, but, as with theatrical representations, each rolegaming session is unique."

Their wine arrived. They toasted each other and sipped, exchanged smiles across the table, and sipped again.

"Gilbert's original, nonmusical version of 1880," he said at length, continuing the small talk, "comprises three acts. In adapting and polishing it for the operatic stage of the Savoy, he dispensed with most of Act Three—despite many scenes of rare comedy, its absence is no indispensable loss and, indeed, rather beneficial to the dramatic unity and balance."

"How did it all end, then?"

"Oh, the Venerable William simple amputated the denouement from Act Three and dovetailed it neatly into the end of Act Two."

"I think you just mixed a metaphor there, Cory."

"Did I? Kindly explicate."

"'Amputate'—a medical operation. 'Dovetail'—isn't that carpentry?"

"So it is, and so I did! I stand—or, more accurately, sit—corrected."

It might not have seemed all that excruciatingly funny to anyone else, or even to themselves at another time and place, but that Saturday in that favorite restaurant, after that particular Friday night, they laughed until they became slowly aware of other late lunchers turning to smile at them.

"Walkinshaw," he mused at last, with another sip of wine, "might prove a more fertile character than the eponymous Foggerty to roleplay. Walkinshaw at least enjoys a bit of being knocked comically about the stage."

Angela asked softly, "Were you *too* disappointed yesterday, Cory, when I made you promise?"

"Disappointed? I felicitate myself on negotiating a transaction beyond the most cherished dreams of a Rockefeller or a Carnegie—who according to legend dealt only in mere financial dross. Angela, Angela, you are so far above my merit... I postulate that in the mysteries of space and eternity, the angels must have been named after you rather than vice versa."

From anyone else, it might have sounded like overblown parody. From him...

"That's very pretty, Cory, but —" She was saved from figuring out what to say next by the waiter bringing their food.

And she found she was ravenous. Cory must have been, too. For a few minutes they ate saying nothing except the occasional short comment about how tasty it was and how they thought they would order these dishes again.

Eventually, when their plates were about half full, she fed him a few bites from hers, and he fed her a few bites from his, reaching across the table with their carefully laden forks. Then, at last, she said, "But the angels were certainly not named for me! If you're looking for a saint on earth, you should meet my faculty advisor up at Minnemagantic U. He once told me that the most heroic thing of all is just to live an ordinary, decent life."

"That notable Professor Czarny who may or may not be an authentic, if compassionate, vampire?"

"Opinion up there runs about half and half. *He* certainly honestly believes that he is."

"Your epistolary communications imparted the tale to me, embellished with numerous salient details. Some accident in pre-adolescence which caused the hospital to despair of his life until, as he later recounted, an older vampire preserved it with the existence-altering bite, following which alleged incident the medical personnel discovered that nothing, to all appearances, provided him nourishment save raw blood from the blood bank, prescribed to be administered orally."

"And before that, as a kid, he'd never been much interested in vampires. His favorite childhood horror story was *The Phantom of the Opera*."

"I further garnered from your missives that he follows the diurnal schedule of his professorial profession."

"Oh, yes. And eats regular meals, as well as his prescription blood-bank blood, usually after it passes its 'use by' date for transfusions. He thinks he only eats regular food for the sociability, the flavor, and to keep his digestive system in order with enough bulk."

"As I recollect, you related somewhere that he regards vampires, not as the immortal 'undead' of legend, but as exemplars of living humanity with, at utmost, somewhat extended mortal spans? As, in fact, among the earliest known shamans of our race? Adducing the 'Body' and more especially the 'Blood' of his and our own Catholic heritage, as well as of assorted other religions, as surviving pointers to rites of the Upper if not even the Lower Paleolithic?"

"And good vampires don't need to worry about any of the usual taboos—sunlight and crosses and garlic and all that. Only the stake through the heart."

"Which would hardly prove salubrious to the illustrious Dr. Van Helsing himself."

"So whenever sunlight or garlic or the silver cross he always wears in his right earlobe start to bother him, he knows it's time to get himself to Reconciliation. That's why he has to live such a good life—simply to go on living normally."

"'Some are born saints, some achieve sanctity, and some have sainthood thrust upon them.'"

"Oh, exactly!" Angela applauded the doctored quotation. "Professor Czarny says there might be vampires living all over—only without dressing the part the way he does—you're like him that way, Cory, always wearing black."

"Although with neither swishing cape, nor silver cross in my earlobe, nor luster of holiness."

"And it's only the wicked vampires who give them all a nasty reputation."

"As do those members of any religion, from Wicca to Islam inclusive, who, quite coincidentally to their creed, dip too deeply into the deceptively alluring tarns of sin and evil."

"As did the Spanish Inquisitors," she teased him. "Shall we go direct to Sam's tomorrow afternoon, or take in 'Foggerty's Fairy' first?"

"'Foggerty's Fairy' tonight, in any event. For tomorrow…I relinquish the final determination to you."

CHAPTER 13

STILL SATURDAY SEPTEMBER 30

Dave lived about a kilometer and a half outside town, in an old frame farmhouse he was remodeling in his spare time. For what shelter they could get from winter winds, the original farmers had set it in a slight hollow among their rolling fields and enclosed it with rows of windbreak firs atop the nearest ridges, far enough away not to threaten the house, even large as the trees had grown by now. Closer to the building gathered a small orchard of half a dozen twisty old fruit trees and half a dozen young ones recently planted to replace predecessors that, too old for bearing, had been retired to glory in the fireplace. Closest of all to the front door grew immense lilac bushes that must be wonderful in springtime. Behind the house were raspberry bushes and what had been a small kitchen garden, for the past several years planted exclusively with the kinds of herbs that could pretty well tend themselves. Taken together, it all must make a gorgeous nest of greenery and blossoms throughout the growing seasons. It was still gorgeous now: for some tastes, even more gorgeous with the autumn colors coming out.

Well to one side of the house were grouped a big old barn, a couple of silos, and some smaller outbuildings designed for assorted uses—these last now dangerously though not yet terminally picturesque. The barn itself was still sound, and the old sign on its side, facing the road, was not so badly flaked off but that people in passing cars could still make out the ad for Old Wabash Brand, though the product itself was no longer available.

Dave had picked Julie up, wearing casual clothes and her black pearl, at the Pankhurst Arms about 1430 and brought her out here early saying that he wanted a little time to show his renovations off to her before starting dinner.

As they went through the front door, she saw they could either go straight to the living area, or turn left down a short corridor. He guided her first to the left: to what had been a downstairs bedroom and old-fashioned small bathroom and now was a large bathroom with diamond-shaped tub big enough for two.

Then back to the living area, where he had knocked down a few nonbearing walls to open most of the downstairs up into one big living room with a kitchen side and a seating-by-the-fire-side, with long, tiled counter semi-setting off the kitchen appliances and work area, dining table in the middle, and, in the wall adjacent to the fireplace, French doors leading to what would eventually be a sunporch but for now was a raised floor and window framing covered in heavy sheet plastic, with ladder, boards, and assorted building supplies piled around.

"Oh, Dave, please don't tell me you're fixing this place up to resell at a profit?"

"What, lose the legacy that brought me here to Forest Green in the first place? Then maybe have to settle for some second-rate crackerbox in town? Not likely! No, I figure I'm here for the duration. Fixing it up for myself, not for some tridol-laden stranger."

The walk-in pantry leading off from the kitchen was the only part of the interior Dave had left more or less in its original condition, just cleaning it up, fitting in a freezer, and adding a modern light fixture. It looked large enough to hold winter supplies for a family of six, and was currently about a quarter stocked. Besides canned goods and canisters for dry staples, it boasted two shelves of Dave's own canning: glass jars of jams, jellies, peaches, tomatoes, green beans, and so on.

"Dave! You never brought me that raspberry jam you promised!"

He grinned an apology. "Gee. In the excitement of Date Number Three at the Geldhoffer and points south, it clean plum' slipped my mind. Well, we'll just have to load you up with your pick of the stuff tomorrow."

"Tomorrow let it be! Speaking of tomorrow, how about filling up a few hours with a little rolegaming on our way back to my shabby, crowded little place with its big bed?"

"Sure. I've rolegamed a little. Hasn't everyone? Not seriously since school days, but I don't guess it'd be too much hardship swimming back into it again with you. We may need a break between sessions, anyway."

They squeezed each other's arms.

Upstairs was still pretty much the way it had been built, six bedrooms and a half-bath, but he explained to her with expressive gestures how he was going to knock the three on the side into a single large master bedroom, with a jumbo-sized bed if they could figure out how to get it up the stairs. On the other side, the present three rooms would become two, one a guest bedroom and one his den. At least, that had been his plan…

"If not a regular jumbo-sized bed," Julie suggested, "how about a waterbed, or an airbed, or one of those foam things you can roll up when you want to transport it?"

"Great ideas! And I could put the frame and headboard together right up here." A promising peck on her cheek. "Thanks, Dragon Lady."

For now, he had an army cot, alarm clock, and his clothes in one of the bedrooms, assorted unpacked boxes and new building supplies in the others. But the couch downstairs in front of the fireplace, he assured her, made out into a luxury-sized bed, and could be very cozy. For now, how about a quick tour of the rest of the property?

It would still be daylight for another hour or so, but she noticed he picked up a heavy-duty flashlight on their way out the back door.

Through the yellowing raspberry bushes, past the overgrown herb garden, here an old deserted chicken coop, there an empty tractor shed…and now they were in the big old barn. Julie could almost picture the fine golden motes that would have been dancing in sunbeams, if the daylight had been strong enough, the sun still high enough. As it was, shadows cloaked the interior. Late autumn afternoon outdoors, deep twilight inside the barn. And smelling surprisingly clean and sweet, for an old barn so long past its working days.

"Not quite sure yet what I'm going to do with the barn, eventually, beyond repainting the outside with a big mural. Maybe open it up to square-dance groups. But I got the inside all cleaned out and ready. Like Hercules cleaning whichever stables they were."

"The Augean. He rerouted two rivers to run through them. Did you do the same with the Vigo?"

"Well, not exactly. I didn't think the City Parks Commission would be wild about the idea, so I just got in a team of helpers and made a barn-cleaning party out of it, complete with picnic table.

"Better than a river any day. Maybe that's what Hercules really did and his PR came up with the rerouted rivers idea." She sniffed. "But isn't that fresh hay or something I smell? Timothy?"

"Gives the place a good, clean, barn scent, doesn't it?"

A long staircase, ladderlike but permanently anchored and having waist-high handrails on both sides, led up to the hay loft. Here the sweet smell of fresh hay was stronger, the daylight brighter. And there…yes, there, against the far wall, beneath the window, she saw the fresh hay—a wide, generous pile of it and…was that a folded sheet there on the floor near it?

"Dave?" she said, turning to wink at him. "But what about dinner?"

"Salad, bottle of wine, and a steak and kidney pie ready in the fridge. Take the pie half an hour to heat up in the oven, or we can eat it cold. Meanwhile, I've heard a lot about tumbling in the hay…"

"And no time like the present for testing those stories, my Dragon Prince," she finished for him, snaking her arms up around his shoulders as he seized her round the waist and squeezed her breasts into his chest.

And they tumbled in the hay.

* * * *

"All this, and a gourmet chef, too," she remarked, much later, as they ate steak and kidney pie, with wine and tossed salad, before unfolding the fireside couch into a luxury-sized bed.

CHAPTER 14

When they arrived at Sam's about 1350, Julie proposed beginning the afternoon with The Seven Cities of Cibola. It was a good, versatile scenario red-blooded enough for Dave—in a good, manly adventure kind of way, yet Saturday-matinee enough that even Angela might agree to join the living-room group this time. Sam would rulemaster from the role of Awitelin Tsita the Zuni Sun Father; Dave offered himself for Coronado; Julie claimed the not-always-used role of Running Antelope, a sort of pre-Sacajawea Indian guide with, perhaps, secret designs of sabotage on the Vanilla invaders; Paul took Hosteen Coyote; Curly the conquistador second in command; Carmine Jones was proud enough of his Native American ancestors to ask for the Apache Chief hungering for these strange new equine beasts of the invaders; and so on through a baker's dozen of players. Corwin and Angela being late this afternoon, Julie suggested that Fray Marcos de Niza be a non-player character until he arrived, and Angela, if she could be persuaded to join the quest for Cibola, might be—say—a Fray Angelo to sidekick Fray Marcos, maybe keep his character alive a little longer than usual.

But they didn't arrive.

And didn't arrive.

Well, Julie mused to herself, maybe they'd rather be alone together today. She hoped he didn't think his decision not to join Dante's Delight meant that he should also drop out of the Sunday rolegames.

It was past 1500, and the game had lost only three player characters, who promptly went out and brought back snacks for everyone from the refreshments table, one of them staying to see whether or not Cibola would be found this time. They thought they were coming within sight of the seven cities of gold… Hosteen Coyote had planned a wonderful new trick of some kind… Awitelin Tsita was about to roll his die and see how well it would succeed…and Corwin Poe hurried into the room, looking flushed and pale both at once.

"Angela!" he demanded of everybody in the room. "Is she here?"

Julie took one look at his face, and stood up. "Weren't you and Angela coming together?"

"So I thought—or else to see 'Foggerty's Fairy' one last time and here for the evening, but the house of her honorary Aunt Sally Fulbright is locked and no one seems to be within. A note on the door, obviously printed in haste, says only, 'Family Emergency.' The hand does not resemble Angela's—it may be Aunt Sally's. I have telephoned everyone whom I could think of—fruitlessly! The utmost I have learned is that she was seen at Saint Martha's for the earliest Mass—as is her custom—but M. Fulbright failed to appear at her own church—the First Presbyterian—for its service at ten-thirty hours. Last, in desperation, I come here. You are my final hope. I—approach being frantic!"

The game was forgotten, except that Sam still sounded like rulemaster as he stood and said, "Everybody, start checking all the downstairs game rooms, just in case she went straight to another scenario without looking in on us first. Don't forget the snack table and the bathrooms. Paul and Curly, help me check upstairs."

"She's been playing, these last two Sundays, with the group in the library," Julie said.

Dave stood up. "I'm a police detective. Where's your phone?"

Angela was nowhere in the house but, as the searchers reconnoitered in the lounge, Dave came in and told them, "It can come in handy, being a pollydeck. Angela Garvey and Sarah 'Sally' Fulbright caught the oh-nine-forty flight to Miami from Forest Green Airport."

"Are you sure?" Corwin insisted. "There can be no error?"

"Tickets were issued in those names, anyway, just as boarding commenced. The counter lady doesn't know them by sight, and didn't get too good a look at them today because of the rush, but she remembers having the strong impression of a pretty young blond woman and a middle-aged brunette one. Does that fit them both?"

"It does." Corwin visibly relaxed a little. "I breathe easier. And Angela's father and siblings reside in Miami. The fear remains— what emergency can have summoned them away with such dispatch as to prevent all but the most rudimentary communication of the situation?"

They all returned to their rolegames. After trying to put a call through to Angela's father's number in Miami and getting only forty sets of three chimes into nothingness, Corwin joined the quest for the Seven Cities of Cibola. But he played so absently that his character ignored several chances for melodramatically painful martyrdom at the hands of either the Apaches or the lost tribes of Cibola, and actually survived to the end, when with one abstracted wave of his hand he assigned Fray Marcos' fair share of the golden booty to the Church.

CHAPTER 15

MONDAY, OCTOBER 2

Morning. Julie yawned and stretched luxuriously, then turned on her side to gaze in sheer contentment at the long, healthy, muscular manshape sleep-breathing beside her beneath the sheet. "My Dragon Prince," she whispered.

Rather a shame about Corwin Poe. She really thought she might have found herself a good replacement for Dante's Delight. Today she'd better tell Sam and the others. She hadn't really had a chance yesterday, getting there with Dave just in time for setting up the rolegame scenario, and ducking out again so shortly after Seven Cities finished up.

She sighed. And how about Dave keeping his head like that, calling on his workline expertise and authority to find out where Angela had disappeared to, while all the rest of them were still running around Sam's big house like corn in the popper? She wondered if Corwin had ever gotten in touch with Angela and her family in Miama. Whatever happened, it must have been serious; but her own workline had taught Nurse Julie Whitcomb not to waste too much time speculating on the million medical and other kinds of emergencies that always could happen. Just take care of the ones that actually happened.

She turned over again for a look at her bedside clock. Oh six hundred hours. Monday morning, October Two. A little ironic that she had awakened first, when he was the one who needed to go in early, his work day starting at 0730.

She felt grateful for last night's tumble. There wouldn't be time for another one this morning. Not if they wanted to do it right. And they did. Always and forever.

Carefully, so as to let him have another half hour, she eased herself out of bed and into the bathroom. When she had finished up, shower and all, and opened the bathroom door, there he stood waiting, with his bathrobe on as if to guard against temptation.

"Good morning, Dragon Lady!"

"Good morning, Dragon Prince!"

A quick mutual grope—just a lick and a promise—and she shoved him into the bathroom, shutting the door and calling through it, "Coffee in five minutes, eggs and bacon in fifteen."

But it wasn't to be fifteen minutes.

By the time the coffee was ready, she had the bacon leisurely browning, the eggs whipped up in a bowl ready for scrambling, and the bread in the toaster ready to be pushed down. Taking her first cup of coffee, she moved to the living room so she could look down at Pankhurst Lake early on an autumn morning while waiting for her Dragon Prince to come out of the bathroom.

Something was floating in the pond that wanted to be a lake.

Something strange and whitish.

Julie frowned at it for a moment, her coffee forgotten in her hands and a very odd feeling in the pit of her stomach.

She put her cup down on the end table and got her old binoculars out of the drawer. Put them to her eyes, adjusted them, found the floating whitish thing again.

So nearly white in the fall dawnlight. So...shaped...a mannequin of some kind? A crash dummy? A —

The binoculars jolted away from the spot as Dave's blue-sleeved arms clamped around her waist. "Okay, Dragon Lady, how about those eggs and bacon?"

"Dave." She handed him the binoculars. "Look there. In the water."

Seeing how sober she was about it, he dropped his playfulness at once, took the binoculars, squinted through them a moment, and said, "Oh, my God! Oh, my Lord and God!"

"Dave? What?"

"No—no—no—NO!" he was repeating. "Please, Lord, not another one! Julie, we've got to get down there!"

He was already halfway to the door. He was mostly dressed, she was still in her long fleece bathrobe, where she had planned on staying most of the morning. She didn't wait to change. The only side trip she made was to dash down the hall and knock on Paul

Osaka's door. "Paul! Come down to the lake right away!" Then she followed Dave.

He was at the nearest dock, untying one of the rowboats. She climbed in after him, cold water soaking her robe to her knees. He rowed. In a few minutes that seemed like hours, they reached the floating thing.

It was a body. A corpse. Floating face downward.

"Keep the boat steady," Dave told her. "Sit on the other side, over there."

She obeyed, leaning farther back in one direction while, in the other, he leaned forward, got hold of the body beneath the armpits, and hauled it up over the side into the boat.

Where it lay face up.

"Oh, sweet Jesus!" Julie gasped, her hands at her mouth, her nurse's training useless. "Oh, sweet Jesus! Is it—Is it *Angela*?"

"Can't be. *Can't* be! She's in Florida. She and her aunt flew down to Miami yesterday."

"*Somebody* went to Miami—tickets in their names. Corwin didn't recognize the printing on the note, hadn't been able to get in touch... Oh, *Dave*!"

"Can't be," he repeated, sounding as if his police training had dropped off him like her nurse's training had dropped off her. "Death...makes them look different, Julie."

"But—? Oh, Dave!"

He snapped back into a policeman, rowed back to the dock. Paul stood there, waiting for them.

"Paul," said Julie.

He took one look down into the boat and gasped.

"Paul, is it...? Does it look like her to you, too?"

"What? Oh...you mean her face. I was looking at... Yes, you mean... Oh my God, Julie, my God! Her or her alter ego!"

"Look," said Dave, "I only saw Angela Garvey once, on that double date, and then I had eyes mainly for my own date. How often have you people seen her?"

"Twice," Paul answered. "A week ago yesterday and the Sunday before that, at Sam's."

Julie did a rapid mental review. "Three times. Twice at Sam's and once on our double date."

"All right. None of us knew her well enough to make even a formal identification."

"I know who does." Julie wiped tears away with her fingers. "Oh, poor Corwin!"

"Let me get back to your phone and call this in right now," Dave went on. "You two stay here with the body. If anyone else should come by, try to wave 'em off."

Dave left.

Paul said, "Julie. Have you looked near the hollow of her right shoulder?"

No. She had been too concentrated on the face. She looked now. Gasped again. Shuddered. Looked at Paul.

He looked back at her.

Her hand went to roughly the same spot above her own right breast. "Paul...*what's going on?*"

"Think your Dave noticed?"

"I don't know... He hasn't said anything, made any sign... Maybe mine looks so much like part of the big dragon design..."

"Well," said Paul Osaka, "I'm not sure you should even think about getting naked again with him. Not in the light, anyway. Not till we—*and* the pollies—know what the hell is going on here."

* * * *

Lestrade and Clayton picked him up. Corwin Davison Poe, Davison being the birth surname, Poe a literary nick-surname. Come to think of it, like her own. Maybe it was affectation, maybe just fashion. No, more than a fashion. Nick-surnames had been around a little too long for mere fashion. Pipes without tobacco had been a fashion. Now hers was just a prop, a toy to fiddle her fingers around. Tattoo stamps...not around long enough yet to tell. Nick-surnames...probably never were universally popular enough to be called a fashion fad, but they were hanging on, they were hanging on. She never even thought of herself as Lozinski anymore, just as Lestrade. Plodding little cog in a law-enforcement bureaucracy, dotting all the i's, crossing all the t's, on her way now with her partner to devastate one more poor floater with the bad news that they needed him to identify a corpse.

It was ironic that yesterday Dave had thought he'd traced down this new victim's whereabouts to safe with family in Miami.

So now they had a second murder victim. Two in as many weeks. M.O. looked too close to the one used on Harry Jackson for coincidence. Forest Green had its own serial killer. National news, here we come. Lady God!

A dozen apartments in the Marquette House, including the housekeeper's, and half of their mailboxes had cutesy tags instead of residents' names. The Hideaway, the Tree House, the Menagerie, Hoosier Arms, Arnheim, the Hobbit Hole… Of the surnames, no Davison and no Poe.

They chimed up M. Esther Florsheim, the housekeeper.

A plump, smiling lady in a floral-pattern housedress, her grizzled hair just visible in rollers where they peeked out from beneath a black and brown babushka. "Corwin Davison Poe?" she answered Lestrade's question. "Oh, yes, he's in Arnheim, second floor, first door on the left. It's only ten hundred hours, though. He always sleeps till noon."

"Police business, M. Florsheim," Lestrade steeled herself to say. "Won't wait."

"Police?" The woman's eyes widened. "Now, don't tell me that one's broken some kind of law, because I won't believe it! The kindest, gentlest, quietest, most generous young soul I've ever seen living here. He'll do almost anything for anybody, just so long as it's in the afternoon, and so long as you let him talk. Of course, he does like his fifty-tridol words, but everybody needs a hobby of some kind. He may grow out of it. Or the rest of us may catch up, if we do enough crossword puzzles."

"Wordy, is he?" said Lestrade.

"Wordy," Dave affirmed.

"But, Officers, whatever *has* he done—do you *think* he's done?"

"So far as we know, M. Florsheim, nothing illegal," Lestrade told her. "Pollies don't always show up to make arrests. That's just one of the easier jobs in our workline."

"Can we borrow your key?" Clayton asked. "In case he's sleeping too soundly to hear the doorchime?"

It turned out they didn't need the housekeeper's key, after all. Davison came to his door at the first chime, fully dressed. Sure enough, as Lestrade had already started to suspect from Florsheim's description, he was her eccentric young library acquaintance who always wore black and saw nothing strange about a middle-aged woman reading children's picture books for her own amusement. Why did it have to be him? Right now, he looked like he hadn't been to bed all night. Face pale, clothes rumpled, limbs trembling slightly.

"Dave!" he exclaimed, looking first at Clayton. "I've been trying to telephone her at her father's house all night—it only chimes and keeps chiming into a void. And I've been telephoning all the hospitals and police stations Information will give me numbers for—have you any notion how many hospitals there are in Miami and its immediate environs?—no one can provide me any information at all…"

Clayton laid his hand on Davison's shoulder. Lestrade said, making her voice as gentle as she could, "M. Davison. Can you come with us?"

He looked from Clayton to her, back to Clayton, back again to her, his dark eyes flicking back and forth searching their faces. He grew a few shades paler. A tortoiseshell cat came up from somewhere, peered around his leg, and meowed.

"If I might just get my jacket," he said shakily, picked up his cat, stroked it a little, and carried it back into the apartment. He was out again in half a minute, catless but having apparently forgotten all about the jacket. Well, his tunic looked warm enough for the day, so Lestrade decided not to remind him of the jacket, and told Clayton as much with a lift of her eyebrow and a slight shake of her head.

Glancing behind and down, apparently to make sure his cat was still out of the way, Davison closed the door and came with the two pollies. Lestrade noticed out of the corner of her eye that Clayton had a supporting hand on his arm.

She felt like a murderer herself, just doing the job they had to do.

CHAPTER 16

STILL MONDAY, OCTOBER 2

Davison was silent all the way to the station, all the way through the station to the morgue. Almost corpse white himself, he stood trembling as they rolled the slab out of the cooler. Clayton helped him into viewing position beside the slab. Thinking back enviously to when they had the family dentist in for identifying Harry Jackson, Lestrade said, "I'll warn you, M. Davison. Death can change people's appearance." Then she pulled the sheet back to uncover the head.

Davison gave a choked little cry and might have fallen if Clayton hadn't been holding him.

Then Davison looked again. Shaking all over, he bent forward, carefully picked up a hank of the blond hair, peered at it very closely. Then he touched one of the closed eyes, jerked his fingers back from the feel of dead flesh, grasped his right wrist with his left hand to help steady it, reached forward again... Lestrade nodded her partner to open the eye for him. Clayton did so.

Davison bent over and peered hard at the eye, looked up at the fluorescent overhead morgue light, looked back at the eye. Hands trembling, maybe, a little less, he picked up the edge of the sheet and started to uncover more of the body. Clayton looked about to stop him, but Lestrade signaled No with a shake of her head. Right now, an accurate identification was the most important thing. They could caution Davison afterward to keep quiet about the tattoo. If the media, and Clayton's friends Whitcomb and Osaka, could cooperate about it so, she figured, could Davison.

He wasn't even looking at the tattoo. He was staring hard at the spot on the breastbone right over the heart. Lestrade guessed he hadn't even noticed the tattoo at first. When he saw it at last he gave a violent start, but made no comment. Like he was already promising to keep the secret, without being told.

Shaking harder again, he lifted the hands, each one in turn, and studied the fingers, frowned as if concentrating on which hand was left and which was right, and studied them again.

Then, at last, he slumped to the floor, put his face in his hands, and sobbed. Almost soundlessly. Shoulders heaving.

"Corwin," Clayton said very softly, laying one hand on his back.

Davison shook his head. "*It's not Angela!* Oh, God, it's not Angela. It's *not* Angela!"

Clayton looked at his senior partner helplessly.

"I understand it, Detective," she told him in a firm voice. Give him the years she'd had with this kind of thing, maybe he'd understand, too. Now she laid her hand on Davison's shoulder. "People also cry when they're relieved."

"I...I..." Davison choked. "It's not Angela, but it could have been! Now someone else will have to...go through this...and *not* find relief. Only despair. It is still a dead young woman...who looks so much like her...and *where is she?*"

"Probably in Florida," said Lestrade. "Probably hidden by big-city shufflework and semi-competence. Maybe not even in the Miami area. Now. Explain how you know this isn't Angela Garvey."

He got out his handkerchief, wiped his eyes, blew his nose, let them help him to his feet. "Angela has a pink birthmark," he began, pointing, "here. Above her heart. More or less in the shape of a Valentine-style heart, if one applies imagination. I have not actually seen it...since our childhood...but she assured me only— Lord! was it only two weeks ago? that she had never seen reason to have it surgically removed. I searched for it because...because neither the color of the hair nor of the eye appeared quite to match Angela's—Angela's hair is a lighter gold, I think—it is difficult to be sure in this light—her eyes more definitely blue...these seem grayer...but, again, it could have been the lighting in this room. And here...on the left cheekbone near the temple...a mole just large enough to be distinctive...Angela has no such mole."

"You also checked the hands," Lestrade observed.

"Many, perhaps most people hold their pens and pencils squnched so...may I borrow a pen?"

Clayton supplied the pencil that fit in the spine of his notebook. Davison took it and demonstrated how many or perhaps most people curled their fingers into a fist and held the pen clamped down beneath crooked thumb and forefinger, resting hard on the first joint of the middle finger.

"A few years of this forms a pronounced callous here, on the knuckle of the middle finger." As if unwilling to touch the corpse's hand again, he pointed at it, resting where he had let it fall on the sheet. "There the callous is, on the left hand... Yes...the left hand. This poor woman must have been left-handed. Angela lacks such a callous—our penmanship instructor was a martinet in making us hold our pens and pencils so..." He demonstrated holding Clayton's pencil in a looser hand, using only the tips of forefinger and middle finger to guide it..."but if she had one, it would be on her *right* hand. No, this must be...Angela's doppelganger—whom she told me—God! only last week!—of meeting in town." His own hand started shaking again as he passed the pencil back to Clayton.

Lestrade felt like making some comment about recruiting Davison as a detective; but not here, not now. It wasn't the time or place for any such comment. Instead she fell back on formality. "Thank you, M. Davison. You've been a great help. We almost made a misidentification here."

"Wait! Perhaps I can help you further...Angela mentioned the name... Oh, God! She even told Angela she had been planning for a necklace-style tattoo—it would have rendered them easier to tell apart... But her name..." He closed his eyes, murmuring, "A world globe, anthropomorphized...a bottle of cola in one hand, a lute in the other...Gaia Soderstrum!" he cried aloud with a half-sob.

"Gaia...G-A-I-A...Soderstrum?" But even as Clayton was writing it down in his notebook, Desk Officer Hogan opened the door and said, "Dave, telephone."

"Go take it, Detective Clayton," Lestrade told him. "I think we're finished here, anyway."

Clayton left with Hogan. Lestrade started to shove the slab back into its locker, but Davison caught her hand, pointed at the stamped tattoo above Soderstrum's third rib on the left side, and whispered, "Sergeant Lestrade, I know that symbol!"

"Yes, I thought you blinked at it." She had been going to press the point as soon as her junior partner came back. "What can you tell us about it?"

"It is the…the badge, the equivalent of a membership card…for a group calling itself Dante's Delight Purgatorio. A group which I…have been invited to join."

"Lady God, don't!"

"But am I not uniquely placed to…to help you gather information concerning this group…from the inside?"

"M. Davison. Don't. Even. Think. About. It. You want to risk ending up lying on a slab in here and putting Angela through what you just went through yourself? Just tell me who's in this group. I assume you must know at least some of them."

He seemed to hesitate a couple of nanoseconds before replying. "It is quite a small membership, as I understand. M.'s Samuel Imani, Paul Osaka, and Curly Friedman—I assume 'Curly' to be a nickname, but cannot remember ever hearing her called by any other."

"Samuel Imani, Paul Osaka, Curly Friedman. Anyone else?"

Davison shut his eyes and then shook his head. "Not to the best of my knowledge."

"Hmm," said Lestrade. She might have said something else, but at that moment Dave Clayton thrust open the door.

"Okay, here you are," he announced. "Still. The floater she's really calling for is you, Cor —" He suddenly remembered to be formal inside the station—"M. Davison."

"'She'?" Davison pushed past him and out the door at a run.

* * * *

It had all been so hectic…and then that horrible news—Angela had caught just a little of it on the television someone had left on in the hospital visitors' lounge, when she went there to collapse for a few minutes. Another murder in Forest Green! And it looked like the work of the same sick person who had committed the one two weeks ago.

Her reason said, "There are more than thirty-five thousand people there!" But she had caught just the tail end of the report, barely more than the "further details as they come in" part. If they'd even mentioned this new victim's gender…but the first one had been a man, Harry Jackson. And those smasters—however they tried to pretty it up with religious-sounding excuses—had been after Corwin. And she still couldn't reach him, and they kept calling her back to the intensive care ward...

Finally, the next chance she got, well into the morning, she asked Information for the number of the Forest Green Police Station and tried there. What was the name of the pollydeck they'd set her up with on that double date? Dave...Dave... She heard the receiver lifted at the other end, the officer asking her, "Hello? Forest Green Police Department." She had to say something.

"Do you have a...a detective there named Dave...something?"

Dave Clayton. Yes, he was there, the officer thought he was still back in the morgue helping... "Well, I guess maybe you've heard the news, M.? We have a body to identify."

Of course she had known that, but...that Dave was back there... Yes, he was a police detective, but she couldn't help thinking of him more as a friendly acquaintance, after the way they'd met on a date...the body...the body...

She was nearly frantic by the time he got to the phone.

"Dave! Oh, Dave, I can't get in touch with Corwin! Busy signals all night long—and this morning, when he should be home sleeping, it just goes on chiming and chiming —"

"Angela, calm down. He's safe. We have him right here —"

"Oh, thank Mother Mary! But—under arrest?"

Dave's sigh was audible even over the phone. "Why does everybody always jump to that conclusion? Like that was the one and only reason we ever had civilians in here? In fact, he's been helping us out."

"Oh, Dave!" No—she was weak with relief—shaky—how long since she had slept?—and Dad and Barb were still in intensive care—but she *would not babble.* "Dave...can I speak with him? Can you put him on the phone?"

"Right away. And, Angela...lady...we've been sick with worry about *you.* You really *are* in Florida, after all?"

"Yes—Boca Raton. Dave —?"

"Yeah, just like I had it pegged yesterday. Only Boca Raton, not Miami. Okay, on my way back to get him right now."

Sick with worry about *her*? But *she'd* been perfectly safe... She shook her head, trying to clear it. It seemed so long since the last time she had slept… No, that's right—how could he have known she and Aunt Sally were perfectly safe, when she hadn't been able to get in touch with him till now?…

And then he was on the line. "Ange…Angela?"

"Cory, oh, Cory, it's so good to hear your voice!"

"Angela, it is…it is manna from Heaven to hear yours!"

"I kept calling and calling, every time I could, but every time yesterday you must have been out—and I wanted to try Sam's house but I couldn't quite remember his last name for Information—and then last night, nothing but busy signals—I finally thought your phone must be out of its cradle—and then this morning…"

"All easily explained. Your family emergency?"

She drew a deep, shaky breath. "Accident. A terrible accident! They were all together in the car, on their way to Gumbo Nature Park—when a truck…speeding, they think…hit a tree or something and slewed around and crashed into them head-on—it's 'under investigation'—truck driver's okay—Dad and Barb almost killed —"

"My God! No wonder you… Will they live?"

"They're still in intensive care. The doctors say Dad is 'stabilized,' and they think Barb's out of danger now. Charley was in the back seat, they were able to move him direct from emergency to a regular hospital room."

"Your whole… Oh, God, Angela!"

The prayer and empathy in his voice helped her pull herself together. "Now you. Why couldn't I get in touch with you?"

"The busy signals—I was trying to get in touch with *you*. When your father's telephone number drew no response, I bedeviled Information for the numbers of every hospital and police station in the greater Miami area —"

"You didn't know we were in Boca Raton! How could you have known? Faith Lutheran—it was the closest big hospital to where the accident happened. But there wasn't any direct flight from Forest Green to Boca Raton till Sunday evening. Our quickest way was direct to Miami and then catch an intercity tubetrain."

"All very simple." He gave a shaky little laugh. "All very lucid, when explained."

"Cory—Dave said you were there helping the police—How? With what?"

"Angela…" He hesitated so long she started to panic again. "Angela…this second victim…it is Gaia Soderstrum—your doppelganger."

"Oh, Blessed Mother!" She almost dropped the phone. "Oh, no, Cory, no!" The image flooded her mind…him standing there, staring down, maybe thinking…imagining.

He was asking if she could not have called him Sunday morning before she and Aunt Sally took their departure—had their need for haste…?

"But it was oh-eight-thirty! You'd have been in bed, fast asleep."

As he made no immediate reply, she babbled on,

"Aunt Sally has been wonderful! I couldn't have held up without her! She's been my anchor. She…Cory?"

"Angela, if any similar circumstances ever—*ever*—arise—and please God they won't—but if they *should*…promise you will telephone me at once, regardless of the hour."

She swallowed. "Yes. Yes, of course. I promise…. Now we're even on promises, aren't we?"

"For a moment, but the advantage is about to swing to you as I beg a second promise. Angela—please—please—rest there safe in Florida until whoever is perpetrating these things has been captured!"

"What about *you*? Cory, why don't you come and join us here?"

Another hesitation before he answered. "There may perhaps be…something further…I must do here."

"What, you can worry about my safety and I'm not to worry about yours? There are research libraries and things down here, too, you know. Indiana isn't the only civilized state in the R.S.A."

"The research I could leave behind in less than a heartbeat. This is…"

"Cory, it has to be just coincidence that it was…was poor Gaia!"

"Very well, let me reconsider it. Faith Lutheran Hospital in Boca Raton, you said?"

"And the Good Samaritan Inn next door. That's where we're staying. It's especially for the patients' families…. Cory, come down right away—you can surely catch a plane tonight or tomorrow morning."

"I…may. I cannot promise but…perhaps…I may."

"And I can't promise to stay here until they catch whoever is doing these…these things. Sometimes they never catch them. I couldn't promise to stay down here for the rest of my life! People go on living in other cities when there are murderers on the loose in them. I can't leave here while Dad and my sister are still in danger, but I won't promise to stay away from my own home town until they catch this—this sick creature."

"Yes…I…appreciate your argument. The ancients dreaded banishment above all forms of mere bodily death. I cannot blame you for withholding this promise. I —"

A tap on Angela's shoulder. She turned and saw the nurse with Caramel skin and green eyes. "M. Garvey?" the nurse said. "Your sister Barbara is awake —"

"Oh, Cory! Barb's awake! I have to go now! Come down and join us. Please!"

"Hurry to her side. Good-bye for now."

She blew a quick kiss into the mouthpiece, hoping he heard or at least sensed it. Then she cradled the receiver and hurried back with the nurse to intensive care.

* * * *

Julie had watched the ambulance arrive, the corpse bagged, loaded in, and taken away. She had fed Dave a hasty breakfast, burned bacon and all, and he had said, "We'll want your witness statement as the one who first spotted the body."

But she had neither the heart nor the intention to see Corwin brought in to identify his Angela's body. Dave had understood. He told her she could write her account here at home, or even speak it into one of the wire recorders at Wallace Library, and they'd transcribe it for the files later. One light kiss, and she watched him drive off.

Then she went back inside to her apartment and conferred with Paul. The police would want a witness statement from him, too; but first he and she had to decide definitely whether or not they should include anything about the stamped tattoo they had seen on the corpse.

By now Julie had half made up her mind it might look less suspicious, down the road, if they told the police. Besides, wasn't there the chance it was *not* identical? Neither she nor Paul had really gotten that good a look at it. But it was a decision that belonged to Dante's Delight as a whole. Paul took the job of phoning Sam and Curly, while Julie stayed inside her own apartment, waited for Dave's call, and began drafting her statement.

Paul eventually came back and reported that Curly inclined to "No." Sam seemed to like Julie's arguments; but long experience had made him very cautious in all things touching the Purgatorio's privacy, and he preferred to decide the question by consensus at a face to face meeting.

Julie thought that if they were going to tell, they should do so as soon as possible. The longer they delayed, the more questions would be asked about why they hadn't come clean sooner. The longer they waited, the likelier their consensus would come out "No." But Sam was hereditary leader and most senior member, and, besides, he had a strong argument about their need to get together face to face for this.

She put her head down on the draft of her statement and cried for several minutes, Paul rubbing her shoulders. Dave, Dave! However this came out—would she still have him when it was finally over? Her Dragon Prince, her wonderful, wonderful lover…

Her phone chimed. She jumped for it, snatched the receiver up in trembling fingers, demanded with thudding heart, "Hello? Dave?"

"Julie, it *isn't her!* It isn't Angela."

"What? Oh, Dave! Dave, is he sure?"

"Young floater could probably make detective right now. She's almost a dead ringer for Angela, but he spotted five pretty clear differences, one of 'em a birthmark, and just about the time he finished listing them for us, Angela herself clinched it by phoning from Florida. Boca Raton."

While Julie sat and let her breathing slow, her heartbeat steady, and her shaking stop, with Paul listening in over her shoulder, Dave explained why Angela had gone there so suddenly, and how she and Corwin had kept missing or crossing each other's calls, finally driving Angela frantic enough to phone the Forest Green Police Station.

After Dave's call, Julie and Paul hugged each other, laughing and crying in pure relief. They had had a summer of Sundays to get to like their Thesaurus Kid, half a month (if only two Sundays and, for Julie, one double date) to come to love Angela, and no chance at all to meet this double of hers.

And Dave still hadn't mentioned a thing about the stamped tattoo. Maybe he really hadn't noticed. Maybe Julie was safe…at least for now.

But maybe that would only make it worse whenever he did find out.

* * * *

like all cats and a few dogs caterina understands almost every word her human says even if cats act on it only when they choose now he is back from wherever he goes with those other humans caterina lets him hold her in his lap and pet her and stroke her over and over he is a good human very gentle he puts out nice things for her to eat he strokes her whenever they both want she thinks she stays with him he is saying caterina my reasoning powers are so fatigued and exhausted and i am so puzzled and perplexed and exhausted my thoughts pursue one another around and around these arguments like hamsters on a running wheel like rats in a maze i can no longer cogitate i must let dea fortuna resolve the dilemma for me if angela telephones first then you and i will be with her tomorrow perhaps even tonight in boca raton and evermore will be with our good em esther florsheim but if julie telephones first ching ching ching the telephone makes its sound like the doorchime only three chings in a row then a little silence then three more chings in a row he stands up and goes to the telephone while caterina jumps off his lap wonders boca raton what is boca raton is it the same as heaven and starts washing her face

CHAPTER 17

STILL MONDAY OCTOBER 2

"Corwin!" Julie began. "We're so grateful it wasn't Angela!"

"Thank you," he replied in a strange, subdued voice. He must be worn out with emotion and lack of sleep. "Julie," he went on, "is that invitation still open to me?"

"What?" For a moment, she felt taken aback. "Yes, yes, it is—I haven't even had a good chance to say anything to the others about your decision—but what about your promise to Angela?"

"There may perhaps be matters of...greater importance than mere pride in personal oath-taking. We are in public crisis. Your work, though private, is invaluable. Trusting that now, following this latest tragedy, Angela will come at last to understand, I seek to assist in your efforts with as little delay as possible. If you would be so kind as to furnish me with the consent form, you will have my signature on it at once."

"You...you have thought about this?"

"Of course. How could I not?"

"Long and carefully?"

"Too long, and with overly intense care. I beg initiation as soon as the Purgatorio can make all ready."

"You...you saw our symbol on the body?"

"It served as the ultimate deciding factor for me. Not only may Forest Green be approaching a state of public panic, not only does a murderer remain at large among us, but Dante's Delight Purgatorio itself could be targeted, endangered."

She thought as rapidly as she could. He must have considered this from every angle, probably had his statement polished, his arguments ready and waiting. And he had noticed the symbol—and hadn't said anything about it to Dave. Yes, he was shaken—who wouldn't be?—but she felt he would have signed and joined by now anyway, if Angela hadn't protested. And he was right about the public crisis. Whatever happened eventually, she herself could hardly go emeritus until things were balanced again.

"We're having a special meeting this afternoon," she told him. "No penitential activity, just emergency planning. I can bring you the form on my way."

"I will sign and return it without delay. How quickly can you expedite my initiation?"

"How long ago have you eaten, what, and how much?"

"Last night, a sandwich—I misremember what kind, I paid it too little attention even while slapping it together. Also, I have a hazy recollection of swallowing a pear, or a banana, or some piece of fruit. This morning, before leaving the police station, two cups of coffee with cream and sugar, and a doughnut. And strict instructions from the admirable Detective Sergeant Lestrade—which I have yet to implement—to eat a good meal and then get a long sleep."

"All right. Make that meal broth and clear gelled salad, maybe one small glass of milk, if you need it to help you sleep this afternoon. Then, nothing but three hundred milliliters of plain water—hot or cold, your choice, but I'd advise spacing it out. Up until midnight, clear hard candy is permissible if you feel any great need for an energy boost. After midnight, nothing more, not even water."

"In the manner of the old style Communion fast. To which I was accustomed as a young boy."

"Do you still have that instruction sheet I gave you?"

"I fear not. I do, however, possess an excellent memory."

"I'll bring you another copy. Are you on any prescription medications?"

"No."

"Good. Don't take any over-the-counter stuff, not even asprik. I should be there in an hour, max."

* * * *

This time when Lestrade called Chicago, she learned that Chris Grunewald was already on the way, having taken official leave of absence and started down as soon as the first report came in.

They got James Soderstrum in for the formal identification of his daughter's body, and Lestrade paid for such job satisfaction as she'd had earlier this morning, by going through the process all over again with no relief at all except the ironic reassurance that there was a better than even chance those apparent torture marks had been inflicted after a relatively quick death. The young woman was still dead, and her father was still devastated. Like the rest of the family. In this kind of case, next-of-kin's permission wasn't really necessary for autopsy work, but Soderstrum numbly volunteered it anyway. He was on his way out as Chris was coming in.

Doc Grumeister didn't mind the second opinion. Living people got them all the time, so why should just being dead cancel the privilege? But all Chris could say, even with a body this fresh, was almost the same as for Harry Jackson. Better arrange to ship this one up to the Chicago labs right away. And by now Lestrade herself was starting to wonder how much difference pre- or post-mortem was going to make in any event, other than throwing the survivors some piddling little grain of half-comfort: "At least they didn't suffer anything else but plain, healthy death."

* * * *

Even after one stop along the way at her preferred drugstore, Julie reached the Marquette House in fifty minutes. She found Corwin drinking a cup of orange gelatin mix, hot. His haggardness shocked her, and she felt a twinge of guilt when she handed him the consenting adult form. "It doesn't need to be signed right this minute," she assured him. "You can always wait till tomorrow, just in case you have second thoughts, after all."

"Second thoughts are a dim memory," he replied. "I think I am well into seventy-second thoughts by now." He spread the form on his desk, got out a fountain pen, signed his full name—Davison and all—with an extravagant flourish, and presented it to her once more.

She folded it, put it back in her satchel, and got out the replacement copies of Dante's Delight mission statement and instructions, along with the three small bottles she had purchased at the drugstore. Putting the statement and instruction sheet on the table, she opened the first bottle and shook out one tiny blue pill. "Sedative," she explained, rolling it onto the table. "It won't make you sleep, but it should relax you enough that maybe you can get a more or less natural nap this afternoon. I'd like you to swallow this one now. Do you have your water measured?"

He held up a glass. "Behold the first hundred and fifty milliliters. The second I guard in reserve to serve me in lieu of supper."

"Good." She watched him fumble the blue pill up into his fingers, lift it to his mouth, and swallow it. Next she shook out one tablet apiece from each of her other two bottles. "This one really does make people sleep," she pointed out, "and this pink one is a good laxative. Take them both at bedtime, which tonight, even for you, should be no later than 2200 hours."

He produced a smile. "One of those chocolate-candy laxatives might have seemed a rare treat by twenty-two hundred."

"This kind is better. It'll cooperate with the sleeping pill. And you understand, these and your measured water and maybe a clear hard candy or two are *all* you should put in your stomach from now until midnight. Nothing at all tomorrow morning. I'll pick you up here about twelve hundred hours. It's extremely important that you swallow *nothing* else. Tape your medicine cabinet shut if you think you might forget. Your fridge and pantry, too. Swallow anything else—a*nything*—and we may have to postpone your initiation."

"May I swallow my saliva?"

She laughed, hoping he had intended that as a joke. "Oh, yes, we'll allow that, if you still have any left to swallow by tomorrow midday. I'll also let you have fifteen more minutes—time yourself—to finish that cup of hot gelatin."

"Thank you. Any small favor appreciated."

"Appreciate it while it's still hot. Now, do you have any further questions?"

"I remember, from my earlier perusal of your informative sheets, that you long ago abandoned loincloths as being too awkward and unreliable for persons not born to them, and substituted swimwear?" Turning to the couch, he located something in a paper bag, and handed it to her. "Herein is contained the least generously cut of all my swim trunks. I fear it may still prove unsuitable: the waistband hides the navel."

"It will at least give us your size." She took it with a reassuring smile. "Anything else?"

"Yes…" A longish hesitation. "Understanding you to practice seven levels of initiation, I seem to recollect some mention of the possibility of accomplishing more than one in a single session?"

"The record is Constance Washington thirty-nine years ago. She took five in her first session: levels one, two, three, five, and six. Level four—angel duty—has to be taken when the candidate is at full strength, for obvious reasons. And seventh level, the cross, always comes last and must have a session to itself. So Constance's record could be tied, but not broken."

"At what level the tattoo? It is described and pictured, but without mention of when applied."

"We never got around to mentioning that because you'll be our first new member since we adopted the stamp a couple of years ago. Before that, we practiced minor scarification, seven rays in a circle, one ray added at each level. The stamped tattoo is a great improvement, I think." Julie smiled as she tried to search his eyes without seeming to do so.

He gazed back guilelessly and said, "Very much an improvement, but certainly applied, unlike the earlier scarification pattern, all at once. At which level?"

"The fourth, we plan. That's the level candidates have always dreaded the most. If they didn't, the Purgatorio wouldn't want them. But if they can make it through their first angel duty, they've earned full membership status even if they never take the higher levels."

"You ought to covet me greatly, then. Like most candidates, I also dread level four above all. Nor would I aspire to tie the record of Constance Washington. But…might I request the first three levels in tomorrow's session?"

"I don't see why not. And now, Corwin, on a different subject, I have a question for you."

He regarded her in expectant silence.

"I'd like to do something for our Forest Green police—something to show our community support for the hard work and long hours they're putting in on this…horrible case. I thought maybe a couple catered trays from Delimart or the Wabash House—assorted sandwiches and finger salads—veggie sticks and the like— a few bowls of fresh fruit and about, say, three big cakes? Four?"

She hadn't seen his eyes light up quite like this since the time she had first described the Purgatorio and its goals to him. No— once, even brighter—yesterday, Sunday at Sam's, when Dave had first brought them the news about Angela being safe in Florida, the news that had turned out to be right, after all. Now Corwin said, "Allow me a share in the offering: engaging the caterers as your task, writing the check as mine."

"Oh, no, Corwin, I didn't mean...I was only asking for your advice, your opinion."

"As I solicit the favor of participating in so far as I can. Besides, I should like to take full advantage of my recent practice in signing my name."

Further protests would be rude. She simply agreed with a "Thank you." He returned briefly to his desk and came back with a signed check...the amount still to be filled in.

"This is very generous of you," said Julie, secretly resolving to let him cover only half the amount.

"If there is any other assistance I could offer—carrying the trays, for example... No, you spoke of having them catered —"

"The best thing you can do right now," she told him firmly, "is spend the rest of today resting up. Get as much sleep as you can. You need it desperately. You'd need it even if you weren't..."

"Facing tomorrow?"

"Facing tomorrow." She checked her wristwatch. "That gives you about twenty-three hours. You'll need them. And so..." She spoke lightly, but at the same time pressed his hand in a warm handshake, "thank you, Corwin, and try to lay in a store of pleasant dreams."

* * * *

caterina is prowling for spiders her human is sitting at his thing he calls a desk and rubbing his little stick over pieces of paper the stick leaves swirly black tracks when he has filled up a paper with swirly black tracks he folds it and puts it inside another folded paper and rubs the tip of his big human tongue over one edge of the new paper and folds it down and makes it stick and rubs his stick on it to make more black marks and puts it on one side and picks up another paper and does the same caterina watches evermore and dreams but she is not to eat evermore her human puts out many nice things for her to eat he likes listening to evermore caterina does not mind

CHAPTER 18

STILL MONDAY, OCTOBER 2

The first Wabash House delivery van surprised the station with three trays of assorted sandwiches and veggies, gifts of M.'s Whitcomb and Poe. "That's my Julie," Dave said happily, helping himself to a roast beef and cheddar on whole wheat.

"Hmm," said Lestrade. This morning's work had left stones in her stomach, but she knew she had to eat, so she made herself swallow half a ham on rye. Chris took time for lunch before heading back up to Chicago, commenting about this Wabash House stuff holding its own any time with big-city catering.

That little break in the day over with, Lestrade told her partner, "Your car, Detective. I want another chat with Dupont and O'Toole."

They reached Vadnais Estates and started watching the name plaques. Lang…Van Geldman…at Imani, she said, "Stop here… No, between here and the next old manse…and bury your face in a road map."

He gave her a curious glance and obeyed. While they sat there in Dave's red Rambler, pollies and car both plainclothes, and he unfolded the road map, she skewed around on her seat and studied what she could make out of the Imani mansion through its surrounding trees.

Big, Victorian, and gingerbread. He even had it painted a pretty shade of gingerbread brown, with trim like icing in pastel blue, green, peach, and creamy white. Lots of spaces in there. It even had a round tower. No doubt a lot of old basement as well.

And maybe a lot of panels of very modern interior sound-soak?

Dave spoke up from behind his map. "I was just in there… sheboy! Was it only yesterday? Seems a lot longer ago than that."

"Everything seems longer ago today, Dave."

"Sam Imani's. Nice floater. I liked him. Good gang of roleplayers he gathers there, Sundays."

"Hmm. Detective Clayton. I've just been dealt an ace in the hole, but I think it's the wrong suit."

The road map made a paper-rattly noise. "You aren't asking me how you should play it," her partner stated.

"No. I'm playing it so close to the vest I'm not even letting the rest of our team in on it. Not yet, maybe never."

"Risky, Sarge. Career-wise, if nothing worse."

"If I lose my job over it, I lose my job. Frankly, after a morning like today's, I don't give a damn. Let 'em have fun finding someone to replace me."

He sat with his face in the map, waiting.

"The question I've got for you, Dave," she went on, "as my partner, is this. Do *you* want to see my new hole card and maybe risk your own career? Because I'm not showing it even to you until you swear yourself to secrecy. If you'd rather stay safe in the dark and hang onto your own job security, fine. No, don't answer me yet. Take a few minutes to think about it. 'Yes' commits you. 'No' can maybe be rethought later."

After a few minutes, he said, "If they fire you, I could find myself next in line for senior detective. And I don't think I want to be there, not just yet. So lay it on me, Old Woman, lay it on me."

"Hmm." She had long been aware he called her "Old Woman," in a proud-sonny kind of way, behind her back. She felt a twinge flattered that he had finally used it to her face. "Thanks, son," she said—for her, that was raw sentimentality. "All right. M. Davison recognized the stamped tattoo. Seems it's the membership badge of a group that calls itself the Dante's Delight Purgatorio."

"Sounds like smasters. How did he know about it?"

"Invitation to join."

A low whistle came out through Dave's lips. "Huh? Corwin? That high-minded, word-spouting young floater? Well, I guess you never know."

"No, Dave, you don't. Not about psychomystiques and rarely about anything else. Yes, they could be smasters, plain and simple. Or they could be… Lady knows what."

"Whatever, I hope you told him not to take them up on that invitation."

"In no uncertain terms. As forcefully as a polly can give orders to any civilian not actually under arrest."

"That's good, anyway," Dave said in a relieved voice. "No floater in their right mind is going to disregard that kind of order from Detective Sergeant Lestrade. Did he tell you who they were, these smasters who invited him in?"

She jerked her thumb back to the gingerbread Victorian. "Sam Imani, Paul Osaka, Curly Friedman."

He whistled again, louder. "Sheboygan! I met Paul and Curly—Osaka and Friedman—there yesterday, too. They seemed okay. I guess you never do know. Sarge, I don't see why you want to keep so quiet about this, withhold it from the Department."

"Use your Goddess-given brains, Detective. We've got two corpses that look like they could have been tortured pre-mortem. And we've got a nest of smasters...or whatever, but they'll be 'smasters' as far as everyone else sees—you're a case in point yourself. And we've got a stamped tattoo on both victims that looks like the same design our smasters use on themselves. Now. Let the whole Department in on this, and how much effort do you think any of them are going to put into investigating any other leads we might have? As far as the Department would care, we'd have our 'prime suspects' and any others would automatically be innocent, not worth a second look. How many juries do you think the best defense lawyer in heartland America would be able to line up who might—*might*, on the farthest outside chance—give this case a fair and impartial hearing on the merits of any other evidence besides the obvious?"

"With all respect, Sarge, sometimes the obvious evidence is the correct evidence."

She waved her hand in annoyance. "Okay, okay, so maybe I'm riding my pet hobbyhorse again. Maybe I've hatched my own suspicions prematurely and just don't like to see them upset by facts. But you asked to come in this far, Dave, now humor the Old Woman. Keep quiet about Imani and his gang at least until we can get enough grounds together for a thorough search of the tattoo artists' premises."

"On what we've got right now, Judge Farquhar would sign a search warrant for Imani's house and grounds in a heartbeat. Osaka's and Friedman's, too."

"Congratulations, Detective, you have already grasped the point I've been trying in my bumbling sidekick way to get across to you."

That gave him pause, but just for a moment. "We could search Naismith's premises any time we want. Strong evidence of an illegal business."

"Which we've known about for years, and been letting slide because the floater hasn't caused another infection in decades, and what happened before that, when he was in some other jurisdiction, we've figured is between him and the International Association of Body Artists. Search his place now, out of the blue, and we telegraph a warning to the other tattoo artists in town. After which we might as well forget about searching *their* premises. No. Either we get enough general grounds to search all three at once, or we get really specific grounds—present, here and now grounds—for zeroing in on just one."

"Good plan, Sarge, as soon as we figure out how we're going to pull it off. Sam Imani," Dave mused on, his voice going soft and introspective. "...Paul...Curly...how many others, I wonder..."

"You can fold the map up and drive on to Dupont and O'Toole's now."

Refolding the map, he gave a sudden jerk so hard the paper tore a few centimeters. Then he relaxed, shaking his head and grinning. "Naw. *She* can't know a darn thing about it. Of course not!"

His Julie, he obviously meant. His Julie of the catered lunch. Lestrade decided this wasn't the time to remind him that good detectives never ruled anything out, and they drove on to Dupont and O'Toole's.

Where nobody was at home except the dog Pango and a by-the-day groundskeeper who told them the owners were up in Milwaukee for an IABA convention, but should be back by late tonight.

* * * *

caterina is prowling in the dark there are no mice she finds a spider to play with ching ching ching the telephone makes its noise ching ching ching it is loud in the quiet ching ching ching both the telephones sound the noise ching ching ching the one here and the one where her human sleeps ching ching ching humans are so strange about sleeping ching ching ching he lies down on a special soft thing humans call a bed ching ching ching and sleeps from when it is still dark to when it is bright for half the day ching ching ching he does not sleep in little naps and wake up often when he is on his bed ching ching ching with his head on a softer thing that they call a pillow ching ching ching and sheets and blankets up to his big human chin ching ching ching so that if he is not clever when he throws them aside ching ching ching they tangle when he gets up ching ching ching caterina pads into the room where he is stretched out on his bed ching ching ching she sits and watches the telephone ching ching ching it does not move while it makes its sound ching ching ching she leaps up onto the bed ching ching ching and pats his long human nose with a velvet paw ching ching ching pat pat pat ching ching ching pat pat pat ching ching ching and he stirs a little but he does not wake now the telephone goes quiet humans sleep too hard how do they survive she thinks evermore sleeps like that too in his high cage with the cover over it but she is not to eat evermore her human gives her nice things to eat but he is sleeping very very hard caterina curls up to his chest and feels it going up and down and up and down and listens to him breathe it is so soft and nice she naps a little and wakes up and hops down off the bed to prowl again for mice there are no mice but maybe another spider and a sip of water from her bowl and a nibble from her other bowl

* * * *

"But he said to phone any time of the day or night," Angela told Aunt Sally, "and this is even the time of night he's usually still awake."

"Well, dear, his usual pattern could be off a little. Apparently he wore himself out yesterday worrying about us. He may have taken a sleeping pill and gone to bed early."

Angela said, "I hope you're right. And this is good news—Barb in a regular hospital room and they think they'll be able to pronounce Dad out of danger and move him to a regular room, too. So maybe it doesn't quite fit the conditions when I'm supposed to call him day or night, only…"

"Angie, dear, you should get a little sleep yourself. Let me drive you to the inn."

"Yes, yes, you're right, Aunt Sally. We both need…a few hours of sleep."

She only hoped, as Aunt Sally led her away, that she could get it.

CHAPTER 19

it is daylight now caterina curls up on the bed beside her human ching ching ching the telephone makes its noise ching ching ching she lifts her head and listens ching ching ching she gets up and pad-pads on the springy bed ching ching ching and puts out a velvet paw and taps his nose ching ching ching pat pat pat ching ching ching pat pat pat and he wakes up and turns and gropes for the telephone but it has stopped making its noise but he gets it into his hand anyway and tells it hello hello hello and then he puts it back and says i thought it was chiming i must have dreamed it i must want so intensely to hear her voice that i dreamed it and it is too late now but i should have liked to hear her voice once more and he yawns and stretches and strokes caterina his hand trembles a little on her fur it is early for him to get up he says allow me to slumber on and dream again and he lies back down and turns and twists and groans and twists and sighs and get up

* * * *

"And he *still* doesn't answer!" Angela cried. "It's oh nine thirty—even if he took a sleeping pill last night, it should have worn off enough by now, the phone should wake him up. He *has* to be in Arnheim! Where does Cory ever go at oh nine thirty hours? Aunt Sally, Dad's officially out of danger now. I'm going to fly home right away."

* * * *

After getting off her 1600 to 2200 shift, Julie had come home, taken her own sleeping pill, and caught her full eight hours, then showered, swallowed toast and coffee, and gone with the fasting Paul to Sam's. Curly had already arrived.

It was their second emergency planning session in two days. Yesterday afternoon's had accomplished little except speculation, worry, and the outline for this afternoon's special meeting. Paul, who was next in rotation, would share penitent duty with their new initiate.

"Though I'm still not sure we really want to go ahead with this for a while," Paul repeated. "Not with the pollies knowing about the tattoo."

"Yeah," Curly said in an unusually neutral voice. "You really sure your Dave floater never noticed yours, Julie?"

Julie had been asking herself the same question several times an hour since yesterday morning. Now she replied, "No, I really don't think he could have. It's so well incorporated into the dragon design. And then the shock of finding that poor young body—I think it just drove...other things...out of his head for the moment. If he'd made the connection, surely he would've said something about it when he cautioned Paul and me to help the police keep it secret about the stamped tattoo."

"Well, that's still a point," Curly agreed.

"Not the sharpest point I've ever heard," said Paul. "He might be your Dragon Prince, Julie, but he's still a pollydeck. They can keep things pretty close-lipped when they want. Maybe what we should rethink is our decision not to take it to the police ourselves."

"Little bit late for that," said Curly, echoing Julie's old thoughts. "Already they'd wonder why you never spoke up about it yesterday morning."

Julie protested, "Just the two of us couldn't make that decision for the entire Purgatorio."

"There's always danger," Sam rumbled. "There's always been danger, coming up on half a century now. In fact, even with the current situation in town, there was probably more danger in normal times back when my grandfather started the group. But there's also a special need in Forest Green right now. However, we're not going to do anything without a consensus. Julie? Go ahead with it this afternoon, or lay low a while?"

She swallowed. But if Dave *had* made, or ever *did* find out about the tattoo connection, she might lose him anyway, no matter what they did now. "I say, providing our recruit is fasted and ready, let's go ahead."

"Sure," Curly agreed before Sam could ask, her grin strong and ivory across her Chocolate face. "What's life worth without a little spice of danger?"

"Paul?" asked Sam.

Paul replied, "I haven't broken my fast. Kind of a shame to let all that effort go to waste."

"And I say yes, too," Sam concluded. "Well, gang, we've got our consensus."

* * * *

Lestrade and her partner sat in their office. He was going through phone books, city directories, and maps. She was taking another good stare at the photos of Harry Jackson.

"Well," Dave announced, putting down his pen, "of the three whose names we've got, they almost have to have their den somewhere in Sam Imani's house. Curly Friedman has to be living above the Good Times Deli on Second—I think those are two- or three-room apartments—and of course Paul Osaka is just down the hall from Julie in the Pankhurst Arms. Paul..." Dave's voice trailed off uneasily. "He would've recognized it... Well," he finished, brisk again, "unless there's somebody else in this thing that Davison doesn't know about, we've got to be looking at Imani's big old Victorian."

"Mmm," Lestrade muttered. "Before we look at that, take another look at this, Detective." Reaching across the table, she set the photos down on top of the city map.

He picked them up and studied them closely. "Harry Jackson. What else am I looking for, Sarge?"

"See any resemblance?"

The frown line between his eyebrows got deeper. "Yeah... maybe...just a little...Sheboygan, Sarge, you don't think...?"

"Jackson was just about the right height, too. Yes, Detective. I mean that at a little distance, Jackson could maybe have looked like Davison. Of course, so could about a quarter of the young floaters in town."

"Yeah. Yeah, I guess so. The Thesaurus Kid does maybe look a little generic. Until he opens his mouth, of course."

"Most of us look more or less generic, Dave. It's the psycho-mystique that makes us different. Okay. One victim a ringer for

Garvey, the other one more or less Davison's physical description...getting a little close to write off as coincidence."

"And they've both been at Sam Imani's—Garvey and Davison, I mean."

"Yes. And what else do they have in common? Jackson and Soderstrum, I mean."

"I don't know. Have we found anything in common yet, besides the way they were murdered and that stamped tattoo? He was a local boy, just home from college...she just moved to town with her family about a year ago... As far as we've learned, the families didn't even know each other..."

"Are we going to have to get Davison back in here to help you out, Detective?" Lestrade snapped. "You've had exactly the same information in front of you all this time that I've had. Both Jackson and Soderstrum were thinking about getting themselves tattooed."

"So are a lot of people. Maybe half the population. Where are you going with this, Sarge?"

"At this point, Detective Clayton, I'd rather test my theory by seeing whether you come up with the same idea independently."

"Same theory you've had in mind before? As in the reason you want to get search warrants for all the city's tattoo artists at once?"

She nodded.

"And this new stuff—possible mistaking of both victims for someone else, and all that—doesn't shake it?"

"Strengthens it, if anything. Damn!" Lestrade added softly, half to herself. "If I'd only found enough to act on, right away that first week, Gaia Soderstrum might still be alive."

"You've got your eye on one of our tattoo artists, don't you? Or two? Which one or ones?"

"You've got the same information I have," Lestrade repeated.

"Sheboy, Old Woman! Sometimes, as your slave-driven junior partner, I wish you didn't treat me quite so much like Holmes treated Dr. Watson."

"Holmes? Wash your mouth, boy!" It was about as close to humor as she usually went. The strain must be telling on me, she thought. "I'm no Sherlock Holmes, you whippersnapper. I'm not even an honest and reasonably intelligent Dr. Watson. I'm just a poor, bumbling, by-the-book Lestrade."

"Old Woman," Dave said with an appreciative grin, "you are anything but 'by the book.'"

* * * *

caterina is searching for mice there are no mice maybe spiders her human makes more black tracks on more papers and folds them and piles them all up and puts another piece of paper on top he starts to move the telephone and roll down the slidy cover of the desk and then he stops and leaves the cover up and puts the telephone back he bends down to stroke caterina she likes being stroked sometimes not always she arches her back and purrs and strolls away he goes out and caterina has all the rooms to herself except for evermore who is making chirpy sounds but caterina does not mind them

* * * *

When Julie pulled up to the Marquette Apartments at 1130 hours, she found Corwin waiting in the lobby. He looked much better than he had yesterday: a good night's sleep would do that. Pale and apprehensive: hadn't they all been *that*, going to their first session? Paul still got pale and worried-looking every Friday morning, even more so yesterday afternoon and this morning.

At the same time, Julie's recruit acted resolute, eager, a little too determined to be cheerful, and...slightly guilty? Well, they were breaking some of the most automatically accepted of modern society's unwritten guiderules. That was why the Purgatorio had always been kept private almost—not quite—to the point of secrecy.

"Now," she asked him, just to be sure, "have you slipped up and broken your fast?"

He shook his head. "Neither sip nor sup has passed my lips. I might have, had I brushed my teeth this morning; but, having brushed them well last night, in the process using up the last of my measure of water, and having actually masticated nothing at all since yesterday morning, I judged that an additional brushing upon arising would be superfluous."

"And has the laxative worked?"

"From anyone other than a medical professional, I should probably resent that question as embarrassing, impertinent, and overly personal. But, yes, it has, and, as you intimated, in pleasant cooperation with the sleeping dose."

"And…" She laid her hand on his forearm, "Corwin, are you still sure you want to do this?"

"I shall not renege."

So they got into her car. As she pulled away from the curb, he remarked, "Your otherwise informative sheets fail to mention where, precisely, we are going."

"Sam's."

"Ah. So the self-same house that hosts our Sunday rolegaming does indeed enclose Dante's Delight Purgatorio as well. Beneath our very noses, down in the cellars?"

"Above our very heads, up in the highest tower room. '*Mount Purgatory*,' you know. It's really a very comforting place. Clean, all painted in whites and pale purples, walls hung with gilt-framed quotations done in illuminated calligraphy, dayglow wall lights—though on sunny afternoons we slit the window shutters a few centimeters open and get a surprising amount of real daylight. The cross is light green composite and stands on a dais between two of the windows. The raised bar stands facing it near the opposite wall —"

Corwin suddenly shuddered, with a sharp indrawing of breath. "No, no," he assured her at once, waving his hand. "I am all right. It sounds…unexpected, as a place of purgation. Julie…would you be so good as to repeat to me those quotations on the wall?"

"All—except our motto, of course, and the verses from chapter twelve of Romans—are taken from the middle part of Dante's *Divine Comedy*, the *Purgatorio*."

> '*I say our pain, and ought to say our solace,—*
> *For the same wish doth lead us to the tree*
> *Which led the Christ rejoicing to say 'Eli,'*
> *When with his veins he liberated us.*'"

Julie quoted from memory.
"And,

> '*God's lofty fiat would be violated,*
> *If Lethe should be passed, and if such viands*
> *Should tasted be, withouten any scot*

Of penitence, that gushes forth in tears.'

"And, of course,

'To drink of the sweet wormwood of these torments.'

Corwin remarked, "Dante's vision furnished Mount Purgatorio with less...lurid penances, did it not? than those of his Inferno."

"Yes, but they aren't very adaptable to people with this-world bodies and regular worklines. As it is, I had to get Friday nights off written into my hospital contract. Probably three quarters of the staff assume I go to AA meetings. I just let them think so."

"This is, after all, not so excruciatingly different from awaiting certain medical procedures.... Julie...this *will* be safe, will it not?"

"Oh, yes. Definitely. You won't be comfortable, Corwin, but you will be perfectly safe."

"What an exquisitely delicate piece of phraseology!" He closed his eyes, leaned back in the car seat, shuddered again, and began to murmur, like a mantra, "'Pain enjoyed is hardly penitential.... Pain enjoyed is hardly penitential....'

Actually, he was having a very healthy reaction to the time closing in. Julie was glad to see it. Also glad that her own angel duties today would be somewhat lighter than usual.

* * * *

Angela had to change planes in President City, which according to a brochure from the stand in the airport had been renamed that from "Parsonsburg" in 1938 at the height of the nation's Mount Rushmore fever, for the fourth great face, the face of the "Greatest Future President," the face purposely left blank. There had been talk in 1946 of carving it into the likeness of Santina Raincloud, the first Native American president, who had seen the country through the Great Depression, the Dust Bowl, and most of the second act of the Last Great War; but two factions of public opinion had united to defeat the plan: the people who said it would be like shutting the door on the possibility of an even greater president sometime down the road—in effect, saying that the R.S.A. had already passed its great days; and the people who said the blank face had always been meant to be purely symbolic. Symbolic of what? Angela had thought, ever since fifth or sixth grade, symbolic of all the great presidents after Lincoln? Corwin preferred the idea that it was symbolic of any president—any person, really—who had done something great without being specifically recognized and honored for it…but now the public phone was finally free, and she had time to try another call to Arnheim.

* * * *

ching ching ching the telephone makes its noise ching ching ching but her human is not here ching ching ching he goes out ching ching ching the telephone makes its sound a long time ching ching ching caterina does not like it ching ching ching she leaps up on the desk ching ching ching she bats it with her paws the loose thing of it flies off it falls over the edge of the desk it hangs there by its cord the telephone in the bedroom stops making the noise too caterina nudges the rest of the telephone off the desk as she springs down many folded papers fall down too they are the ones he takes so much time with it is too bad about them falling down and scattering over the floor but what can caterina do pick them up in her mouth and jump back up onto the desk carrying them she likes to jump but to carry the papers up is work let the humans do it they are much better at it with their hands with the long wiggly things that are nice for stroking caterina when she likes being stroked she goes searching for mice there are no mice maybe a nice fat spider

* * * *

Angela counted seven sets of chimes. Then she thought she heard him lift the receiver, and she started to cry Hello—but there was a clinking and a thudding, and then just a busy signal…

What had happened?

Oh, Mother Mary, Mother Mary, Blessed Virgin Mother, let my next plane come soon, let me get there in time!

CHAPTER 20

STILL TUESDAY OCTOBER 3

They were headed out to pay Dupont and O'Toole another visit, this time in Lestrade's blue Fairfield. When they reached Vadnais Estates, Lestrade told her partner, "I'm going to pull up and park when we get about ten meters past Imani's place. I want another look at it."

"Want to figure out where they have their smastering den? I swear, I don't see how it can be anywhere on the ground floor, not unless all their gear is hand-carried and hidden out of the way when not in use. Rolegaming pretty well fills up most of the ground-floor rooms Sundays, and the few it doesn't, are left open for the guests anyway. So are the second-floor comfort stations. Seems to limit smastering to the third-floor or higher, and the basements. I'd bet on the basements."

"Yes," Lestrade said dryly. "Anyone would think so, wouldn't they? Listen to yourself, Detective! You met these floaters, you liked them just fine, you had an innocent good time with them, but one faint hint of smastering, and your whole attitude to them changes, presto! What happened to all this Christian sermonizing about 'judge not or you'll be judged yourself'?"

"Hey, Old Woman, I never thought the *whole* Sunday crowd could be in on it. I just wondered where Sam and his cronies lead their double lives."

"Save 'Old Woman' for when I like you again, Detective. Look. You don't like this kinky stuff, and maybe I don't like it either, but as long as the floaters involved are doing it of their own free will and nobody is getting seriously hurt, the law says—maybe reluctantly, but it's still on the books—to leave 'em alone. And the Old Woman says, If you stop socializing with everyone, Republicrat or Democritan, who does anything in the privacy of their own homes that you don't happen to like or approve of, sonny, you're going to live a lonely life."

"Sarge," he said after a moment, "I'd sure as hell hate to get in the way of a genuine scorching from your tongue."

Must be her tone. Okay, let it be her tone, as long as it got her point halfway across. "Okay, Detective, stop worrying about it. I only scorch the floaters I like."

Imani's estate was on the other side of the road. About a car length past the corner of Imani's fence, Lestrade pulled the car over, parked it, got out and strolled back, making a careful survey of the area. Clayton followed her.

"Looking for something, Sarge?"

"A good place for a stake-out."

"What happened to live and let live?"

"Not to stake out Imani's place," she growled. "To place one or two or our own to look for anybody else who might be staking out Imani's place."

"You mean you think our murderer maybe zeroed in on Jackson and Soderstrum because he thought they were floaters he'd seen going into Imani's?"

"Or coming out."

"Sarge, that's just... Sarge, that's a really long shot."

"Maybe. Cheer up, Detective. If your personal prejudices are spot on here, we'll have somebody right on hand either way. Let's see. Rise of land over there across the road from Imani's. Good. Stargazers. A couple of pollies in plain clothes, acting like stargazers. Let's hope we get some clear nights, especially next Sunday. Use an unmarked car...yes. Now, who? Little Bird and...Vergucchi complaining about his rheumatism these days...maybe we can get Brown reassigned."

Having settled it in her mind, Lestrade turned for another look at what they could see from here of Imani's Victorian. Not much visible through the trees, except that round tower. Were its top windows shuttered up? She thought about getting the binoculars from the car, decided against taking the time and maybe looking conspicuous.

Something about the place...gave her an odd feeling. Not nasty, just...unsettling. Young Davison might have a word for it—some word known to him and maybe three or four other people in the world.

All her fine talk about live and let live, and now she was reacting exactly like ninety-nine point nine percent of the population? Rosemary Lestrade, she scorched herself with a hard mental shake, you big hypocrite! Haven't you learned anything from what your own Wiccan people have had to put up with from good, fundamentalist Christian citizens? With that, she rejoined her partner in the car and they drove on to Dupont and O'Toole's.

Today it was him they found home alone with Pango, the dog who had the size of a small pony and the psychomystique of a box turtle on tranquilizers. O'Toole explained that his wife Hilga a.k.a. Fleur was out looking for something with Rottweiler or maybe Timberwolf blood—maybe a pair of them—to punch up home security.

"In that case, you'll need a Beware of Dogs sign," Lestrade observed. "City guiderule. Any reason to think this neighborhood is threatened more than any other place in Forest Green?"

"No…not really. But isn't that enough? Aren't the whole city and all the surrounding farmlands threatened? Ask me, I'd say everybody around needs a good, fierce watchdog or two."

Clayton picked right up on it. "What, exactly, do you mean, M. O'Toole, by 'not really'?"

"Well…first thing we saw in this morning's paper was the photo of this new victim. The photo asking, 'Did you see this woman alive at any point before yesterday morning?' And, well, Detectives…"

"If you saw her anywhere, M. O'Toole," Lestrade told him, "you've got a serious duty to report it. Finding the last person to see her alive—and leave her that way—helps us trace her movements."

"Yes. The thing is, we never saw her this last wraparound. How could we? Being up in Milwaukee for the IABA convention. So… we couldn't figure out if this counted or if reporting it would only clutter up your desks… You've been in touch with her family, obviously. So why would you want to go earlier than the last time *they* saw her alive?"

"To the point, M. O'Toole," snapped Lestrade. "When and where did you see the late M. Gaia Soderstrum? Let us judge how relevant it is."

"Sunday before last. Her and that young floater in black—must've been her date—heading in for the rolegames at Sam Imani's place. Hilly and me were out walking our dog. Didn't know them from Adam and Eve—except that we've been seeing him Sundays all through the summer—but we said hello when they stopped to pet Pango. You know how it is."

Lestrade thought about asking O'Toole how many fancy words the young floater in black had taken to say hello, and decided it was beside the purpose. She also decided, and signaled Clayton with a raised-brow nod, not to explain that the young woman they had seen was just a look-alike of the actual victim. "Okay, M.," she pronounced, "you're off the hook. A week ago yesterday, at a place her family knew she was going, doesn't help us much. We came to see you about something else, anyway."

"Something else, Detectives? There hasn't been another…"

"We're always working on several cases at once, M. O'Toole. This one concerns possible copycat use of a tattoo stamp."

O'Toole visibly relaxed. "Afraid I can't help you there, Detectives. We don't make tattoo stamps, my wife and I. If we needed any boost to our income, we might. But we don't. But isn't copycatting a tattoo stamp more in the line of IABA than police work?"

"A stamp marking members of a gang possibly involved in illicit activities looking a little too much like the group mark of a perfectly innocent club." Lestrade had figured it out ahead of time. No use getting O'Toole and his wife suspicious of their near neighbors if there turned out to be no cause. Suspicions, once planted, died too hard.

O'Toole was shaking his head. "Still can't help you, Detectives. Like I said, my wife and I just don't do stamps."

Clayton asked, "Not even for a friend? By special request?"

O'Toole spread his hands. "Sorry. Not a question of business policy. As I think my wife may have mentioned on your earlier visit, we don't even have the equipment for stamp-making. You can search our place if you like."

Lestrade and her partner exchanged quick glances. "Thanks, M. O'Toole," she said, carefully casual, "that won't be necessary."

"Say someone—a friend, say—asked you," Clayton went on. "Would you recommend any of your fellow artists for the job?"

"Partly depends how soon they wanted it. For probably the finest craftship, Colliers of Colorado or Bob Yovill of Washington, D.C. But Colliers usually takes six months to a year, and with Yovill the wait could be a couple of years. For a competent quick job, Elias Hammer right here in town is probably as good as anybody."

"Thank you again, M. O'Toole," Lestrade said before Clayton could add anything farther. "I thank that'll be all for today."

* * * *

"We don't need a search warrant when somebody hands us permission on a silver platter," Clayton was saying as they got back in the car.

"But we do need more than two pollies to give a property that size any halfway decent search. As O'Toole could have guessed when he made the offer." Damn! she wished he hadn't.

"We could at least have gotten it in writing."

"What's the point? Anything suspicious they might have had is going to be gone before we can get back with enough people to search the place."

"So you played it for the least chance of tipping off Hammer and Naismith?"

"Minimizing the damage. Maybe there's hope for you yet, Detective."

"Sarge, you're looking hard at Hammer, aren't you?"

"We aren't labeling anyone 'Prime Suspect,'" she answered, reminding herself as much as him. "Not yet. Not with what little we've got. Still too early. Start labeling anybody 'Prime Suspect,' and you stop looking hard enough at everybody else." But, yes, she admitted to herself, in some secret part of her brain, and not too happy with her own psychomystique, she was looking hard at Hammer. And she couldn't shake the guilt of feeling that, if she'd only found enough to work with right after Harry Jackson's murder, Gaia Soderstrum might still be alive.

She also couldn't help taking another frown at Imani's tower as they drove past his Victorian on their way out. What *was* it about that place?

CHAPTER 21

STILL TUESDAY OCTOBER 3

The country being on Winter Time, it was after dark when Angela's plane got into the Forest Green airport. Luckily, she had no checked baggage, and the snack on the plane had given her more than she could eat today, so all she had to do was hurry out to her old Mason, which they had taken Sunday morning rather than leave Aunt Sally's beautiful new Bakersfield in the airport parking lot.

She came as close as she had ever come in her life to deliberately breaking speed limits on her way through town to the Marquette House.

Very grateful, now, that he had given her his keys—thinking at the time that *she* might sometime be the one in need of a safe place—she fumbled herself in through the front door and then the door into Arnheim.

It was all clean and neat. Everything looked okay. Could Aunt Sally have been right? *Could* he have been flying down to Boca Raton even while she was flying up to Forest Green? Could their planes have passed each other in the air?

"Cory!" she shouted into his apartment. "*Cory!*"

No answer, only his tortoiseshell cat came padding delicately out at the sound of Angela's voice.

He would never have flown off to Florida for who knew how long and just left Caterina alone in the apartment. Or Evermore. Looking around again, she saw the telephone lying on its side on the floor at the foot of the desk, its receiver out of the cradle. Caterina must have jumped up and knocked it off. Yes, that explained the busy signal. The cat must have knocked all those envelopes off at the same time. Angela went over, replaced the telephone on the desk, started gathering up the scattered envelopes.

They were letters. Sealed and addressed, but only with names, not street numbers. And no return address, no postage stamps. To Corinna Olmstead Casanova—that was his older sister, up in Arbor City; Patrice Davison Whitman and Michael Olmstead Hawthorne—his parents; M. Esther Florsheim…his landlady, Angela *thought*; Detective David Clayton, F.G.P.D.; Detective Sergeant R. Lestrade, F.G.P.D.… and—here was one for her, Angela Garvey! And…and…one labeled "Corwin Davison Poe, His Last Will & Testament"! And a single slip of paper—it must have been on the top, that was why it was on the bottom now—reading, "In the Improbable Eventuality of My Premature Demise."

Angela hardly even spared a glance to make sure Caterina stayed in the apartment. She broke every speed record on her way to the police station. She would have welcomed any polly who pulled her over.

* * * *

what is that all about caterina wonders the human who is here before the one her human likes so much she grabs up all the folded papers and runs away is she chasing a mouse there are no mice but there are always spiders here is a nice big spider beneath the couch caterina plays with it until it stops moving she eats it and goes and drinks water from her dish

* * * *

Angela sat in the small waiting lounge of the Forest Green Police Station, turning the letter with her name on it over and over in her hands. All the other letters, even his Will, she had given to the officer at the front desk, to use however the police judged best. She assumed Sergeant Lestrade and Detective Dave Clayton were already reading theirs.

As for her, she would not read hers until they knew for certain… Even to open it now would be like admitting in her heart that they were too late.

* * * *

Dave and the Old Woman sat in their office, reading. He was trying to act like a good police detective and check any personal feelings of his own at the door. Just the facts, M. Just the facts.

"Detective Clayton—or may I without impertinence continue addressing you as 'Dave'?

"Your perusal of this epistle signifies that in all probability my corpus delecti no longer houses my soul—essence—psychomystique—call it what you will, which, for all any of us can know, perhaps hovers near you even now, searching and aching to render whatever further assistance might prove possible to its present condition.

"I append only this hope, this last prayer: some member or members of a group may prove guilty of an—extracurricular, let us call it—outrage, without the other members necessarily being tainted."

What the Sheboygan did he mean by that last sentence?

"Lady God!" Lestrade exploded. "All right, Detective, listen to this. Translation. He begs pardon for disregarding my 'suggestion'—pretty way of putting it!—but at least his remains give us more evidence. He lists about a dozen indicators we can use to help identify his body—big of him!—along with the names of his dentist and personal physician, and hopes this spares us any need to call Angela Garvey back from Florida. If so be we have to get somebody in to formalize the identification, his sister Corinna Olmstead is handy in Arbor City. He'd even enclose a set of fingerprints—holy martyr Silverstairs!!—if he had such a thing as an ink pad handy. All right, M. Davison, if we get you back in one breathing piece, we'll see whether we can't accommodate you *there*. And—well, praise the Lady you finally saw your way through to come clean about this one! Just a little bit tardy, wouldn't you say?—" She cut herself off, slammed the letter down on her desk, got up, came around to her partner's side of the table, and put one hand on his shoulder. Very gently, considering. "Dave...I'm sorry. I hate telling you this...or maybe he put it in your letter, too? No, I see he didn't. Dave...Julie Whitcomb is one of them."

"Julie? *Julie?*" He started up, almost grabbed his senior's hand. "*JULIE?* No! She can't be —"

"She's the one who recruited him," the Old Woman answered in a tight voice.

"No. No. Oh, no." So that's what Corwin was getting at with that last sentence of his. Looking back, Dave guessed he should have seen it coming, if he'd been any kind of an objective detective. If he hadn't let his blind spot take over.

"Come on, Detective Clayton." She was all Sergeant Lestrade again. "Get Vergucchi and Little Bird. And everybody else we can round up. We don't need a warrant this time. Emergency rescue mission. We'll try Imani's place first."

"Right, Sarge!" The only way he was going to get through tonight, Dave saw, was by turning the man off completely and letting the professional shell carry him.

* * * *

One side of the lounge was open to the front office, so Angela saw the tall woman come in, saw her hand something to the desk officer while saying, "Everyone on hand to this address. Bring the security limo. There are at least five of them. Maybe more."

Angela got up and went out of the lounge to her. "Are you Sergeant Lestrade?"

The tall woman turned, looked at her. "And you'd be Angela. M. Garvey."

"Wherever you're going—is it about Corwin?"

Muscles tightened in Sergeant Lestrade's jaw before she answered. "It's about M. Davison, yes."

"Let me come with you!"

"M. Garvey. It'll be no place for civilians. I want you safe here."

"Sergeant—p*lease!* I can't just wait behind and…worry. I've been worrying since midnight! All last night in Boca Raton—all day on the airplanes! I won't get in the way. I'll stay back. Only—Sergeant Lestrade, I *can't* just sit here doing nothing! I'll—I'll follow you in my own car, if I have to!"

Sergeant Lestrade glanced at the envelope in Angela's hand. "What did he write to you?"

"I don't know—I haven't even opened it. That would be like admitting he's…he's… Please, Sergeant! Woman to woman?"

"Come on," said Rosemary Lestrade. "Stop wasting time."

* * * *

They took the marked police cars this time, sirens and all. Lestrade put Clayton behind the wheel because he was the speedier driver, sirens or not. Maybe not quite as speedy as Little Bird and

Vergucchi, whose car could have passed theirs five minutes from the station, if it wasn't for protocol and the city traffic they were already sending scuttling.

All three of them—Lestrade, Clayton, M. Garvey—sat mostly in silence.

Out of my Lady-damned mind, Lestrade was thinking. Won't get in the way, my Auntie Henry! Oh, no, she'll stay well back out of our way, all right, just like that double-blasted sweetheart of hers obeys a direct "suggestion"—as he so self-servingly puts it—from police authority. Holy martyr Silverstairs! However tonight plays out, I lose. Let's see, any way I can excuse bringing a civilian along? Okay: she knows the house, she's been in there before, I figured she could help us out as a guide. And if we hadn't brought her along in the police car, she'd have followed us in her own, for double the trouble. There. My excuses when Chief Grayling rakes me over the coals about all this. Lady God! If we can't salvage anything else tonight, at least let us salvage Davison alive. Preferably in mendable condition. Because he's going to need his strength when *I* light into him!

Be nice if we can salvage Whitworth, too. Dave's department.

When they reached Vadnais Estates, they shut off the sirens—no point announcing a raid too early—and slowed down just enough to avoid any unexpected after-dark traffic, motor or pedestrian, on the winding residential roads.

They pulled up quietly beside Imani's grounds. Two police cars and the security limo with Brown and Wentworth. Six officers. Should be plenty, unless this "Purgatorio" group had a lot more members than Davison knew about. And one civilian, more likely to need protection than give them much help, no matter what Lestrade's cover story for Chief Grayling was going to be. She turned her attention to Imani's Victorian.

It seemed to get bigger, the closer they got. Big and dark. Should be lights on somewhere... Lestrade squinted up. Was that a faint glow, there in the tower windows? Lightblock drapes? Shutters? Den in the basement, lights probably wouldn't show at all.

"'Purgatorio,'" M. Garvey was whispering beside her. "Dante's Delight. I just read the Divine Comedy last year. *Mount* Purgatory."

Lestrade saw that M. Garvey was looking up, too. "Right," the detective sergeant said in a voice just loud enough to take in her whole squad. "We're trying that tower first."

She got out her police ring of skeleton keys. The second one fit Imani's lock. They made it inside with minimum noise, started pointing their flashlights around. Six thin beams of light, weaving around like some kind of crazy cat's cradle. The whole house seemed quiet, dark. But it didn't feel deserted. It felt like somebody at home somewhere in here. Probably that blame tower, so Lestrade decided a light or three downstairs would be safe enough. She found a light switch and tabbed it on.

Fine vestibule. Victorian style, well kept up. Like stepping back into the era of Holmes and Watson, for sure.

M. Garvey looked around, frowned a little, and led the way into the house, waving them to follow. Not pushing it. Polite and shy and right in the spirit of silence. The Old Woman's leathery old heart warmed to her a little.

They proceeded as a group, Lestrade first behind their blond Sacajawea, tabbing on more lights here and there, Clayton beside her wherever space allowed. She noticed he looked pale but determined, and every now and then pressed his lips into a tight line.

"Here," M. Garvey whispered, bringing them to the foot of a wide staircase with a smooth wood banister. "I'm not sure how high these go," she confessed.

Well, it was a start. Nodding to her, Lestrade took the lead.

Lady, they damn well better leave enough of him for me!

The staircase continued to the third floor before stopping at a corner where two corridors met. Lestrade shut her eyes and mentally checked her orientation before turning down the hallway she thought led to the tower side of the house.

Bingo. Another stairway. Going down as well as up. Treading carefully, they went up. By now they were back on flashlights rather than risk stairwell lights.

The last three steps to the next landing up had been stripped of all carpeting and painted: looked in the beam of the flashlights like black, some midway color—red?—and white, in ascending order. Fortunately, pollies wore rubber soles they could keep quiet on bare wood.

The staircase made a ninety-degree turn and continued past this landing one level higher, but all she could see up there was one more landing, in front of a blank wall, with maybe above it a ceiling trapdoor to the roof. And there was something about those three painted steps... Softly and cautiously, she mounted them and tested the doorknob. Felt unlocked, well oiled. Turned without making a sound.

She glanced around behind her. Clayton at her right shoulder, good. M. Garvey pushing up at her left shoulder—not so good, but trying to get her back and an officer into her place could cause more noise pollution than Lestrade wanted to risk right now. She waved the flashlight in her left hand to signal "Be Ready," tabbed it off, thrust open the door, and announced into the sudden flow of light:

"Everyone in this room is under arrest."

CHAPTER 22

STILL TUESDAY, OCTOBER 3

There were three of them, sitting on the floor beneath a full-sized green cross, other pleasant apparatus scattered neatly around the edges of the chamber, fancy framed mottoes or something—bless the Prexy!—hanging on the walls. The ceiling was high, the windows shuttered, the floor sunken to the depth of three steps down—painted white, red, and black—giving Lestrade a good view of things. The far side, facing the door, was closed off with heavy purple theater-type curtains. The trio sitting on the floor looking up at her were a solid brown-haired man approaching middle age, an attractive—to say the least—black-haired young woman, and a hefty Chocolate Pureblood who could have been either gender. All fully dressed and ready for public appearance. The man and woman had white neck-scarves, the Pureblood a white vest. All this Lestrade saw in a couple of heartbeats.

The man said, "We've all signed consenting adult forms, Officer."

"You're not under arrest for all this nonsense, M.'s." Lestrade waved around at the room. "You're under arrest on suspicion of murder and kidnapping —"

"Sergeant, no!" And look who came waltzing out from behind the purple curtains, bandages peeking beneath both sleeves but otherwise acting cozily at home and none the worse for wear. "They are inno-"

"SHUT UP, M. DAVISON!" snapped Lestrade, aware that at the same moment M. Garvey was crying,

"Oh, Cory, your *solemn promise!*"

"I said everyone in this room," Lestrade went on. "That includes *you,* M. Davison."

"-cent," he finished in a whisper, closed his mouth, and mechanically held his hands up for the bracelets. But his shocked gaze never left the doorway. Where, Lestrade verified with one quick backward glance, M. Garvey no longer stood.

Noticing the bandages were elastic, neatly wound halfway up over the heels of his palms, she pulled the steelplas cuffs just tight enough not to slip off. He ignored the whole process, still staring toward the place where M. Garvey had stood. Only when Lestrade stepped back, probably blocking his line of vision, did he seem to pull himself more or less together, lifting his wrists to examine the handcuffs with what looked like abstracted curiosity.

A second man had come through the curtains. Tall, skinny, with a broken-crooked nose, about thirty, carrying a half-eaten sandwich. As Officer Little Bird approached him, he stuffed the last of it in his mouth and held out his hands. Vergucchi was taking care of the middle-aged man, Wentworth the Pureblood—maybe not quite a Pureblood, with that shoulder-length straight hair. "Detective Clayton," Lestrade told him, jerking her head at the woman, "cuff her."

* * * *

Julie stood up and watched Dave approach through a wavery film of tears. Looking away to wipe her eyes, she saw that Curly had turned around and deliberately held her wrists out in back to her polly. What an inspired idea! To salvage as much purgatory as they could out of the situation. Besides, Julie didn't really want to risk looking Dave in the eye. As he got close, she followed Curly's example.

Instead of cuffing her hands in back, he put one hand on her shoulder and turned her around to face him again. His touch was neither gentle nor rough, just…businesslike, impersonal.

"Dave," she whispered, trying after all to look up into his gray eyes.

Completely the police detective, he slid his gaze neutrally down, picked her wrists up one at a time, and cuffed them together in front. He never said a word to her. Just one glance at her face, too quick for her to read his expression, right before he turned back to the one who had to be his "Old Woman," Sergeant Lestrade.

* * * *

Lady Goddess Mother! Lestrade was thinking. Any more pairs of lovebirds we can manage to split apart tonight? Seems unbalanced to leave all of three hearts unbroken. "Now," she demanded, "how many more of you are there to come out of the woodwork?"

"Nobody else, Officer," the middle-aged one replied. "You got us, all four."

"Five," Lestrade corrected him. "You'd be M. Imani?"

"Sam. Sam Imani. And it's four. That one —" he did a double-handed gesture at Davison, "shouldn't fall under your arrest. He was just joining us tonight. Not even a full member, yet."

"He stays arrested. All right, Officers, let's take them away." Gripping Davison by the shoulder, she watched the others file out first.

"Sergeant Lestrade," he said softly, "I had...labored under the impression that Angela—M. Garvey—was safe in Boca Raton."

"Giving you your chance to break a promise to her as well as a direct command from me. You young idiot, she flew back today out of worry for your questionable hide!"

"'Questionable' has my full endorsement." He took one shaky breath and said, "Will you grant her police protection?"

Lestrade relented, just a little, and just for the moment. "To the best of our power. Now come on!" and propelled him out at the end of the line.

They found M. Garvey waiting beside the front door. Davison came to a stop. "Angela..."

"How long did your solemn promise last, Corwin Poe? Two days?" She held up an envelope with her name on it.

"Have you...read it?" he asked.

For answer, she tore it in four and thrust the pieces back at him before she stormed out the front door.

Only one of the pieces stayed in his cuffed hands. He ran his fingers over it as if checking whether the flap was still sealed down, then let it fall beside the other pieces and exited the house into Officer Brown's waiting custody. Lestrade lingered long enough to gather up all the pieces of envelope and letter. Evidence, you plodding drudge of a pollydeck. Evidence to sift and comb and try like hades to make something out of.

That was the excuse she handed herself.

* * * *

The police security limo had four wide back seats separated from the driver's section by a plate of steelglass. Julie had never ridden in one before. It was as comfortable as any regular car, or would have been, apart from the fact of being under arrest, with Dave...

Beside her, Corwin suddenly yanked his fists apart until the cuffs bit into his bandages, winced, and broke the silence. "An ant striving to play croquet with no height to swing the mallet and no access to the rulebook!" he exclaimed.

"Make that mallet a live flamingo," Sam remarked from the next seat back, "and you've just about got it."

"Your forgiveness is naturally rescinded," Corwin continued.

"What?" said Sam. "Why?"

Curly pointed out, "You tried to insist it was just four of us, Sam."

"Hey, Corwin, I didn't mean—" Sam began... "Look, I was just hoping to keep you out of it. Everything considered, why should you be under suspicion with the rest of us? Anyway, pretty poor argument for the ideals of the Purgatorio, if we started rescinding forgiveness now. What about it, gang?"

There was a murmur of agreement from Curly and Paul. Julie added her Yes to complete the consensus.

"After I have served as your Cassius and Brutus and Judas? It is thanks to me that we sit here now."

"Just don't hang yourself on us," Paul spoke up from the back seat. "Judas' problem was, he couldn't accept being forgiven."

Sam added, "And try making that Shakespeare's Brutus instead of Dante's."

Corwin bent forward and put his face in his linked hands.

"It was probably bound to happen sooner or later," Sam went on philosophically. "I think we got a little bit too complacent when the consenting adult laws came in."

"Adult..." Corwin murmured, and Julie remembered he was just twenty-two. Still getting used to being grown-up in the grown-up world. She remembered when she was that age. That had been about the time she joined Dante's Delight. With Dave still years in the future.

After a few more blocks, Julie said softly, "Corwin. We've lost them, haven't we?"

"I fear I have.... Let my comfort be that Angela can do far better."

"No, she can't." Scooching across the seat, Julie groped for his hands and got them into her own. "And call me selfish," she went on, "but I don't think Dave is going to do better than me. Not that I'm so good. But we fit together, Dave and I."

Corwin returned the pressure of her fingers. They sat, two pairs of cuffed hands layered together, awkward but comforting.

Another short silence. Curly broke this one. "Next time I play it smart like the rest of you and let 'em cuff me in front. This isn't penitential, it's just darn uncomfortable."

"Uncomfortable counts," said Sam. "I think we're almost there, anyway."

"It's embarrassing to own to this," said Corwin, "but I have never before been under arrest, never hitherto experienced serious embroilment with the legal authorities."

"None of us have," said Julie.

"You're wrong there," Paul announced. "I was arrested once. When I was a kid in high school. For shoplifting."

"What are we to do?" Corwin asked. "How comport ourselves?"

"Just let the pollies take the lead. Go where they push you, do what they want, don't give them any backtalk. We don't have anything much to worry about tonight. It isn't like screenshows about the bad old days before pollies got paranoid about lawsuits for false arrest and/or police brutality. And they make doggone good coffee."

"It's what comes after tonight that we have to worry about," said Curly.

"What comes after tonight..." Julie murmured. She thought she was going to cry again. Oh, Dave, Dave, my Dragon Prince!

"I think we're there, gang," Sam observed as the limo pulled up to the police station.

* * * *

At the station, Lestrade grouped her team, except Wentworth, who was herding the arrestees from the limo into the station.

"Body searches on these, Sergeant?" Vergucchi wanted to know. If it hadn't been a case of murder, the question wouldn't have been asked, even by an old-timer like Vergucchi. Nobody did body searches nowadays for any crime less than arson and armed robbery. Even in those cases, if one was done on a floater who turned out to be innocent, the automatic monetary recompense could put a big dent in the year's budget. But this was suspected murder and kidnapping—no, strike the kidnapping, the idiot had run into it with arms open.

"Just prints and photos," Lestrade decided. "This lot might *enjoy* body searches. Process Davison first, then bring him straight back to Interrogation. I'm taking his statement myself. Personally." She glanced at her partner—she had had him brief her on who was who during the drive back. "For the others. Detective Clayton, you take Imani's statement. Officer Little Bird—Whitcomb. Officer Vergucchi—Osaka. Officer Brown—Friedman. I don't think they'll give you any trouble."

"Sarge," Dave asked, a little shakily, "do you want me in there, with…"

"No, Detective, I do not. No 'good polly, bad polly' games tonight. It'll be 'bad polly' all the way."

"Old Woman…if you decide to see Whitcomb…can you go just a little bit 'good polly' on her?"

Lestrade searched his face. Almost—not quite—gave him a tiny smile of reassurance. But all she answered in words was, "We'll see. We'll just see. Anybody keep track of what happened to M. Garvey?"

"I think she went back to the waiting room, Sergeant," said Little Bird.

"Good. Keep her there. Officer Wentworth," she went on, as he came out to join her squad. "I haven't given you anything else to do. Take M. Garvey some sandwiches, coffee, whatever she wants. Go out and buy her a paperback book if she doesn't like our choice magazine selection. Anything that makes her happy." As if anything could. "I'll be in Interrogation. Waiting for Davison."

Once in the interrogation room, she turned her back on the never-curtained steelglass picture window, shook the pieces of M.

Garvey's letter out on the sink counter, fitted them together, and read the message. Mush. Flowery, overblown mush. Sydney Carton, take a back seat.

Good Lady God! Why wasn't there anybody to write *me* mush like that, back when I was M. Garvey's age?

Pocketing the torn letter again, she leaned back and waited.

CHAPTER 23

STILL TUESDAY, OCTOBER 3

In good time, Lotus Blossom Lee delivered Davison to Interrogation, left him there, and shut the door behind her. He stood near the door, looking around uncertainly, never quite venturing to meet Lestrade's eye.

"Take a seat, M. Davison," she told him in a calm, emotionless, carefully controlled voice, with a gesture at the easy chair facing the window.

He crossed the room, sat down in the chair as if it was Gojira ready to chomp, and looked to right and left at the nailed-down snack table and the wire recorder on its stand.

"Coffee, M. Davison?" This time she made her voice almost motherly.

"Thank you. That would be extremely welcome."

She poured a cup. "Cream? Sugar?"

"Of the former…two dollops, if you please, and…tonight… I think…two spoonfuls of the latter. For the caloric energy."

She added the sugar, stirred it well, poured in the cream, brought the fine china cup and saucer—nothing too soft for the interviewees, at all costs avoid any appearance of police brutality—and set it on the snack table beside the chair. "Cookies? Petits fours? Maybe a sandwich?"

"Thank you again. A sandwich would taste delectable."

She got the sandwich plate out of the mini-fridge. "Egg salad, ham salad, liverwurst, or chicken?"

"The first, please. Eggs are, after all, the youngest and tenderest of chickens."

She took off the cellophane, put the sandwich on a fine china plate—different pattern from the cup and saucer; even for luxury interrogation rooms, the budget extended only to discontinued floor-sample place settings—cut it into four neat triangles, added a linen napkin, brought them over and set them beside the coffee. By now anyone could see he was starting to relax.

A couple of teenage girls happened to stroll by, at their ease in the back alley. It being as wide and well lit as the front walkway, and almost as full of shop windows. They looked in, grinned, pointed, poked each other lightly in the upper arm, exchanged a word or two inaudible through the sound-soak-treated steelglass, then waved at somebody or something out of sight of the occupants of the room, and hurried away.

Taking her post well to the side of the chair, Lestrade got down to business. "Well, M. Davison," she said in abnormally friendly tones, "suppose you tell me why, exactly, you saw fit to disobey my direct 'suggestion.' Didn't I make it plain enough?"

"Craving your indulgence, Sergeant, if I might beg enlightenment as to what final, comprehensive, and absolute authority the police enjoy over the licit activities of free civilians?"

That tore it.

She scorched him royally. She excoriated him raw. She dragged his bloody carcass through red-hot embers and laid him out in lilies. She personally escorted him through every monotheistic hades she had ever heard anything about, and tossed in the Buddhist and Etruscan hells for good measure.

His coffee sat cooling beside him forgotten, his sandwich untouched, his mouth hanging half open like a stunned puppy's.

She never even thought about relenting until she saw him trying to blink back tears. She didn't actually wind down and finish up until he fumbled his handkerchief out of his pocket and blew his nose.

"Your coffee is probably cold," she observed, making a sudden shift to Polite Hostess. "Hotten it for you?"

He answered not a word. Just sat still with his head bent down. Well, Dave always told her, out of the depths of his mercifully limited experience with it, that she had the most scorching tongue of his acquaintance. Came in handy now and then. She picked up the lukewarm cup, took it over to the sink and emptied it out, refilled it, added the sugar and cream, and brought it over to the easy chair.

By now he had his head back on the cushion, eyes closed, breathing still a little ragged, but obviously hard at work pulling himself together again. The teenage girls were back, peering in and giggling. The beauty of a scorching tongue was the way you could apply it across the room and never lay a finger on the honored recipient.

Too bad it didn't work on the really hard scumbags.

"Well, that did *me* some good, anyway," she remarked. "Here's your hot coffee." She set the cup back down in its saucer.

He picked it up with extreme caution, took a few sips, and said in a small voice, "Overblown? Pompous? Pretentious? Puffed-up? Conceited?"

"Use your famous memory, M. Davison. That was the least I called you."

"…These may perhaps comprise the adjectives I most fear true of myself. Apart from those which I already knew to be justified."

"Oh, you've justified everything I called you."

"Hyp…Hypocrite?"

"Okay, on that one, I guess maybe I could have stopped with 'lying.' You're going to give me your statement now, and you're going to tell me the truth. I want to know exactly what you were doing to get yourself arrested. I'd say, 'in your own words,' but I strongly suggest that for once in your life, just for the record and the comfort of the stenographer, you stick with words the rest of us don't need to look up in unabridged dictionaries. And no hearsay, no interpretations of anybody else's motives. Or movements that you didn't witness directly. I'll also take it as a personal favor if you leave out any mention of that mild little scorching I just made you a present of. Oh, by the way," she added, to get him a little more at his ease, "thanks for understanding how a middle-aged female bachelor can get a kick out of reading kiddies' picture books. All right, your turn to talk, my turn to just listen." She tabbed on the wire recorder, gave it the date and the "statement of" tag, stepped back, and got out her pipe.

He looked at the turning wire and then at her. "Where… Where shall I begin?"

"Begin with whatever decided you to sign that consenting adult form." She stood back to be silent, only tapping the bowl of her pipe with her fingernails sometimes, raising an eyebrow at him now and then, and listening in amusement whenever he stopped and groped for a simple word in place of a perfectly good complicated one.

Yesterday morning, she mused, when we brought him to the morgue, he was talking more or less like any ordinary floater. Must have been the stress. Now he's only got himself to worry about...

"Why did I sign it?" he began, and shook his head helplessly. "I sincerely wish I could answer that. The thought of Angela's—M. Garvey's—safety *seemed* to be uppermost in my mind. If poor M. Soderstrum had indeed been murdered in mistake for her...and if the Purgatorio's symbol indeed betrayed their involvement...Yet *that* I could scarcely believe. But I had already, in some sense, betrayed them to you, so the consi-...the thought of clearing them was also present in my mind, of clearing them and thus freeing your attention to find the real murderer...who might be attempt-... trying to frame Dante's Delight. In either case, it still seemed to me that I was ideally situ-...placed to discover the truth about them, and that knowing the truth must benefit us all. But...there is also the fact that I...had earlier been strongly moved to accept their invitation on my own count, before any of those other factors obtr— arose. So, forgive me, I really can neither understand nor eluci-...explain my own psychomystique in this case... Is 'psychomystique' a word common enough to be admitted?"

Lestrade gave him a nod. He continued,

"Please understand... If I may insert a few words of explanation? In the Purgatorio's own concep-...self-image? its activities are neither immoral nor perverse, but of altr-...of social benefit. I won't argue the point here and now. Misled they well might be, but depraved in the usual sense of that word they are not. Their guiderules are almost monastically stringent—I mean, strict—and forbid anything of a...of a sexually carnal nature.

"At every meeting, two members play the role of 'penitents' and suffer, the others accept the role of 'angels' who administer... I'm sorry, I cannot quickly think of a simpler word—the sufferings. The roles trade off, and every member dreads 'angel' duty above 'penitent' duty. Before each meeting, the desig-...the penitents whose turn it is must fast quite strictly for about a day. My fast began yesterday, as soon as I had signed the form. Paul—M. Osaka—undertook the role of my fellow penitent, for they do not believe that anyone, even during initiation, should suffer alone.

"Arriving at M. Imani's home about midday, we found a light colla-...meal waiting on the dining-room table: five plates, each holding a peanut butter and jelly sandwich, some carrot sticks, and an olive, with a tall glass of cold water at each plate. The angels naturally needed their energy. M. Osaka and I, of course, must maintain our fast, and had our hands bound to the arms of our chairs, to prevent inadvertencies—apologies—absent-minded nibbling. In truth, peanut butter and jelly sandwiches have never appealed to me, and at this time I felt no pressing desire for any kind of food; but the glass of water I thought I could have drained thrice over and requested more.

"This mild version of the torment of Tantalus formed no official part of the purgatorial ceremonies. It was a mere informal…may I use the word 'prelude'?…a last time of socializing before the business of the day. Among their guiderules is that mealtime conversation be always kept light and diverting. Certainly, the sight of that glass of water, coupled with the awkwardness of conversing without the use of one's hands, helped divert my mind from what was to come. It distracted me sufficiently that by the time Sam, Curly, and—that is, M.'s Imani, Friedman, and Whitcomb—had finished their repast, even peanut butter and jelly had begun to look more or less tempting. M. Osaka and I may actually have carried the bulk of the conversation, being unburdened by any need to work in bites and sips.

"A quarter of an hour after the conclusion of the luncheon and clearing away of the dishes—M. Osaka's and mine being covered with cellophane and set aside for later consump-…for eating afterwards, we were unbound, M. Whitcomb gave me a purple candle, herself took a white one, and led me up the stairs. There are seven levels of initiation and, in my foolhardiness, I had requested the first three in one session, which is allowable. The membership tattoo is given only after the fourth level—the new member's initial angel duty—and I had originally thought that only then would I be able to penetra-…to learn the full secrets of the Purgatorio. Although dreading that fourth level above all, I hoped to…speed things up as much as lay within my power. Sergeant Lestrade, I wish those young women just outside the window would take their departure."

Lestrade broke her silence long enough to say, "They've got the legal right to stay there as long as they like, M. Davison. Don't worry, the soundproofing is good unless we scream. I think they're window-shopping you."

"Thank you. It lends one a certain empathy with merchandise on display. Well!" Turning to face as much as possible away from the window, he cleared his throat and continued, "Where was I? Oh, yes! Every member must of course repeat the fourth level at alternate meetings. Of the six penitential levels, five can be re-peated more or less at the penitent's own choice. The first level, however, must be experienced once only. I...cannot testify for certain as to how M.'s Imani, Osaka, and Friedman whiled away this interval, but I glimpsed them setting up a three-player chess board as I followed M. Whitcomb out of the room. I must confess to a moment of envy.

"Gaining the Purgatorio, M. Whitcomb had me lie down, still fully clothed, on one of the two cots they have in the withdraw-ing room—behind the curtain—and adminis-...gave me a dose of some hallucinogen...commonly called...let me think... Dream-dust? Visionquest?...ah! Visiondust."

Lestrade nodded. Safe enough stuff, as substances went.

He went on, "As I closed my eyes and lay quiet while it took effect, she began murmuring me through a kind of guided medita-tion. Bit by bit, as the illusion deepened into seeming reality, I lost awareness of the sound of her voice, so that after a certain point I can no longer testify how much of the vision was due to her guid-ance and how much to my own psychomystique.

"I shall not prolong the description of that hallucination. Some of its details mercifully blur in my own memory. It involved my slow roasting through being forced by hideous demons to crawl on my hands and knees over glowing embers, my piecemeal dis-memberment and consumption at their hands before my very eyes, the rattling and shaking together of my bones beneath the gaze of my impaled head. I suppose that some part of my mind must have remained aware of the visionary nature of the whole experience, or it could not have been borne, nor would my subsequent actual and physical experiences have seemed more than pallid anticlimax. At last there followed the reassembly and reclothing in flesh of my skeleton—in itself, a painful process enough—the reattachment of head to neck, and blessed resurrection into wakefulness. All very shamanic.

"After questioning me as to the unfolding of my vision, M. Whitcomb was—no, that is interpretation—appeared quite satisfied, and allowed me half an hour to rest, along with one small piece of candy to suck, while she went to summon the others. I suppose, had I been the competent spy I had set myself out to be, I should have seized this oppor—...chance to search the Purgatorio. I did not. I simply rested, in both body and mind.

"The others arriving in the tower chamber, M. Osaka joined me in the withdrawing room—behind the curtain—where we changed into swimming trunks, somewhat more hip-hugging than my own preferred style for beachwear. When we emerged, M.'s Imani and Friedman bound my fellow penitent face downward to a sort of inclined frame—you may have noticed it—then led me to the raised bar, stood me on a three-legged stool, and enclosed my wrists in a pair of metal rings above my head. They then removed the stool and left me hanging by the wrists while they returned to flog M. Osaka with rubber hoses."

Lestrade raised her brow and tapped her pipe, but made no vocal comment.

"To my astonishment—for is not this the device one so often sees apparently applied in screenshows and suchlike entertainments—the pain of hanging by one's wrists is immediate and pervasi-... I mean...runs through—the entire body. I can only hope they have means of faking it for the actors. I drew some comfort from the reflec— the thought that at least this was not the more infamous suspension by the thumbs, nor the hands-behind-the-back strappado, nor being yanked up and dôwn. I could not, however, bear even to imagine what it must be to a heavier person, like M. Imani or M. Friedman. The sound of the hoses falling on M. Osaka's back, I think I found to increase my own suffering more than it fostered any comforting sense of fellowship. From time to time, M. Whitcomb wiped my face with a dampened cloth and murmured a few words of encouragement; but, taken all in all, up until half an hour ago, I should have called it the second to the longest five minutes of my life."

The longest, Lestrade figured, being any five-minute segment of yesterday morning before the second victim turned out not to be M. Garvey. Okay, what bumped this hanging by the wrists episode out of second place? The scorching *I* just gave him? Rosemary L.

Lestrade, you must be even better at it than you thought! Maybe it wouldn't be such a waste of time to try it on the real scumbags.

"When it was over at last—some of the more experienced purgatorians endure up to ten minutes, never longer, but to me as an initiate they were merciful—my fellow penitent and I were helped back to the cots behind the curtain, where M. Friedman massaged M. Osaka's back with oil, and M. Whitcomb bandaged my wrists. The suspension process creates a groove, you see, with the flesh mounding up on either side." He held up one wrist, as if Lestrade could see through the bandage. "It is not permanent. We were given one swallow of water apiece, and half an hour to recup-...to recover somewhat, during which time I tried to persuade M. Osaka that he had done more than enough for one day, that I could endure the third level without the camaraderie—I'm sorry, the companionship? of a fellow sufferer. He refused.

"When we were called forth again, M. Osaka mounted at once to the cross, stretched out his arms, and allowed M.'s Imani and Friedman to bind him to it hand and foot, while M. Whitcomb guided me to the side table—you may have noticed it, Sergeant Lestrade? It may at first glance suggest the infamous rack, but it is simply a kind of plaswood bed with restraints and a hard headrest in the ancient Egyptian style, nothing more. She had me lie upon it face upward, strapped me down with bands around the chest, forearms, and lower thighs, and produced a supply of very long, very slender needles in an antiseptic-soaked pincushion. She explained that this third level of initiation was a hygienic and minimally scarring reproduction of perhaps the most ancient shamanic ordeal on record, as seen in Paleolithic—may I use the word Paleolithic? cave painting which show bodies transfixed with arrows protr-... sticking out in all directions like so many human pincushions. You were already aware that M. Whitcomb is a highly skilled nurse? Taking a pinch of epidermis near my navel, she stitched her first needle through it.

"I fainted.

"When I came to myself, I was lying once more on the cot in the withdrawing room, a light blanket covering me to the chin, M.'s Whitcomb and Imani bending over me. Seated on the other cot, M. Osaka was having his wrists bandaged by M. Friedman: both are paramedics. All assured me that I had successfully achieved the first two levels, that three in one afternoon had been quite ambitious for someone with a rather low threshold of pain, but that they would welcome me to repeat the third level in a week or two—depending on how many extraordinary—in the sense of emergency—sessions they put in during the present citywide crisis.

"So far, every event of the long afternoon had confirmed my belief in the complete innocence of Dante's Delight. Yet I felt I must make assurance doubly sure...are quotations from Shakespeare acceptable? Besides, my duplicity—apologies, I cannot find a simpler word for it on the spur of the moment—weighed more and more heavily on my conscience the more my doubts of these people's sincerity dissipated. Also, I may have grown somewhat giddy and reckless."

Lestrade shot up both eyebrows and grunted.

"Weighing—rather hastily—all these factors, I confessed to them my uppermost reasons for signing the consent form: that the second victim had so much resembled M. Garvey; that I had seen the tattoo stamped on the body and recognized it, from its picture in their information sheet, as the symbol of Dante's Delight Purgatorio; that I had felt pressed to learn whether they were completely innocent or somehow involved.

"M. Friedman asked if I were working for the police, to which I could with a perfectly clear conscience answer 'No.'"

Lestrade tapped her fingernails on her pipe. Davison had the sense to look a little shamefaced about that whopping understatement, but put it behind him and went on,

"And they forgave me! I had played Judas to them, and they forgave me, all of them in unison, with neither long discussion nor voting. They even emphasized that I remained welcome to join their circle. Even after our arrest, they refused to rescind their forgiveness. Sergeant Lestrade, does this not sufficiently prove their innocence?"

All she said was, "Stop editorializing and finish your statement."

"I...thought I had finished. What more of any importance...? As far as we knew, there was nothing to mark me as a missing person, and I think... May I say that much? My own thought remains a fact, whether or not accurate... In any case, I saw no sign that any of them feared interruption that evening. How could we have known or guessed that M. Garvey had returned from Boca

Raton and found—to her pain, which I cannot regret more—the letters I had penned simply to insure against any outside chance of the Purgatorio's guilt, expecting that in all probability I would return home to laugh at and destroy my needless precautions. M. Osaka and I were left alone to reclothe ourselves, while the others brought us the luncheon we had not been able to eat earlier. The other three repaired to…went to the outer room while we ate. I had the impression they began discussing whether they should not go to the police themselves, though they kept their voices low so as not to disturb our digestion, and we overheard no more than a word or two here and there, by accident. This was the state of affairs when you…honored us with your unexpected visit. Can there be anything else?"

Lestrade said, "You mentioned seven levels of initiation. I counted six. What's number seven?"

"Oh. Compression. That is…the opposite of stretching. It is actually the sixth level, the seventh and highest being quasi—… I might say, temporary crucifixion."

"Nails and all?"

"Usually ropes. Sometimes cilices."

"Wounds? Bleeding?"

"Small ones. Comparable to the pricks of thorns."

"Hmm." Nothing so far to cause any wounds of the kind found on the two murder victims. In fact, compared with some real smasters of Lestrade's passing acquaintance, all fairly restrained. "Any other practices?"

"Some. Proposed by the penitent in question and allowed or rejected by consensus following discussion. Rarely proposed by any penitent not already old in the five repeatable levels already mentioned."

"Detective Clayton has told me that there are in fact scars on M. Whitcomb's back, which she claims resulted from an accident involving a fall on broken glass. Never mind how he knows."

"Until about a lustrum…that is, five years ago, they did employ scourges, blades, and occasionally various forms of heat. M. Whitcomb may have earned some scars in the earliest months of her membership, before they went to lighter equipment. Or she might actually have fallen on broken glass. I have never seen her other than fully clothed."

Lestrade walked over and tabbed the recorder off. "You enjoyed that, didn't you?"

"*Did* I? Not, I assure you, at the time!... But, in retrospect, I suppose...recounting it to—in some sense—a captive audience...yes, perhaps I did enjoy *that*. Do not people both normal and healthy relish describing their operations, dental experiences, and other ordeals once safely past the same? And it distracted me from..." Letting his voice trail off, he stole another look toward the window. "They are still there."

"Yep. Still giggling and poking each other and ogling you."

He mused, "It must be the deplorable—unfortunate—human fascination with the criminal element. Are they not aware that a citywide alert remains in effect?"

"Should be safe enough this close to the police station. Relax, M. Davison. They're how the public protects you from police brutality."

"With only partial success."

"I never laid a finger on you. 'Sticks and stones' and all that."

"Whatever philosopher added 'words will never hurt me' clearly had never had the privilege of your acquaintance, Sergeant."

"I'll take that as a compliment. Now. I hope you understand that as a witness for the defense, you're every prosecutor's dream come true."

"What?" It was almost a whisper.

"Fact: you've established that we have here a cozy little knot of people who get together regularly for the purpose of torturing one another. I don't care what kind of noble-sounding rationalizations they're come up with, the general population—and that includes the jury pool—is going to see it as smastering. Fact: this cozy little knot of smasters—as everybody is going to see them—uses a stamped tattoo as their membership mark. Fact: this same tattoo has been found on both murder victims. Fact: tattoo stamps are registered. Artists can't legally copy other artists' designs, or ethically sell stamps with the same design to different and unrelated buyers. Fact: both our victims show marks of either torture or mutilation. Hard to be sure which, after the time they spent with water rinsing the wounds clean of any blood there might have been. Our consulting forensic examiner puts the highest probability on post-mortem mutilation, but people, including juries, are going to ignore that and assume 'tortured to death' because it's more shocking, therefore, to the disgrace of our species, more fun for most people to believe. At least when they think whoever did it is safe in custody. And when it only involves strangers. Now: put these facts together, and how do you think any jury—outside, *maybe*, Vegas or Frisco or possibly selected parts of New York City—is going to vote? And any conceivable element of doubt be damned."

"But...my own experience with Dante's Delight..."

"Can't very well murder *all* their recruits, can they? You were just one of the luckier ones. That's how the prosecution will call it, anyway. Of course, they might allow, M.'s Jackson and Soderstrum *could* have died accidentally, maybe from initiations that got too enthusiastic. The difference in the sentencing will be life plus ninety-nine years or life plus fifty."

"Cannot I testify at least as a character witness —"

"Oslo Syndrome."

"But it was *not* Oslo Syndrome! They in no sense kidnapped me! I signed the consent form of my own free and unconstrained will. Had I changed my mind at any point, even on my way upstairs with M. Whitcomb, they would have allowed me to tear up the form and leave without further argument. M. Whitcomb even attempted to dissuade me, in light of my promise to —"

"Pity she didn't succeed. We're not even talking facts any longer, M. Davison. We're talking twisty little prosecution arguments. They can make it Oslo Syndrome without blinking. And your own safest course will be to let them."

"My...own..."

"Make yourself out to be one of the victims, and you walk home a free man. Or turn State's Evidence. Your testimony won't be any more damning as a witness for the prosecution than as one for the defense, and you'll get off with a suspended sentence."

As he sat digesting the information, which might never have occurred to him before, that today's initiation nonsense had put him in almost as much danger from the law as the rest of the idiots were in, Lestrade glanced out the window and remarked, "Our giggling girls have finally left us. Probably got bored when I took over."

"No," said Davison.

"No?"

"To pass myself off as a victim would be a lie, and I have already told too many lies in this affair."

"And told them too damn well."

"Rolegaming experience. And to turn State's Evidence would imply that I believed them guilty. These people have befriended me. I will not turn traitor on them yet again."

"Then you'll be sitting at the defendants' table right alongside them. I hope today's little escapade was worth it."

He passed a shaking hand in front of his face, sat silent for a moment. Finally he said, "Even so. I...have lost her in any case.... Please ask M. Garvey to take my cat into her home. I think M. Florsheim might like my canary." He looked back at Lestrade and tried to crack a joke. "Possibly prison will knock some of the pomposity out of me."

She would've been disappointed in him if he had gone down either of the safe roads.

"All right, M. Davison," she said, leaning back against the wall and tapping her pipe again. "In confidence. I agree with you. I think they're being framed, too."

He looked at her hopefully.

She went on, "Trouble is, the idiots—including you, after today's little picnic—have made themselves so double-damned easy to frame! I've even got a fairly strong hunch who's framing them, but plain hunches don't buy search warrants. Not without something hard to back them up."

"You need evidence in order to procure evidence?"

No point spelling it out for him that his stunt had upset all her plans and hopes. One way and another, he'd been through enough for now. "See?" she said. "You *can* put things in a nutshell, after all." She tabbed the chime to signal 'done with this one' and added, while they waited, "First offense, no previous record—I assume?"

He shook his head.

"New recruit, not yet part of the group when the murders happened. A good lawyer might be able to get you off with ten to twenty. At least hire your own lawyer."

"A 'good' lawyer, as opposed to the lawyer the others will have?" he protested.

"A *separate* lawyer, just to underline the situation for the court. Courts can be slow on the uptake. Ah, here!"

It was Dave who opened the door.

"Cell number two," she told him, jerking her head in Davison's direction.

"Number two, Sarge?" It was the VIP cell, the one the pollies themselves sometimes sneaked into and used when they needed a lie-down during long hours. Davison didn't need to know that.

"Number two, Detective. Lock him in, and come right back. Or send me Little Bird…Brown…anyone who's available."

CHAPTER 24

STILL TUESDAY, OCTOBER 3

The Old Woman must've given him a hard time, Dave thought sympathetically on their way to the cellblock. Young floater was staggering against his arm. Must be fresh out of adrenalin.

"Yo! Kim," Dave said, passing her. "The Old Woman wants someone in Interrogation."

"Right, Detective." The rookie didn't actually salute, but her tone of voice did. She turned and hustled away, all Official Police Business.

"Very…very aesthetically pleasing…young officer," Corwin murmured into Dave's shoulder. He didn't say anything else until they reached the cellblock. He was the next thing to sleepwalking.

Once inside cell number two, it was Dave who broke the silence. "Corwin…"

"Call me prisoner number…yet to be assigned."

"Hey, don't even think that! Sergeant Lestrade will pull something out of her hat."

"I hope it is not myself."

"Scorch you, huh?" Dave asked sympathetically.

The other nodded.

"And you're still in one piece? Impressive. Well, try not to let it get you down too far. She only scorches the ones she likes."

"I refuse to make an obvious rejoinder."

"Your privilege. Corwin…about Julie…"

Blinking himself a little more alert, the younger man looked back into Dave's eyes. "Officer…Detective…whatever you are thinking…there was no…activity of a salacious nature…in the Purgatorio."

"It's not even that. Well, not so much. It's… Well, dammit, boy! It's still unhealthy, dirty. With or without."

Corwin gripped Dave's upper arms and stared him even harder in both eyes. "Dave. This...peculiarity...calling it nothing worse... has cost me my...love. Please, please, I beg you, don't let it cost you yours!"

Then he collapsed onto the cot. Dave spread a blanket over him, left the cell, locked the door as quietly as possible, and stood in thought, looking down the corridor between the two rows of cells.

* * * *

Officer Little Bird," Lestrade said when the rookie showed up. "M. Garvey still in the building?"

"Still in the waiting room, Sergeant, just like you wanted."

"I'll see her next."

Officer Little Bird blinked around at the interrogation room. "Sergeant, M. Garvey is not...?"

"She's a material witness, Officer. But in here is more comfortable than in my office, and I don't feel like moving."

As soon as Little Bird had left, Lestrade finished fitting the pieces of torn letter back together again on the sink counter.

* * * *

The Forest Green Police Station had eight cells, each one large enough to fit four people in reasonable comfort, as far as comfort was possible when you were under arrest. Eight cells were probably overdoing it for a small city as peaceable and safe...usually... as Forest Green. Only two cells, at the far end, had already been occupied, by a separated pair of "drunk and disorderlies." There was plenty of room to stick Dante's Delight each in a separate cell. They would have preferred being together, if they'd been asked their choice.

They were all in a row on the same side of the corridor: cells one, three, five, and seven. The Privcom guiderules still let police bug their own cellblocks, "for safety," but Sam, Paul, Curly, and Julie had nothing incriminating to let slip as far as the police were concerned, and talking things over from their separate cells would have been possible. Still, there were those two drunk and disorderlies in cells six and eight, and prudence remained in order as far the general public was concerned. So the four friends sat—or paced—silent with their own thoughts. All had given their statements, each to a different polly, two pollies with typewriters and two with steno pads. Julie had lost track of Corwin. They had taken his fingerprints and mug shots first, and then led him off to some back area of the station.

She sat on her cot in cell number seven and allowed herself to cry.

She heard someone come in, a murmur of voices…too low and far away for her to make out the words, but she thought she recognized Dave's voice, and Corwin's. They must finally have finished with him, too. Locking him up beside the rest of them. Julie wiped her eyes and wondered whether Dave would come all the way down the corridor to her cell.

He did. She raised her eyes and saw him there, standing on the other side of the bars, looking in at her.

"Hey, M. Handsome," she said weakly.

"Hey, Dragon Lady."

She was at her cell door in three strides, groping for him through the bars.

He leaned in against the side of the cell door, reached his own arms between the bars, and gently seized her shoulders. "Julie. Back there at Sam's house…that was the pollydeck. This is the man, me, your Dragon Prince."

Pressing as close as the bars let them, they clutched each other and managed a long, sweet kiss. A cheer spread through the rest of the cell block: starting with the two drunk and disorderlies, who had the best view, quickly spreading to Sam, Paul, Curly, and finally, she thought, reaching Corwin at the far end.

But all Julie really cared about right now was Dave.

* * * *

M. Garvey came in looking curious, glanced around the interrogation room, started getting herself a cup of coffee, and noticed the letter laid out on the counter. Lestrade watched her staring down at it, carafe in one hand and unfilled cup in the other. The policewoman stepped up behind her and took away the coffee and cup before the material witness forgot and dropped them.

"Interesting, M. Garvey?" Lestrade inquired, filling the cup with coffee.

For answer, the younger woman gathered up the four pieces of letter, folded them carefully, and tucked them into her breast pocket. She accepted her coffee, walked to the easy chair, and sat down like a china doll trying not to break.

"So now you know," said Lestrade. "The young idiot broke that promise to you because he thought in his muddle-headed way it was the best thing he could do to help keep you safe."

"Don't talk about him like that."

"Just a few minutes ago I called him a lot worse than that to his face. He survived."

"He admits right here in this letter that there were other reasons, too," said M. Garvey. "Psychomystical reasons."

"Everything's psychomystical. You know and I know that all those other reasons wouldn't have been worth a broken ice-cream stick without the concern for your safety. Now. What are you going to do about it?"

"...I always planned to forgive him."

"Glad to hear it."

"I just thought he deserved to squirm a little first."

"He did. Richly. And he has. Between you and me, M. Garvey, woman to woman, the two of us have made him squirm enough for this evening." Lestrade quickly wrote a pass and held it out. "He's in cell number two. Show them this at the desk and someone will take you back there."

"Oh, thank you, Sergeant, thank you! You're a *wonderful* woman!" M. Garvey snatched the pass and dashed out the door, leaving her coffee steaming on the snack table.

"I'm a wonderful woman, am I?" Lestrade muttered dubiously, picking the coffee up and starting to drink it herself. "And you, M. Garvey, just missed acting like a total pumpkinhead. I hope, anyway, you were telling the truth about planning to forgive him all along. Well, I'm heading back to my office now, see if anybody else's statements have reached my desk yet."

* * * *

Angela had never actually been in a cell block before. It didn't look so very different from the screenshows, only a little more pleasant, somehow. The overhead light was turned down to a quarter-moon glow, and the pinpoint lamps at foot level outlined the corridor like a straight-line constellation of tiny stars. Small lamps must be on in two of the cells at the far end, because light shone out between the bars and pooled in the corridor.

"Seems to have settled down for the night," the Cinnamon polly—Officer Little Bird—observed softly at Angela's side. "I understand there was quite a little celebration in here just a few minutes ago."

Not liking to disturb the hush, in case people were sleeping in their cells, Angela whispered, "Celebration?"

"All I can say for sure," Officer Little Bird replied, "is, Detective Clayton went in a while ago, it sounded like cheering, Detective Clayton came out again looking happy and worried both at once."

That would be Julie.

And they had Julie in one of the cells.

The cells had reflective-glow numbers on the dividing walls, even numbers on Angela's right, odd numbers on her left. Officer Little Bird unlocked the first cell door on the right—cell number two—and stepped aside to let Angela in.

It was really much nicer than she would have expected, the little she could see of it in the dimly reflected light. Of course, her attention was on the cot, the form lying quietly beneath the blanket.

"He could be asleep," the polly observed in a low voice. "Would you rather…?"

"No, I'll stay. That's a chair, isn't it?"

Officer Little Bird hesitated, almost as though she was trying to decide whether to leave Angela the key. Finally she said, "Just tab this chimer when you want to come out," showed Angela a night-lighted button on the wall a few centimeters from the cell door, went out and relocked it behind her. It made only the smallest clunking sound.

She tiptoed to the cot, leaned over, whispered, "Cory? Are you asleep?"

"Angela? Is it you? Or a dream?"

"Not a dream, Cory. Or else we're both dreaming it at the same time."

He scooched himself up in the cot and asked, "Still…friends?"

The wistful hope in his voice tore her heart. She groped, got tight hold of his shoulders, bent farther over and kissed him. Hard.

After a heartbeat, he responded, kissed back, got his arms up around her and started squeezing, very gently.

I won't break, Cory, she thought, I won't break! And tried to tell him so by squeezing him harder. And harder. So happy that every time she tightened her grip, so did he.

She thought about teasing his lips apart and sticking her tongue between his teeth, the way she'd heard other people liked to do. But the moment was too perfect as it was. Why risk disturbing it? She felt his bird swelling up and growing very, very solid. Her nest was feeling warmer and softer by the moment, ready to welcome…

Just in time for self-restraint, he pulled back out of the kiss and said, "May I…interpret that as an affirmative?"

"Oh, Cory, you *silly!*"

"…Copacetic! But I need a few moments to…recover somewhat."

They settled side by side on the cot, resting their backs against the wall, his arm hugging her shoulders while she curled her legs up under her and snuggled into his chest. She needed a few moments to recover, too. She wasn't quite sure this was the best way to recover, but he registered no complaint.

"I thought…I feared…I had lost you forever."

"Oh, not that easily, Cory, not that easily!" A breath or two later, she added, "We belong together, don't we? Yin and yang, man and woman…"

"Day and night, light and darkness, sunshine and shadow…"

"We…complete each other. Together, we make a whole."

"The universal unity in microcosm. The eternal recombination of the elements."

"Oh, Cory…"

"Still, it might be better, for you, not to… We might soon be 'free' and 'imprisoned.'"

"Oh, no, Cory, no. I can't believe that could ever happen. When they know why you did it—and the police already know…"

"But neither the courts nor public opinion."

"They'll find some way to keep you out of court. I'm sure they will! If Sergeant Lestrade and Detective Clayton…Cory… That double date… Was Dave *Julie's* date, all along?"

"So I had understood at the outset."

"Then why didn't you correct me when I…"

"Your certitude caused me to question my own former view of the situation."

"Oh, you silly! You mean you just didn't want me to feel embarrassed!"

"Well…perhaps…a modicum of that, also," he admitted.

Anyway, if worse came to worst, they still let people on the outside get married to people in prison. She decided not to say that aloud, now he seemed to be relaxing a little. "Cory, will you be able to fall asleep tonight?"

"Between the joy, the apprehension, the exhaustion, and…this other, it could prove difficult. Angela, this has been a…a very strange day…no, a very strange set of days for me."

"For all of us, Cory. Let me see if I can't get you some kind of sleeping pills."

* * * *

Three of their statements—Imani's, Osaka's, and Whitcomb's—were ready and waiting on Lestrade's desk. Vergucchi and Little Bird took statements directly on their typewriters. Brown and Wentworth used shorthand, but Brown transcribed it into typescript a lot faster than Wentworth.

The three she had before her were in substantial agreement, just enough differences for plausibility. When you got suspicious—if you had any intelligence—was when different people's statements matched too closely, detail for detail. *That* suggested premeditated conspiracy. Small differences in relatively unimportant details suggested everybody concerned was telling the truth as they saw it filtered through their individual psychomystiques.

Imagine Davison worrying about whether "psychomystique" was too fancy a word. Wasn't that he was really trying to show off, just that he loved words and lost track of which ones his listeners might not know as well as he did. I must really have put the fear of something—the dictionary?—into him for a while there. Lestrade almost chuckled, sobered again at once. Lady God! If she had ever wanted to clear any innocent floater…make that plural. Blast if she didn't *like* the idiot lot of them.

She turned her attention back to the statements, shuffled Whitcomb's to the top, tapped it with her pipestem. Okay. This one next. She tabbed her chime.

When Officer Brown answered it, all she told him was, "M. Whitcomb. Interrogation." When Lestrade couched an order that way, the "Right now!" was understood.

* * * *

"Sleeping pills? Sure." The officer at the desk reached into a drawer and produced a small white envelope. "Ol' Doc Grumeister swears by these. We keep 'em on hand for any time we really need to settle anyone down in the cells. Doesn't happen too often."

Angela accepted the envelope. It was sealed and carefully labeled. She thought she could feel two roundish lumps inside.

Good. He wouldn't even have to wait for her to go out and find a drugstore open late. She looked around for Officer Little Bird, who was waiting to take her back to cell number two.

CHAPTER 25

So this was Dave's romantic interest. Yes, now she had time for a closer look, Lestrade could definitely see the appeal. *If I were a man, I might be fighting Dave for her.* That long black hair, red lips, high forehead, skin just a hint of Butterscotch, cheeks just a hint of hollow, long legs in a long gray skirt just flared enough for easy walking, guileless green eyes.

Never trust appearances. Especially guileless. That guileless look can be faked. Or authentic.

The two little giggleboxes were back outside the picture window, this time with a couple of stout lads to keep them company. Lestrade wondered how long before the girls got jealous of the way their young sweethearts ogled the interrogatee, and dragged them away. *Or maybe they were all siblings and it didn't matter.*

"M. Whitcomb," she began, riffling the pages of statement in her hands. "Correct me if I've got any of this wrong. You wanted to retire—'go emeritus,' M. Imani calls it—from the Purgatorio, at least partly for romantic reasons of your own. You thought you had M. Davison lined up for your replacement. M. Garvey objected. Strongly enough to change Davison's mind. But you held off telling the rest of your group the bad news.

"There was M. Garvey standing in your way. There had already been one killing. A second one would be easy to copycat. Next thing we know, there's M. Garvey's ringer floating dead in that little lake right behind the place where you—and M. Osaka—have your apartments. And M. Davison is back in, being geared up to take your place."

Always interesting to watch how different psychomystiques reacted when they saw where she was headed with stuff like this. M. Whitcomb breathed faster and faster, more and more heavily.

Her face started to flush. But she sat perfectly still and composed, letting the pollydeck say her fill.

Lestrade finished grimly, "It's possible for a group as a whole to be innocent, but one or two members guilty. How about it, M. Whitcomb? Did either you or M. Osaka have easy access to that tattoo stamp?"

M. Whitcomb took a deliberate swallow of her coffee, set the cup back down very carefully in its bone china saucer, cleared her throat, and said, "Sergeant Lestrade. I didn't do it. I'm not going to shout and cry and protest that I could never under any circumstances kill anyone. Under certain pressures, I've often thought that anyone with any strength of character at all—even doctors and trained nurses—probably could do anything. But I'm grateful to say I've never felt under any such pressures."

"Not even to make sure of Dave Clayton? From whom you kept all this secret."

"Not even for him. It looked as if Corwin—M. Poe—wasn't going to work out, after all. That was too bad, but recruitment has always been a tricky business for Dante's Delight. It was simply back to the old lookout posts. And—Sergeant Lestrade—Angela is a person you want to coddle and protect, not—not murder! Not for any reason at all. I sincerely wished every happiness for her and Corwin. So would the rest of us—so *will* the rest of us, if we come through this thing. Sergeant, the Purgatorio offers our pain to *help* other people, not hurt them."

"Hmf." Secretly, Lestrade liked Whitcomb. She liked her self-possession, she liked her answers, and she felt satisfied that these damfool pain gymnasts were at least sincere in their lunatic philosophy. And, so far, everything fit in with the hunch she'd had all along. But brilliant leaps of sleuthing insight were for Holmeses and Poirots. Lestrades couldn't afford to rule out any possibility, no matter how plodding. So what she said, without any softening of her voice, was:

"So could the late Gaia Soderstrum could have been a person most people wanted to coddle and protect."

"So could the late Harry Jackson." Whitcomb answered like the registered nurse she was when not purgatory-ing or romancing.

"All right, M. Whitcomb. Let's say, provisionally, that I'm willing to take your story at face value. I'd like to see the tattoo in question on a body that's still alive."

Whitcomb glanced at the teenagers outside. Then she stood up, turned her back to the window, walked over to Lestrade, and took off her white neck-scarf. Her tunic had two mother-of-pearl buttons below a V neckline.

Lestrade also noticed she was wearing a single small black pearl around her throat. Probably for sentiment, since the scarf had covered it from view. Hadn't Dave mentioned giving her something like that?

Whitcomb undid the buttons and eased the tunic aside to bare the area of her upper chest between breast and armpit. Sure enough, stamped there beneath the collarbone, pretty much where it was on both murder victims: a tattoo that looked identical to theirs. Lestrade figured it would probably still be identical, or all but, if placed side by side. Identical as two cookies from the same cutter. There could be tiny, accidental variations, but who was going to look for them? Not as if they were fingerprints, after all. And even identifying fingerprints was a job for the experts in the field, not exactly as cut and dried as most civilians seemed to think.

"I see yours seems to be part of a larger tattoo, M. Whitworth."

"That was done about two months ago, Sergeant. I had the artist incorporate the symbol of Dante's Delight into the larger image."

"Your artist did a good job of it. A good enough job that Detective Clayton never noticed it even when you and he found M. Soderstrum's body."

Whitcomb flushed again and quietly rebuttoned her tunic.

"Pretty much in the same place as M. Soderstrum's. As you would have noticed yesterday morning. Same place as the one on M. Jackson, too."

"But not the same place all of us have ours, Sergeant. Sam's is below his navel, Paul's on his inner right thigh, Curly's on the heel of her left foot. They'll be willing to show you for themselves. Our group is *private*, not *secret*." Readjusting her scarf, Whitcomb turned back toward the window and gave the teenagers a wave as she told Lestrade, "But I hope you can give Sam and Paul a little more privacy when they show you theirs. Because of where they have them."

"Fine. I can check them in Processing—the fingerprints and photos room." Lestrade waved to the teenagers with the hand that held her pipe. At Whitcomb, they had grinned and waved back. At the polly's wave, they turned and melted away. "Who keeps this tattoo stamp?" Lestrade asked Whitcomb.

"Sam. M. Imani."

"At his house?"

"In his box at the bank, I think." M. Whitcomb smiled. "It doesn't get that much use. Our maximum membership would be six—if we ever got there—but it's hard enough just keeping it up to four."

"Any idea who made that stamp for him?"

"I know he tried Dupont and O'Toole first, but it turned out they never do stamps. M. O'Toole gave him some recommendations, but if I ever knew which one of them Sam—M. Imani—went to, I've forgotten. Or maybe M. Imani even found someone else entirely. It isn't exactly a fact I ever needed for my working memory, Sergeant. You'll have to ask M. Imani himself."

"I will. Meanwhile, M. Whitcomb, I don't imagine it'll strain your working memory too much to let me know where you got the rest of that big tattoo about two months ago."

Whitcomb started to answer. At that nanosecond, Officer Little Bird thrust open the door and said,

"Sergeant Lestrade, ma'am! Detective Clayton and Officer Brown are rushing M. Davison to the Emergency Room."

"WHAT NOW?"

"M. Garvey gave him a couple of sleeping pills—the Slumbersound Dr. Grumeister swears by, and we've never had any trouble with them before. But he seems to be having some kind of reaction."

"*Slumbersound?*" Whitcomb looked a lot more shaken than when Lestrade had suggested casting her as the murderer. "Oh, no! Sergeant, it's reacting with the traces of Visiondust still in his system!"

Lestrade took only an instant to make up her mind. "*Nurse* Whitcomb. You're coming along to the hospital with us."

* * * *

Forgotten, the recorder continued turning its spindles round and round in the silent interrogation room until the wire ran out and the machine tabbed itself off.

* * * *

Kim Little Bird kept most of her mind on driving. With the part left over, she was thinking, And the Old Woman always insists she stickles to the guiderules! By the guiderules, M. Whitcomb was still a suspect under arrest. Nurse or not, by the guiderules, she should be back in her cell. Or, at least, back in handcuffs while outside the station. The guiderules were so far behind them now, they'd be lucky to catch up by Hallowe'en.

"Visiondust," the Old Woman was saying, as if they were still in Interrogation. "So that's what you gave him, M. Whitcomb?"

"It's usually very safe, Sergeant. Functionally, its effects wear off in about three hours. But physiologically, enough of it lingers in the system to react with Slumbersound—with a whole list of other meds—for up to forty-eight hours. If this is anyone's fault, Sergeant, it's mine. I should have thought to warn you."

"Or I should've warned the front desk," Kim put in from the driver's seat. "I took M. Whitcomb's statement, Sergeant. I knew what she'd given him. It just never occurred to —"

"I read her statement, Officer. And I took M. Davison's myself. I knew what he told me he'd had, and I know what we keep at the station. I was just clarifying. We'll divvy up the blame later. There's plenty to go all around. M. Whitcomb. Will he live?"

"Yes, if they caught it in time. It's a good thing Angela was in there keeping an eye on him. Sergeant, Visiondust is probably the safest stuff of its kind you can get."

"Except as a mixer," the Old Woman commented.

"It's legal for us Cinnamons," Kim said unnecessarily. "Decriminalized for everybody else."

"Ever taken it yourself, Officer?"

"Once, Sergeant. Traditional coming-of-age ceremony. Never again."

"The experience tends to be rather intense, Sergeant," said M. Whitcomb. "Even when not guided. Physically, it's non-addictive. Emotionally, most people never feel the desire to take it a second time."

"All very jolly. 'Shamanic.' You said the stuff's 'functional' effects wear off in about three hours?"

"Pyschomystically speaking, he was back in full command of himself by the time we went to second level. Otherwise, we would never permit any candidate to go beyond level one in the first session, under no matter what circumstances."

Having taken M. Whitcomb's statement, Kim understood pretty much what they were talking about. She hoped she'd get to read the other floaters' statements.

* * * *

The hospital waiting room was as pleasant as a hospital waiting room could be, which was like talking about "the easiest room in Hell." Between Faith Lutheran in Boca Raton and Mother of Mercy here in Forest Green, Angela had seen too many hospital waiting rooms, visitors' lounges, and cafeterias this week. Purgatorio? These Dante's Delight people were only playing at it! The *real* Purgatory on Earth was a hospital waiting room…your heart in those back regions where they were working on someone you'd trade places with in a heartbeat, if you only could!

"Oh, Dave, Dave!" She couldn't quite think of him as "Detective Clayton." She hadn't had that much contact with him socially, but it was more than she'd had with him in his official workline, even including this long, long, very long, very strange day. "Dave, will he…?"

"I'm no medic, Angie." Dave put his cup down on the magazine table, sat beside her on the overstuffed couch, and took her cold hand between both of his. "But from what I've seen of your floater, he's pretty…to use a word he might like himself…resilient. He bounces back."

"Was it…anything they did to him? Those 'Purgatorio' people?"

Dave shook his head. "I took Sam's statement. If he was telling the truth, Corwin didn't get anything up there this afternoon that all the rest of them haven't been through at least once, most of it every couple of weeks, and come up smiling. Julie's a nurse, Paul and Curly paramedics, they know how to keep things from getting out of hand."

"Then…could it have been…oh, Holy Mother Mary! Could it have been the sleeping pills *I* gave him? Oh, Dave, Dave…"

"Hey, hey, Angie." He had his arm around her shoulders, like a brother. "And who gave you those pills, huh? Not your fault. If anything…"

She glanced up, saw him trying to grin.

"If anything," he went on, "you've got the grounds for a whopping big lawsuit against the Forest Green P.D."

"And what good—what good on earth would that do?" Her handkerchief was sodden through. She pulled a paper one out of the tissue holder on the lamp table at her side of the couch. "How would a lawsuit…?"

"Oh, no! Look, Angie, look—I never meant—people who survive can bring lawsuits, too —"

"What's this about lawsuits, Detective?" the voice of Sergeant Lestrade cut in.

She had just arrived, along with Julie and the young Native American officer. Dave stood up on seeing them. So did Angela.

Julie exchanged one nod with Dave and hurried on through to Emergency. The Cinnamon officer followed her. Angela remembered that Julie was a nurse at this very hospital; the polly must need to keep an eye on her because she was still under arrest.

Sergeant Lestrade came over to Dave and Angela. "Any news on his condition?"

Dave shook his head. Angela said, "Not yet," and took his hand again, for comfort and strength.

They sat down and waited, Angela and Dave on the couch, Sergeant Lestrade in an armchair catacorner to them. They waited in silence. After several minutes, Sergeant Lestrade said, "M. Whitcomb tells me it's an interaction between the sleeping pills we keep at the station and the hallucinogen he took earlier today."

"Oh!" Angela exclaimed softly. "Then it *was*—I *did*—What hallucinogen?"

"It's a no-fault, no-blame situation, M. Garvey. Either of those is harmless in itself. And neither you nor the desk officer who gave you the Slumbersound was aware he had had Visiondust. Or that the two things could still interact after eight or nine hours."

"Visiondust?" said Dave. "We wouldn't even run a pureblood Vanilla in for possession."

Then they relapsed into silence. The seat cushions were incongruously soft. Angela thought they should be hard. That would fit the "no-fault" situation better.

After forty-nine minutes, Julie came back out to the waiting room. "It's all right," she told them. "He's going to be fine. He's up in room forty-three now, sleeping. Officer Little Bird decided to go up and mount surveillance." She looked toward Sergeant Lestrade. "Sergeant, it'd be best if you could let him finish the night here and take him back to jail after breakfast. I'm ready now."

"No." Sergeant Lestrade stood up, shaking her head slowly. "Hold him here awhile. All this gives me an idea. You can stay here, too, M. Whitcomb. Just let Officer Little Bird keep an eye on you, too."

Angela said, "I want to stay, too. I want to stay with him, right in his room."

Julie said uncertainly, "Hospital policy is, spouses only."

"I'm his fiancee."

Sergeant Lestrade said, "That should count. Let the hospital bend a few guiderules for once, keep the F.G.P.D. company. Detective Clayton, you come with me. We've got plans to lay."

CHAPTER 26

WEDNESDAY, OCTOBER 4

Oh seven thirty, and morning light finding its way through the blinds. Angela had finally fallen asleep on the long couch against the far wall. Julie, now in the nurse's uniform she'd had in her locker here at the hospital, was sitting on watch, reading a paperback history of Sumeria, when she heard Corwin sleep-mumble something that sounded like, "Rosemary nodding on the grave." She looked up in time to see him opening his eyes. He blinked several times and stared around at the view from the pillow, a frown line deepening between his eyebrows. She stood up and bent over.

"Julie? Is Angela here? Or did I only dream…?"

"She's fast asleep on the couch over there. All tuckered out, poor dear."

"What is't—as they say in Shakespeare—o'clock?"

"Oh seven thirty-three."

"How odd! That this hour of the morning should find Angela asleep and me awake. Julie, I thought…did I dream *this*, or were we arrested yesterday?"

"Oh, we're still under arrest, boy. Don't worry your head about that. Sergeant Lestrade phoned your landlady—M. Florsheim?— to feed your cat and canary and goldfish. Can she be trusted?"

"With my bonsai, at least temporarily. Remarkable woman, Sergeant Lestrade. Then that, also…" A frown passed across his face—pain? embarrassment?—to be replaced with a rather lopsided grin. "A very remarkable woman, indeed. With a rare gift… Has the Blarney Stone any equivalent when it comes to bestowing the opposite ability?"

"Not that I know of."

"Is today Wednesday?"

Julie nodded.

"Vermeer day. Arnheim reposes in good hands…should I ever see it again. Where are we now?"

"Mother of Mercy Hospital. The Slumbersound they gave you at the station interacted with the Visiondust I gave you yesterday."

He took a few seconds to chew on this. "Then it was not in nightmare that I underwent the interesting experience of having my stomach pumped?"

"No, that was real, too."

"You might consider that as an appropriate supplementary apparatus for the Purgatorio. In substitution, perhaps, for the Tantalusian teasing of binding the penitents' arms to their chairs during luncheon."

It did not escape her notice that he used "you" and not "we."

"Are you hungry now?"

"I could eat. Copiously."

"Copiously, we won't allow you. Not just yet. How about an egg, toast, and tea?"

"All contributions gratefully accepted. Julie—why did the Visiondust not interact with the sleeping preparation you had given me to swallow the evening before?"

"That one was a sugar pill."

"It *was?*" He sounded astonished. "But it sent me into so deep a slumber that not even the chiming of Angela's telephone call awakened me."

"Placebo effect. It was your own exhaustion that put you to sleep and kept you there, once you thought you'd taken a strong sleeping pill, and relaxed into it."

"You left something to chance."

"Not really. I figured that if the placebo didn't work, you'd be too tired to go through with it next day, and we'd salvage your promise to Angela."

"The other two pills? The afternoon sedative and evening laxative?"

"Oh, *they* were real. But blameless of any interaction."

"All in all," he observed, "this has been a very peculiar week."

Julie went out and reported to Kim Little Bird, who was stretched out on a rollaway in the corridor. Taking the whole surveillance thing very casually by now, Kim went with her to get breakfast trays for all four of them. When they returned, Angela was sitting beside the bed, reading Corwin the history of Sumeria.

After breakfast, he went back to sleep, while Angela sat and watched him with a blissful smile. Julie and Kim went to the visitors' lounge two doors away and chatted over second cups of coffee.

* * * *

Judge Al (for Aloysius) Farquhar was a sprightly, elfin little man with a twinkle in his eye, and well aware of all these facts. At seventy-two, he was still going strong. Retirement held no fascination for him and, fortunately, his workline would not force him into it until he was obviously *non compos mentis*, which might never happen. Doctors had it almost as good that way, but Al Farquhar had never liked the sight either of blood or of people's squishy pink inner surfaces—tongues and suchlike—when viewed up close. Hence, the Law and, finally, after decades of work, the Judgeship.

He heard Lestrade through and shook his head. "All very nice, Rosie. Even plausible. Stamped tattoos, placement of. Tattoo artist lined up in your crosshairs. All maybe just a little pat, wouldn't you say yourself? Still circumstantial. Youngster, would *you* sign a search warrant on that, if you were me?"

"Look. We've got five floaters probably to certainly innocent of anything but gross stupidity and over-enthusiastic playacting. But who don't stand the chance of a lame kitten in a forest fire if this thing ever sees a courtroom. Over against one looking guilty as hell, even if so far it's circumstantial. On the arithmetic alone, isn't it worth your signature?"

"Hmm.… No, Rosie, almost, but no kewpie doll."

"All right," she said, "what about…" and outlined her plan.

He tapped his chin thoughtfully. "Mm-hmm. I have seen scifi screenshows in which that might, just possibly, be called 'entrapment.'"

"We aren't talking scifi, Judge. We're talking plain here and now. With you right on the spot to witness it."

"Hmm-mm," he repeated. The notion had its appeal. "All right, then, let's try it. They say a floater's never too old for a little role-gaming."

* * * *

Lestrade arrived with Clayton, ushering in Judge Farquhar, about 1130 hours, in time for her to overhear Whitcomb telling somebody in the visitors' lounge, "The whole trick is learning to put it out of your mind the rest of the week."

Lestrade looked in. The somebody with Whitcomb was Officer Little Bird, who sprang up and snapped to attention as soon as she saw the detective sergeant. Whitcomb also stood, more slowly and gracefully.

"No," Lestrade told them, with a dismissive wave of her hand, "I don't even want to know what you two were talking about. So, Officer Little Bird, you decided it was safe enough to leave your post?"

"Not very far, Sergeant, ma'am."

"Mmf. All right, we won't worry about it. This time. He awake?"

"M. Garvey is with him, Sergeant," said Little Bird.

Whitcomb added, "We left them deep in the history of ancient Sumeria. Among other things."

"How much have you told him about the plan?" As Lestrade had outlined it to them and Clayton before leaving to persuade the Judge into it.

"We haven't told him anything, Sergeant," Whitcomb answered sweetly. "We thought we should leave that to your silver tongue."

The detective sergeant gave her a look that would have quelled any uniform on the force—Little Bird shrank out of its way quickly enough—but Whitcomb acted unfazed. Lestrade decided it wasn't worth the effort to follow up.

"Sergeant Lestrade," Judge Farquhar inquired curiously, "what will happen if the lad refuses to play along?"

"If I know anything at all about this floater, he'll crawl all over himself for the chance to play along. If he doesn't, maybe the shock value of seeing the two women will do the trick. Otherwise, apologies for wasting your time, and we owe you a good lunch."

Lestrade led the way two doors down and into Room 43. M.'s Garvey and Davison were apparently more interested in snuggling than Sumeria. They looked a little like the Babes in the Wood, about to fall asleep with sibling arms around each other. Aloud,

Lestrade commented, "Cozy. Well, M. Davison, how'd you like to get that stamped tattoo, after all?"

While M. Garvey scrambled to her feet, looking slightly embarrassed (for *what?*), Davison moved his line of sight around from Lestrade to Whitcomb, Clayton, Little Bird, the judge, and back to Lestrade and Whitcomb. "To what will it commit me?"

"Nothing, beyond a little charade this afternoon, and a chance to clear all your names." In a few words, she explained her hopes and plans.

His face cleared at once. "An opportunity to redeem myself in some small degree? My duty—*to be saved?* Oh, let us not linger! To cite the Venerable Edgar in new and revised context. I have been told that I can scream very entertainingly on command."

"We don't want 'entertaining,' M.... Poe," Lestrade told him. "We want convincing. Nurse Whitcomb can coach you while we're gone. All right, Detective Clayton."

Clayton brought out the stamp they had taken Imani—not bothering with handcuffs—to get from its bank safety deposit box. Unwrapping it, Clayton handed it to Whitcomb and told her, "Sam says, all loaded and ready."

The nurse looked at the sergeant. "Where?"

"Anywhere," Lestrade told her, "that's far enough away from where you've got yours."

"Over my heart?" Davison asked eagerly. Leaving the sheet and blanket up to his waist, he started working himself free of the hospital gown to bare his smooth torso.

"Lie back," said Julie.

He lay back.

"Right about...here?" she went on, touching the place.

He nodded, and reached for M. Garvey's hand. Sitting down in her bedside chair again, she wove her fingers between his. Whitcomb positioned the stamp, made one sharp downward press. Davison winced slightly, but lay still. Whitcomb lifted the stamp away. Lestrade grunted approval at the neat blue whirligig symbol.

Her approval was nothing to Davison's. Hoisting himself high enough for a look down at his own chest, he told M. Garvey, "Now, with a certain amount of imagination, we can say that at last Raggedy Andy has his own candy heart."

Must be some private lovers' joke, Lestrade decided, watching them continue wiggling each other's fingers.

* * * *

So now Al Farquhar was getting to roleplay a medic. In his borrowed white coat, with his borrowed name tag, and borrowed stethoscope, he stood at the ledge beside the hospital room sink, his back to the bed but positioned so that he could steal sidewise glances without looking too obvious about it. While waiting, he spread the search warrant out in front of him, and arranged a few medical-looking charts and papers on top of it. He was enjoying himself immensely.

Behind him, Nurse Whitcomb and the pretty young blond lady were coaching the game young floater in the bed on convincing jerks and moans.

Officer Little Bird came back into the room and said, "They're at the end of the corridor." She positioned herself at the door. The blond ducked into the bathroom. Judge Farquhar heard its door close. Nurse Whitcomb would have her back turned on the bed, looking like she was busy with nurselike fussing around.

Too much sound-soaking in the hospital to hear footsteps coming down the corridor, but after another minute the room door opened again and the pair of detectives brought in this tattoo artist, M. Elias Hammer. The judge started listening very carefully.

"All right," Hammer was saying, "so they've done for another one. Should've cleaned them out of town a long time ago. What the hell are we paying you pollies for?"

"Just take a look at it, M. Hammer," said Sergeant Lestrade. "All we want is your expert opinion."

"How come you never called me in to look at those other victims?"

As far as Hammer ought to know, neither of the other victims had been tattooed. Judge Farquhar shuffled his papers again, checking the warrant at the bottom. But then, Hammer could have guessed...

Lestrade was answering evenly, "They were already dead, M. Hammer. Beyond any help of expert advice."

A short pause. The judge stole a look around and saw Lestrade and Hammer approaching the bed, Clayton joining Little Bird at the door.

A slow moan from Davison-Poe.

"You seem to be starting with his right shoulder, M. Hammer," Lestrade remarked, probably for Farquhar's benefit.

The judge stole another glance around. Yep, that's what Hammer was doing, all right. Had the snaps unsnapped and was pulling the hospital gown as low as he could. Like he wanted a look at that one spot in particular. Of course, he could just be a little eccentric in how he went about getting one of those blame things off somebody else. Wasn't something anybody outside a hospital staff did every day.

"Hey!" said Hammer. "What..."

Judge Farquhar slipped the search warrant down far enough to uncover the signature line.

"We never said where it was, M. Hammer," Lestrade replied in a polite neutral voice. "Nurse, can you help us here?"

Nurse Whitcomb turned around. So, figuring it was what any attending medic would do, did Judge Farquhar. Hammer probably wouldn't know his face, unless from the campaign literature—and that had been several years ago—and the occasional photo in the papers or quick shot for the screen news.

Hammer wasn't even looking in his direction. He was staring at the nurse. "But that's..."

Judge Farquhar checked his pen, but the suspect got himself under control, only muttering something indistinguishable.

More moaning from Davison-Poe. Nurse Whitcomb making soothing, nurselike sounds as she eased the hospital gown completely off his chest.

Hammer demanded, "What the hell—"

The judge had been there when the signals were prearranged: Lestrade nodding to the nurse, the nurse giving the patient a tiny pinch on the back of the neck, the patient letting go with, all in all, a fairly convincing scream.

Bringing the blond out of the bathroom in a rush.

"WHAT THE HELL!" shouted Hammer. "*You're dead!*"

Judge Farquhar poised the point of his pen touching the signature line.

Rosie Lestrade was saying, "And you'd know that, how, M. Hammer? Never brought around any photos of the second victim, did we?"

"In the paper—Monday—wasn't it?"

"Congratulations, M. Hammer," Lestrade said dryly. "Not too many people would remember a face that well from one newspaper photo seen forty-eight hours ago. Not unless they had already recognized the face from before it appeared in the paper."

Judge Farquhar had already signed the warrant. He folded it and slipped it to Sergeant Lestrade.

Who passed it to Clayton and told the suspect, "Sorry, M. Hammer, but that wasn't your first little slip. Taken all together, you're under arrest on suspicion of two murders."

CHAPTER 27

SUNDAY, OCTOBER 8

Only half a week, and things were already settling back into normal. Dave didn't know—and didn't ask—whether the Dante's Delight gang had held a meeting Friday night. Julie had spent all Friday night with him, while Corwin and Angela had been in Boca Raton Thursday to Saturday visiting her family in the hospital, and come back showing off twin engagement rings, hers with a lozenge of black onyx embedded in a moonstone, his with a circle of moonstone embedded in black onyx.

True, Kim Little Bird had been in private conference Thursday with the Old Woman and Chief Grayling about something or other, and had shown up for her Saturday morning shift wearing her sleeves as far down as they went. And this afternoon she sat in an easy chair catacorner to Sam's, wearing a knowing look on her face. All the same, Dave wasn't even going to ask. After all, Kim was at least half Native American: father one-quarter Vanilla, mother one-quarter Cinnamon.

But whether or not the Purgatorio was up and running again—and, as the Old Woman kept pointing out, it wasn't illegal—Sam's Sunday afternoon rolegame parties had come back strong. Hard as it was to believe after the week just wrapping around, they hadn't missed a single Sunday. In fact, Sam said that the unavoidable ripple of publicity was bringing in more than enough newcomers to replace the few old regulars it had cost them.

Of course, Julie, Corwin, Angie, Sam, Paul, Curly, and Kim Little Bird had already heard all about how Lestrade cracked the case, but Sam's living room was full of people who hadn't, people who were avidly interested.

"Elias Hammer was Sergeant Lestrade's suspect from our first interview with him," Dave was telling them. "It was the way he kept badmouthing one whole class of people, trying to aim us against one group in particular. That kind of prejudice tends to set the Old Woman's back up. Made her think 'frame-up' from the outset. Only, she always makes herself look at all the angles, always says it's bad procedure to label anyone a 'prime suspect' until all the facts are in. And she couldn't get enough for a search warrant of Hammer's premises until we put that charade on in the hospital room.

"Turns out Hammer was the one Sam bought the tattoo stamp from. Also the one Julie went to for her dragon tattoo—and, whatever the floater's faults, and murder is a big one—he did good stuff in his legitimate workline. But he saw the old scars on Julie's back, dating from before the group went to…well, softer techniques, and he figured them for what they were. He also recognized his own stamp design near the hollow of her right shoulder, put two and two together —"

"A little lopsidedly," Julie threw in, "and got five."

"— and couldn't stand the thought that he might have provided a membership badge for a bunch of smasters."

"Not smasters," Julie insisted. "Purgatorians."

Dave pecked her a kiss. "Okay, I think I see the difference… finally…but Hammer, along with most of the world, didn't and probably never will. Seems he had some personal bad experience with a couple of smasters, years ago in Cleveland. Anyway, he started secretly trailing Julie whenever he could, mostly on wraparound days. He had AA meetings himself Friday evenings, but he saw Julie and a lot of other people coming into Sam's house Sunday afternoons, never dug far enough to learn they were just innocent rolegamers, and assumed Sundays were when the smastering was going on—with a lot more people than there ever were in Dante's Delight Purgatorio. On Sundays it outraged him, as a card-carrying Christian, even more. So he made himself a duplicate stamp—of course he still had his original design on file—and used it on the first young floater he *thought* he recognized from Sam's Sunday gatherings who came to him for a tattoo."

Dave noticed Angie hugging Corwin a little tighter.

"Hammer figured all the members of the group wore it in the same place he saw it on Julie," Dave went on.

One of the new faces in the living room asked, "Didn't it tip him off, that Harry Jackson wasn't already wearing the tattoo?"

"He figured, for once correctly, that it had something to do with full initiation. Explained Harry's lack of scars, welts, and similar markings the same way to himself. So in Hammer's own psycho-mystique, it was the smasters—as he saw your group—who were actually committing the murder, and he was saving your victim from sinking any farther into the depths of depravity.

"Harry died very quickly from strong poison in the ink. Hammer started marking him up almost at once, while the heart was still beating slightly, he said, but the victim was as unconscious as if he'd been in medical surgery. Hammer's conscience was still functional enough to keep him from perpetrating the same kind of torture he wanted to stop. Of course, not knowing what the 'Purgatorians' were really doing—knowing only a few of the things they had stopped doing years ago—he got it all wrong, and marked the body up in ways Dante's Delight would never have done, even back before they toned their original techniques down. Hammer wanted to make it look, if not like deliberate murder, at least like smastering gone too far. Then he dumped the body in the Vigo to hide the fact that so many of the marks had been made post-mortem. Our Lady Lestrade was right all along in suspecting that angle, even while the rest of us couldn't see any reason for someone wanting to disguise simple murder, make it look like death from torture.

"Well, we interviewed him, along with the other tattoo artists in town, and he did his best to aim us at the floaters he wanted us to stop. When we didn't seem to be taking the bait, and someone else he thought he recognized from Sam's came to him for a tattoo, he did a repeat —"

Corwin's arm tightened around Angie.

"— and this time dumped the body into the pond behind the place where he knew Julie was living, both from trailing her and from the phone book—he had her full name from his customer records."

"You're lucky to be alive yourself, Julie," someone remarked from the far side of the room.

"He wasn't ready with his poison stamp, yet," she answered, shivering in Dave's arm. "And he wanted to trail me. He was too good at that. I never even suspected…but, in a way, I am the one who killed Harry and Gaia."

"No, Julie," Dave assured her, "never, never think that. It was Hammer who killed them, not you. Never you at all.

"Of course, as soon as we had the search warrant, it was easy enough to find the second stamp. Once Hammer told us what poison he had used, our labs were able to verify its presence in the traces left on the stamp and in the victims' blood."

"What poison was it?" somebody else asked.

"Privileged information," Dave answered him. "Sorry, we never give details like that to the public. Not writing any recipes for wannabe criminals, gang!"

"What about at the trial?" a fourth questioner wanted to know.

"Even if you go to the trial, pal, that'll most likely be one of those details kept between members of the court, safely out of hearing of the general audience. But there may not even be a public trial. Hammer might end up directly in a prison for the criminally insane."

There was a moment of silence.

Corwin broke it. "He must be a man very unhappy with the role allotted him in this world."

"What about poor Harry and Gaia?" said Angela.

"Was not our empathy with them taken for granted?" Corwin sounded surprised. "What can we do, except pray that they were happy until their early deaths, and have returned to happiness beyond the Veil."

Julie shuddered against Dave's chest. "And I'm wearing that man's tattoo!"

"Well," Dave said soberly, "whatever else he was, he was still a good tattoo artist, and gave you a fine dragon. Give it a little time, lover. If it keeps on bothering you, we'll float a loan, have Dupont and O'Toole remove and replace it."

"Let's all chip in for that," Sam suggested. "It can be a farewell purgatory for you away from the Purgatorio, Julie. Or a wedding gift. And I think I can talk my good neighbors into bumping you to the head of their client list."

"Thanks, Sam, thanks."

"What, exactly, did you have to do in all this, Corwin?" Hank Algood wanted to know.

Corwin dismissed the question with a wave of his hand. "I? Oh, I served as a supernumerary in more or less the operatic sense. Simply the one who coincidentally required emergency hospitalization."

None of the other principals contradicted him. It had been his own prearranged choice of cover story: Dave supposedly recognizing Julie's stamped tattoo, added to Gaia Soderstrum looking so much like a young woman known to have come to Sam's role-gaming Sundays, had been enough to bring the police Tuesday; Corwin's presence there had been more or less accidental. He said the full truth would have been more embarrassing than commendatory to him.

Kim Little Bird stood up. "Enough shop talk. Let's get on with the games we came here to play!"

"Right," Sam agreed. "Underground Catholics in Elizabethan England, in here. Who else is rulemastering today?" He looked around the group.

"Knights of the Round Table, anyone?" Hank Algood proposed. "I'll even let Robin Hood into the act for once."

A newcomer got to her feet and said, "How about Zeus versus Odin?"

"I came all prepared to rolemaster a rattling game of Starcatchers," somebody else offered.

Another newcomer, a portly floater like a red-bearded Santa just approaching middle age, stood up and introduced himself: "Oziah 'Ozzie' Prendergast 'Gillikin' here. Anyone for a good game of Oz?"

Glancing from Sam to Prendergast 'Gillikin,' Corwin decided, "I think that I should enjoy playing a villain in the marvelous land of Oz. As I recollect from my childhood scanning of the Oztories, the villains tend to meet…interesting fates."

"Like being melted with a bucket of water?" Curly teased him.

"Ah! To be melted! Slowly to dissolve away and soak smoothly back into Earth's bosom. How restful, how tranquil and soothing, that sounds following certain of the recent events through which we have actually lived."

"Supernumeraries and all the rest of us?" Angela delivered a feather-touch punch to his upper arm. He caught her hand with a barely visible squeeze.

Which inspired Dave to snuggle Julie closer yet in his arm. "What do you say, dear Lady? Shall we join the Starcatchers, you and I?"

"Why not, Dragon Prince? We might even give them a few tips on catching stars."

CHAPTER 28

Rosemary Lestrade had started shedding her shyness of synagogues, mosques, and Christian churches even before she graduated from grade school. She had already decided to be a detective, and qualms about other people's places of worship, especially in a basically monotheistic world, could only have been a handicap in that workline. So she had no trouble at all functioning in Saint Martha's on the day of the double wedding. Not even with three officiating monotheistic clerics on hand, no less: Dave's minister, Julie's minister, and the pastor of Saint Martha's to tie the knot for Corwin and Angela.

Aside from the choice of venue—something about Catholic guiderules—Dave and Julie had had first choice in all the wedding plans. It was only fair. With Angela's father and siblings still in rehab down in Florida and Corwin's parents still world-cruising, the younger pair planned a renewal of vows ceremony a year or two down the road. In effect, a second wedding for the benefit of all the members of both their families.

Dave had his mother to march him down the aisle, Julie her father, Angela a floater named Hank Algood, and today Lestrade herself was filling in for Corwin's mother. At one point, he had suggested they do it handcuffed together. Since he had sounded half serious, she had scorched that idea in a sentence and a half, including a side threat to let his big sister Corinna, who was coming down from Arbor City, take over. He had never mentioned it again.

Today, for once in his life, he was wearing white, a rented tux matching Dave's. He looked good in white. Probably pointless to try talking him into it on other occasions. Both brides wore long white satin dresses with billowy skirts. Christian weddings tended to very oldstyle fashions. As for Lestrade, she put on the rust-colored slacks and tunic she kept for the rare formal occasion, added a white rosebud in the boutonniere hole, and called it good.

The actual ceremony was short and sweet: exchanging of vows, exchanging of wedding bands, exchanging of long kisses. The photo-taking afterwards lasted longer. The reception was at the Wabash House, where Lestrade nursed her champagne for the toasting, drank two or three Scotch-and-waters between toasts, ate about as much good food as everybody else, and never even noticed at what point between cutting the twin wedding cakes and the middle of the dancing the happy couples slipped away.

"Smiling looks good on you, Rosie," Chief Grayling remarked. "You should do it more often."

He must have been celebrating hard. Even in purely social situations, he never called her "Rosie" unless he was getting pickled.

* * * *

The Honeymoon Suite had mellow lighting, a bottle of champagne on ice, a tray of chocolate-dipped strawberries, and a huge, heart-shaped bed with covers turned down. The sprays of greenery on the walls suggested the approaching Christmas season: all evergreens and holly. Red-ribboned sprays of mistletoe dangled everywhere.

Champagne was nice, and chocolate-covered strawberries were nice, but after that lovely dinner at the reception, all Angela really wanted was to hop into bed right away. Corwin, however, had already eased the cork out of the bottle and was filling both champagne flutes.

"Wish me good fortune," he said with an awkward smile, "on *la nuit des amateurs*."

"Only if you wish me the same."

"To wish you good fortune, my love, is to wish the same for myself. And, hopefully, vice versa."

"Oh, Cory!"

They touched their flutes together with a tiny, crystal ping, then lifted them to their lips and sipped, searching one another's eyes over the rims. "Have you heard," he said, as they lowered the flutes, "the reason for serving chocolate-glazed strawberries with champagne? The flavors are adjudged mutually enhancing."

Why, she thought, he's *procrastinating!* So it's really true: men *are* more bashful than women.

"I really couldn't eat another bite," she told him. "In fact, I can't even finish this lovely champagne." She set her flute down on the silverwood dresser. "Cory, let's feel a little naughty! Let's take our wedding rings off and leave them over here."

He gulped down half his champagne and set his flute beside hers. "Our engagement rings, also?"

"Not *that* naughty. We'll pretend we're just jumping the gun by a night or two."

He slipped his wedding band off and set it carefully in the shadow of the flutes. She slipped hers off and balanced it on end in the circle of his. Their engagement rings, they replaced on their fingers. "But we're *really* married, of course. We're really, really married, and it's all right!"

"Indubitably." He caught her and kissed her, careless whether they were beneath one of the mistletoe sprigs or not. A long, sweet kiss that warmed her triangle to a glow.

"Cory," she murmured, as they surfaced and stood fast in a tight hug. "Do you think maybe we should try it with…with our tongues?"

"With our tongues?"

"So many people seem to say that's the very best way to do it."

So they tried it with their tongues. His was slidy, sweet, and sort of nappy, but…After a moment they pulled back and stared at each other.

"I wonder why that's supposed to be so great?" she said.

"You relieve me," he replied, "for I wondered the same. I…trust our mutual reaction does not augur ill for the…whole point of the matter."

"Let's try this, then: we'll undress each other, garment by garment." She began by pulling off his neck-scarf.

"I am grateful you changed out of your bridal gown for the drive across town." He undid her belt and tossed it on a chair. It slithered off to the floor.

"Who would guess we're spending the bridal night just on the other side of Forest Green?" She groped for the buttons of his tunic. "Did Dave tell you where he and Julie were going?"

"I believe that is one of those things gentlemen refrain from mentioning, even to one another." He eased off her scarf as if her neck were blown glass.

"We're all alone, only the two of us, and, oh, Cory! We're really, really married! Lift your arms so I can pull your tunic off."

Garment by garment, they undressed each other until finally they stood stark naked on the deep-piled carpet, rubbing their hands up and down each other's bare skin, starting with her birthmark and his new tattoo. She hoped her touch was thrilling him as much as his was her. By the stirring of his pointer against her thigh, she guessed it was.

At length he observed, "Even the best-heated of rooms may suffer stray drafts in the month of December."

"Let's get under the blankets."

"Which side would you prefer?"

"What difference does it make? Aren't we both going to end up in a tangle in the middle?"

So they both hopped into bed on the same side, bunching up into a cozy knot between the sheets.

Eventually, after several very enjoyable moments, they pulled just far enough apart to straighten the covers, lie down on their backs with sides touching, and tab the room lights off by means of the master switch just reachable over the headboard.

She knew she would never forget the thrill the first time his masculine hand landed in the hairs of her naked nest.

"Angela," he whispered, "take mine into your hand and squeeze."

It was her turn to feel a little bashful, but she bravely groped, closed her fingers around his pointer—how big and round and firm it felt!—and tentatively squeezed.

"More forcibly—I won't break."

"Neither will I, Cory. Rub! Rub hard!"

How long they lay there, working and massaging one another's privates, she didn't know and didn't care. Eventually, relaxing to lie quiet and pant for a few moments, she said, "You get so firm, and I get so soft and wambly."

"Even as nature intended." He rolled over almost on top of her and they found new ways of weaving their limbs together for another half-hour or thereabouts.

But.

"This is preposterous!" he exclaimed at last. "We know where everything is supposed to fit, we are young, energetic, and—I think—both of us fully prepared in every fiber of our being, and yet nevertheless…"

"It's supposed to be so easy in the missionary position… We *are* in the missionary position, aren't we?"

"Perhaps if I had ever studied the *Kama Sutra*—which ought perhaps to be mandated as prerequisite reading for matrimony…"

"Corwin… I can't be…what's that word?… I can't be *frigid*, can I?"

At that, he laughed. "Love, if *you* are frigid, the ice must be melting and boiling away at both poles of our planet! Perhaps it is I who…"

"Never that! Why, I'm not sure I could even get my hand around it by now."

"Could it conceivably be the excitement of the day? Long as it has been, and filled with tension—glorious, pleasurable, ecstatic, but inevitably draining…"

"Maybe we'd better try to fall asleep now? And go at it again when we're fresh?"

It took them a long time, but eventually they slept. Side by Side. Like the Raggedy siblings.

* * * *

Julie lay on top of Dave in the lightly jiggling Pullman bed, tracing their fingers by memory over one another's dragon tattoos, his old and hers so new that the top layer of freshly disturbed skin had barely finished flaking away.

"A full frontal Dupont and O'Toole original!" she mused. "And only a few months ago, my highest dream was just one little design by them—my prince's choice—by my left breast, balancing the symbol on my right side."

"They did themselves proud. Almost a pity…" Dave added… "for my eyes alone. Maybe someday we'll have 'The Naked Julie' done in oils for posterity."

"When we're rolling in tridols and can afford to commission it ourselves."

"When we've got our house remodeled to where we want it."

"Mmm."

"I'm guessing," he added after a while, "Sam and Corwin and Angela were the big contributors."

"It was my wedding gift from everybody who pitched in, Dave. Sweet Jesus doesn't measure contributions by the dross amount, and neither will we. Only by the love of the giver."

"Mm-hmm." Next time they surfaced, Dave pointed out, "And where would a giver be, without a happy receiver?"

* * * *

Angela woke in the drapery-filtered light of dawn. Rolling on her side, she gazed at his face. He was still asleep, of course, breathing softly. Oh! she thought, emphatically if less than realistically. Anyone who tries to annul it on grounds of non-consummation, I'll fight them all the way to the Supreme Court!

She imagined running her finger gently along his profile, forehead to chin, then maybe a tiny little tap. She didn't quite venture to do it, but his eyes opened anyway, of themselves. He rolled toward her, looked into her eyes.

"Awake already?" she said. "How uncharacteristic of you!"

"This is hardly a characteristic morning, gauged against the past. It may perhaps grow less atypical as our days glide by. Oh, Angela, even if there were never to be more than…than there was last night…I would live and die contented."

"So would I! But…let's try again, shall we?"

"Excelsior!"

First, they got out of bed, threw on the hotel's terrycloth robes against the winter chill of the room, breakfasted on champagne—he had worked the cork back into the bottle's neck last night, so the beverage was still sparkly—and chocolate-dipped strawberries, feeding each other and laughing when a bite went crooked and left a chocolate smear on lips or cheeks or chin, which each enjoyed licking off the other. When all the strawberries were eaten, they held one another close in a long, kissing embrace.

"Have you that lubricating ointment handy?" he inquired. "The tube Aunt Sally gave you?"

"In my suitcase. Don't you think it might make us a little *too* slippery?"

"We may as well try the experiment. It can hardly de-prove on last night. At worst, we can remove it again with a wash cloth."

She found the tube of intimate lubricant and brought it back to the bed. Then off with their robes and back under the covers, bare naked between the satin sheets, rubbing their hands over and over one another.

"Skin is so lovely!" she whispered.

"Mmm… The antique Greeks conceived of bodies as the boundaries separating our essences one from another. The Hebrews, conversely, regarded bodies as the vehicles enabling us to interact, soul with soul, on this mortal plane."

A little more rolling and very pleasurable groping.

Next time they paused for a short rest, she said, "I dreamed about…them…in the night. Gaia and Harry. They were hovering in the air above the bed, coaching us and cheering us on. They seemed to be…very happy."

"Remarkable! We may have shared the same dream."

"Is that even possible?"

"Difficult of verification, but I have encountered such things in my reading.… Fondle my nether regions again?"

They got into position and fondled again. For all they were worth. When he was swollen very hard indeed and she was as soft and wambly as she could be without absolutely dissolving, he groped for the tube of lubricant and anointed her generously, ending by working one finger inside her cleft and wiggling gently. And, oh! If it had been a thrill last night to feel his hand on her triangle, this was a thousand times more so!

"I believe," he murmured, "this is what they refer to as 'parting the petals.' The sweet, fragrant petals."

"More!" she cried, her inner muscles spasming around his finger. "Oh, Cory, more!"

Instead, he withdrew his finger slowly, millimeter by millimeter, and handed her the lubricant. "Now…if you please…anoint me."

She did. He lay with eyes closed, his face wreathed in total bliss.

"Now," he went on, "this came to me in dream. Let's try whether it works equally well awake. Lying on our backs, we should arrange our bodies in a V, hips touching, shoulders angled some distance apart on the pillows."

Bubbling with curiosity, she followed his directions. When they were well arranged, he lifted her right leg up over his thighs, leaving her left to follow of its own will, but with her legs spread comfortably apart.

Then he rolled a little bit more in her direction and rested the tip of his pointer—the beak of his bird?—in the rim of her nest.

After a breathless second, he began to push.

"Oh, Cory, oh, it's going *in!* It's really, really going *in!*"

Halfway. He stopped halfway, and they rested. It was the most comfortable sensation she had ever felt in her life. It was right…so very, very *right*. She thought she could have lain like this forever. She was…almost…a little disappointed—but only for a fast heart-beat—when he rolled farther inward and pushed again.

Farther, and deeper, and it went gliding in so smoothly…Care-fully, carefully, working his body up over her legs, he rolled on top of her, hugging her shoulders as his pointer stayed inside… until their crotches were pressed as tightly together as could be… and, oh! at last she understood how a little pain could be very, very sweet…the pain that was all but a pleasure…but it passed and the sweetness did not…the pleasure that's all but pain. She felt his male equipment nesting in her female parts and thought, in rather nonsensical delight: What the well-dressed wife is wearing this season—*her husband!*

And, So *this* is the Sacrament. The ceremony, the witnessing, the signing things—that's all just the sacramentals. *This* is the real, actual Sacrament itself—the oldest Sacrament we have, old as Adam and Eve in the Garden of Eden, old as the Old Stone Age, even older…This is what it means, "With my body I thee worship."

She moved her hands down to the cheeks of his behind, and squeezed. He moved his hands down beneath hers, and squeezed back. Harder…harder…as if nature were taking over their wills, their very beings…Deliberately, she tightened the muscles of her inner nest and hugged his bird as tightly as she could.

He gave her one look filled with astonishment and pleasure. Then he buried his face in her shoulder and started thrusting with his hips.

Up and down, up and down, a few centimeters out and then in again to the…to the hilt? faster, faster…she was quivering, she lost track of whose parts were whose…so this is what it is when "the two become one flesh"…how sweet, how beautiful, how…

And the universe contracted into itself, and…imploded… and spread out again in wonderful, crashing waves…embracing them…ebbing gloriously away…leaving them wrapped together soul blending into soul.

After just enough time, they rolled apart and lay smiling at one another.

"Your eyes are aglow," he said.

"So are yours. Oh, Cory, I never guessed it would be like *that!*"

"Nor I," said Corwin. "There are no words."

ACKNOWLEDGEMENTS, BIBLIOGRAPHICAL NOTES, ETC.

Purgatorial stunts are by specially trained literary characters under carefully controlled conditions. ***Do Not Attempt at Home.*** Ever.

* * * *

On Sept. 30, 2011, I visited Northwoods Body Art on Railroad Street in Hayward, WI, to check various points concerning the use of tattoos in this novel. Many thanks to these friendly people for answering my questions! I was delighted to learn that such a "tattoo stamp" as I envisioned was indeed quite possible in a work of this genre. Even twenty years younger, and I feel sure I would have enlisted them to give me a tattoo.

* * * *

The quotation "Even as you and I" is from Rudyard Kipling's poem "The Vampire."

Quotations from Dante's *Purgatorio* are from the Longfellow translation: Canto 23, ll. 72-75; Canto 30, l. 145-145; Canto 23, l. 86.

In Edgar Allan Poe's poem "The Sleeper" occurs the line, "The rosemary nods upon the grave," which could explain Corwin's sleep-mumble in Chapter 26. The citations "My duty—*to be saved? Oh, let us not linger!*" are drawn from E.A.P.'s poems "To Helen" and "Ululame."

The specific Johnny Gruelle stories cited are "Raggedy Ann's Trip on the River" and "Raggedy Ann's New Sisters" from *Raggedy Ann Stories* and "The Taffy-Pull" from *Raggedy Andy Stories*. Gruelle's books seem more or less identical, with relatively unimportant variations, in both our timelines. True, in our timeline, Beloved Belindy does not talk with a dialect accent in the book named for her; but the real-for-sure human cook Dinah does. In any case, however it may be regarded in our timeline, in those parts of the R.S.A. population who form the main cast of *All But a Pleasure*, attempting any dialect, from "Chocolate" to Brooklynese, is looked on as amiable if not outright complimentary.

The Gilbert & Sullivan operas *The Governess, Foggerty's Fairy, The Tuppenny Prince,* and *The Drood Solution* do not exist in our timeline. *The Governess* and *The Tuppenny Prince* bear certain resemblances to the last two Savoy Operas of our timeline, *Utopia, Limited* and *The Grand Duke*. In our timeline, Gilbert's 1880 nonmusical version of *Foggerty's Fairy* can be found in his *Original Plays, Third Series*. The content of *The Drood Solution* may more or less be guessed at by reference to the last, unfinished novel of Charles Dickens, *The Mystery of Edwin Drood*. Dickens was perhaps Gilbert's own favorite author.

The great historian of the Spanish Inquisition in both timelines is Henry C. Lee. Since the major split in the timelines seems to have occurred about 1868, so that Lee had the same body of material to study in both timelines, his studies in theirs are essentially the same as in ours.

Three-player chess sets exist. I purchased one years ago and still have it around somewhere.

A quick Internet search reveals that something called "Vision Dust" or "Visiondust" exists in our timeline. Any resemblance to the substance going by that name in the R.S.A. is purely coincidental. A similar search seems to turn up "Slumbersound" only as tags for beds; should any soporific appear in our timeline under that name, it is, again, coincidental.

* * * *

Since I have myself been accused, to my surprise, of showing off an overly extensive vocabulary, I may owe it to everyone to point out that Corwin's word choice is indeed toned down by the end of this novel. For example, where the Corwin of Chapter 23 says (admittedly under orders from Lestrade, but at this point they might not make quite so much difference), "Not, I assure you, at the time!" the Corwin of Chapter 1 would have said, "Not, I attest and avow, contemporaneously with the occurrences under consideration!"

Several of the rolegaming sessions Corwin and Angela played with Oziah Prendergast Gillikin as rulemaster have been recorded, appearing from time to time in The International Wizard of Oz Club's annual publication *Oziana* (for 1986, 1988, and in 2012 or 2013). His Oz villain, closely modeled on himself, has not met exactly the kind of "interesting" fate that might have been expected: at last report, "Dr. Corwin Poe," Computer Wizard, was living quite comfortably with his Ozian wife, the jailer Tollydiggle (played by Angela), in the Emerald City Prison, making an annual attempt to conquer Oz, perhaps chiefly to maintain his status as Official Villain and earn some such relatively harmless corrective measure as being dipped in ink. In her illustrations for the earlier Computer Wizard stories, Melody Grandy Keller has given Corwin and Oziah what I regard as their definitive portraiture, as well as providing a delightful Angela who, however, seems to have undergone the widespread phenomenon of gaining weight after marriage.

* * * *

Back in the early decades of the 20th century, when the "rules of the mystery genre" were being set up during the Golden Age of mystery writing, Ronald Knox included as his rule number 4 (of 10), "No hitherto undiscovered poisons may be used…" and probably would have included drug interactions if people had been as aware of them then as we are now. S. S. Van Dine made it his rule number 3 (of 20), "There must be no love interest. The business in hand is to bring a criminal to the bar of justice, not to bring a lovelorn couple to the hymeneal altar." Van Dine's rule, if applied today, would render it impossible to include a mystery element in the romance genre. I consider the "undiscovered poisons" rule equally inapplicable to and especially unrealistic in fiction set in an alternate timeline which would certainly have discovered some different poisons and interactions, while failing to discover some familiar to us.

* * * *

After being put down on somebody's list somewhere as a hunter—which I emphatically am *not*—thanks to ordering dog food from one certain company under the Amazon umbrella, who may possibly have collated my order with my searches on the Wisconsin hunting seasons website (attempting to ascertain when it might be relatively safe to walk my Australian Shepherd mix without putting both of us in blaze orange), there are areas I *will not* research on the Internet. Our local libraries are wholesome and limited, and I shy from using Inter-Library Loan since the time my borrowing privileges were under threat of revocation if I did not return an ILL book which I had in fact already returned well before its due date.

Nevertheless, while using the 'Net to check the definitions and spellings of certain terms, I could hardly fail to notice that practices like those of Dante's Delight do in fact besprinkle our own timeline—and often seem to make those of my purgatorians pale by comparison. I do *not* endorse these practices! Intellectually, I am in total agreement with Lestrade and Angela: these are at best grotesque, at worst incredibly stupid, and always potentially dangerous. Emotionally, I confess to a certain appreciation of the purgatorians' and Corwin's arguments in these matters (*Corwin Poe, apres tout, c'est moi...mais Rosemary Lestrade, elle aussi, c'est moi*). Philosophically and theologically, I cannot quite rule out the idea of the need for a cosmic balance; nor do I find myself able to lay down a blanket condemnation without discarding a very great part of Catholic, Christian, and other religious tradition. Nevertheless, I hazard the opinion that normal living, with its sorrows, accidents, diseases, and natural catastrophes, provides as much balancing element as we need, without our artificially adding to it with wars and artificially-sought penitential practices. Up until the last few chapters, I'd entertained some nebulous idea that the events of this novel would bring down the final curtain on Forest Green's Purgatorian group—Kim Little Bird quite took me by surprise when she stepped up to keep it going. Well, at least Dante's Delight does not attempt to rule its members completely body, mind, soul, discretionary time, and finances.

About four decades ago, in practical research for another novel, I enlisted the help of two understanding friends to try getting myself hung by the wrists, and found it quite as uncomfortable as Corwin intimates. Since that earlier novel never actually got completed, it seemed no more than thrifty to make use of my own experience at last. Virtually everyone knows what it is to get pricked by needles, whether in connection with sewing, splinters, or medical treatment. To try to get some vague notion for the feel of handcuffs with perfect safety, I tried paper-clipping two rubber bands together. The bit about shamanic vision ordeals and sticking with arrows as seen in Paleolithic cave paintings I found in a work entitled *Shamanism: An Encyclopedia of World Beliefs, Practices, and Culture*, ed. by Marika Namba Walter & Eva Jane Fridman [my own Curly Friedman had already been named before I found this 2-vol. encyclopedia], (Santa Barbara, CA; Denver, CO; Oxford, Eng.: ABC CLIO ©2004), vol. 1, pp. 153-160; I located this work in the Dexter Library of Northland College, Ashland, Wisconsin, during a rehearsal break of the Chequamegon (pronounced "che-WAH-m'-gon") Symphony—a "communiversity" orchestra—early in the writing of *All But a Pleasure*. For most of the rest, I pretty well had to wing it.

I must confess to being that *rara avis* among modern writers, a Catholic baptized and bred who has *not* "fallen away," who still attends Mass or at least, in the absence of a priest, Communion Service regularly, who holds a Lay Minister's Certificate in the Diocese of Superior, and when at home lends her flute to the liturgical music ministry. And who perhaps should not be writing a genre nowadays linked so mandatorily with "intimate" scenes at all. I also have ecumenical toeholds in both modern Wicca and my late husband's Congregational United Church of Christ. Thus, any comments in this novel which might look at first blush inimical to Christianity or any other religious tradition, are to be understood either as the personal sentiments of the character involved, or as cries of the Loyal Opposition seeking to bring an essentially good thing up to its highest potential.

The existence of Catholic women priests in this alternate timeline should by no means be interpreted as an argument *contra* the papal pronouncements of my own timeline. It simply seemed inconsistent to postulate that the Rome of a world timeline so shaped by egalitarianism in gender-related as in racial matters would cleave to so strict a rule against ordaining women. Or perhaps the Catholic church of the R.S.A. has actually split off from Rome.

At the outset, I aimed this novel and its immediate sequels at the lucrative or so I understand modern romance market. Months of intensive reading in this genre left me with two strong impressions: (1) graphic sex scenes are obligatory, except perhaps in the "religious" or "inspirational" subgenre, which seems heavily into humanoid angels, uplifting miracles, and edifying certainties (none of which I could write about convincingly); (2) there's a heck of a lot of doggone good storytelling in this modern romance genre anyway, if you get the right ones, which usually seems to mean the thicker ones.

It is clear that the more wildly and passionately intimate graphic sex scenes of *All But a Pleasure* should belong by rights to Julie and Dave. But I have my auctorial limitations, so contented myself with leaving slots where a pen more adept than mine at this sort of thing could, at editorial behest, dash them in. (It seems that even experienced writers may suffer vainglorious daydreams!) When it came to Corwin and Angela, however, I relucted to trust their intimate moments to anybody's pen but my own. If the results make the more naive and innocent couple come across as the wilder, I can only beg readers to supply for themselves the passionate intimacies of the more fluent pair.232